LINUS ™

kaboom! ™

Cover
Art by **Charles M. Schulz**
Design by **Kara Leopard**

Collection Designer: **Kara Leopard**
Editor: **Chris Rosa**

For Charles M. Schulz Creative Associates
Creative Director: **Paige Braddock**
Senior Editor: **Alexis E. Fajardo**

Special Thanks to the Schulz family, everyone at Creative Associates, and Charles M. Schulz for h
singular achievement in shaping these beloved characters.

Ross Richie CEO & Founder • Joy Huffman CFO • Matt Gagnon Editor-in-Chief • Filip Sablik President, Publishing & Marketing • Stephen Christy President, Development • Lance Kreiter Vice President, Licensing & Merch
Aruna Singh Vice President, Marketing • Bryce Carlson Vice President, Editorial & Creative Strategy • Scott Newman Manager, Production Design • Kate Henning Manager, Operations • Spencer Simpson Manager
Sierra Hahn Executive Editor • Jeanine Schaefer Executive Editor • Dafna Pleban Senior Editor • Shannon Watters Senior Editor • Eric Harburn Senior Editor • Chris Rosa
Matthew Levine Editor • Sophie Philips-Roberts Associate Editor • Gavin Gronenthal Assistant Editor • Michael Moccio Assistant Editor • Gwen Waller Assistant Editor • Amanda LaFranco Executive Assistant • Jillian Crab Design Co
Michelle Ankley Design Coordinator • Kara Leopard Production Designer • Marie Krupina Production Designer • Grace Park Production Designer • Chelsea Roberts Production Design Assistant • Samantha Knapp Production Design
José Meza Live Events Lead • Stephanie Hocutt Digital Marketing Lead • Esther Kim Marketing Coordinator • Cat O'Grady Digital Marketing Coordinator • Amanda Lawson Marketing
Holly Aitchison Digital Sales Coordinator • Morgan Perry Retail Sales Coordinator • Megan Christopher Operations Coordinator • Rodrigo Hernandez Mailroom Assistant • Zipporah Smith Operations Assistant • Breanna Sarpy Executive

BOOM! Studios, 5670 Wilshire Boulevard, Suite 400, Los Angeles, CA 90036-5679. Printed in China. First Printing.

ISBN: 978-1-68415-402-9, eISBN: 978-1-64144-385-2

Classic Peanuts Strips by
Charles M. Schulz
Colors by **Justin Thompson, Katharine Efird,
Donna Almendrala & Art Roche**

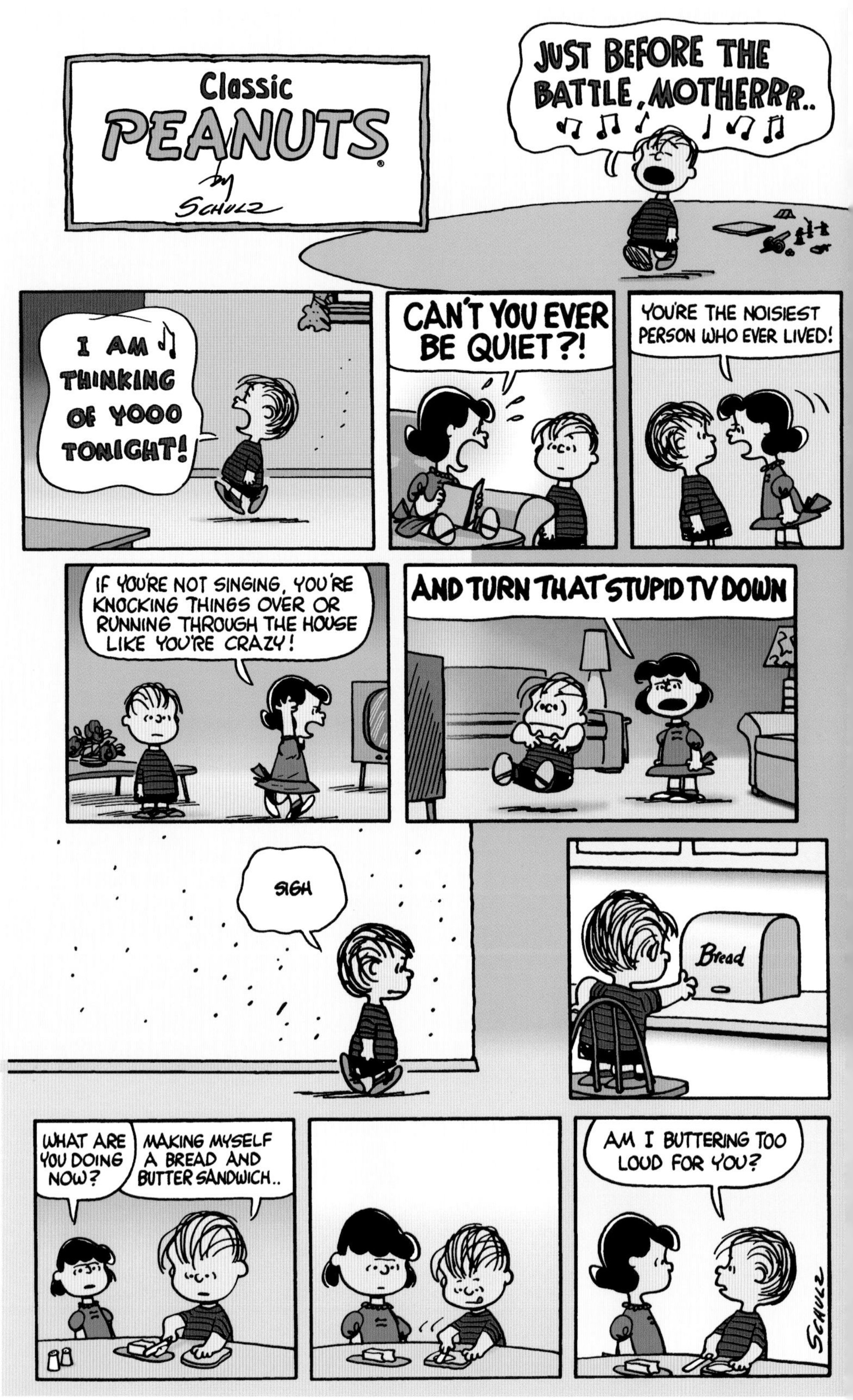
Classic
PEANUTS
by
SCHULZ
JUST BEFORE THE BATTLE, MOTHERRRR..
I AM THINKING OF YOOO TONIGHT!
CAN'T YOU EVER BE QUIET?!
YOU'RE THE NOISIEST PERSON WHO EVER LIVED!
IF YOU'RE NOT SINGING, YOU'RE KNOCKING THINGS OVER OR RUNNING THROUGH THE HOUSE LIKE YOU'RE CRAZY!
AND TURN THAT STUPID TV DOWN
SIGH
Bread
WHAT ARE YOU DOING NOW?
MAKING MYSELF A BREAD AND BUTTER SANDWICH..
AM I BUTTERING TOO LOUD FOR YOU?
SCHULZ

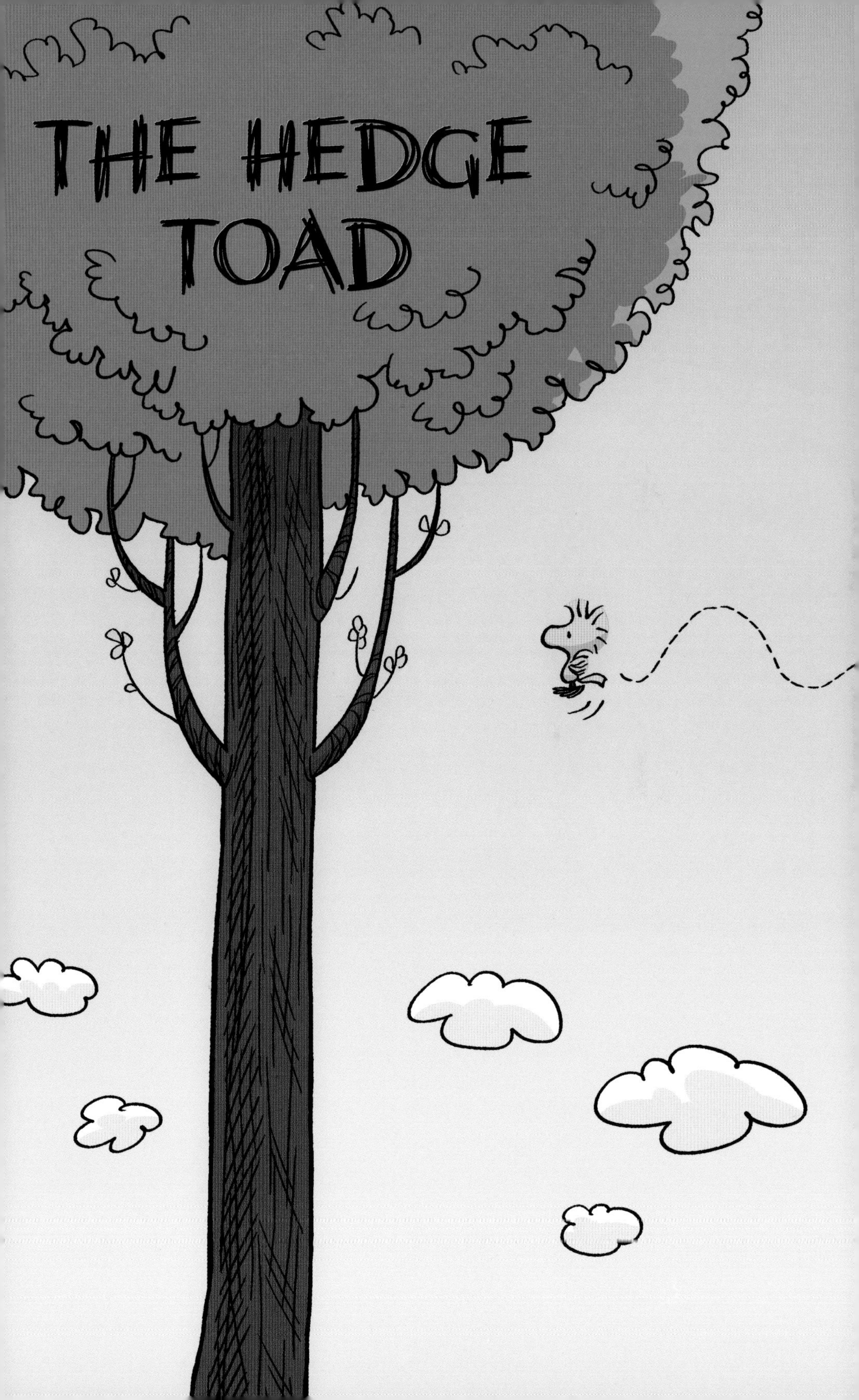
THE HEDGE TOAD

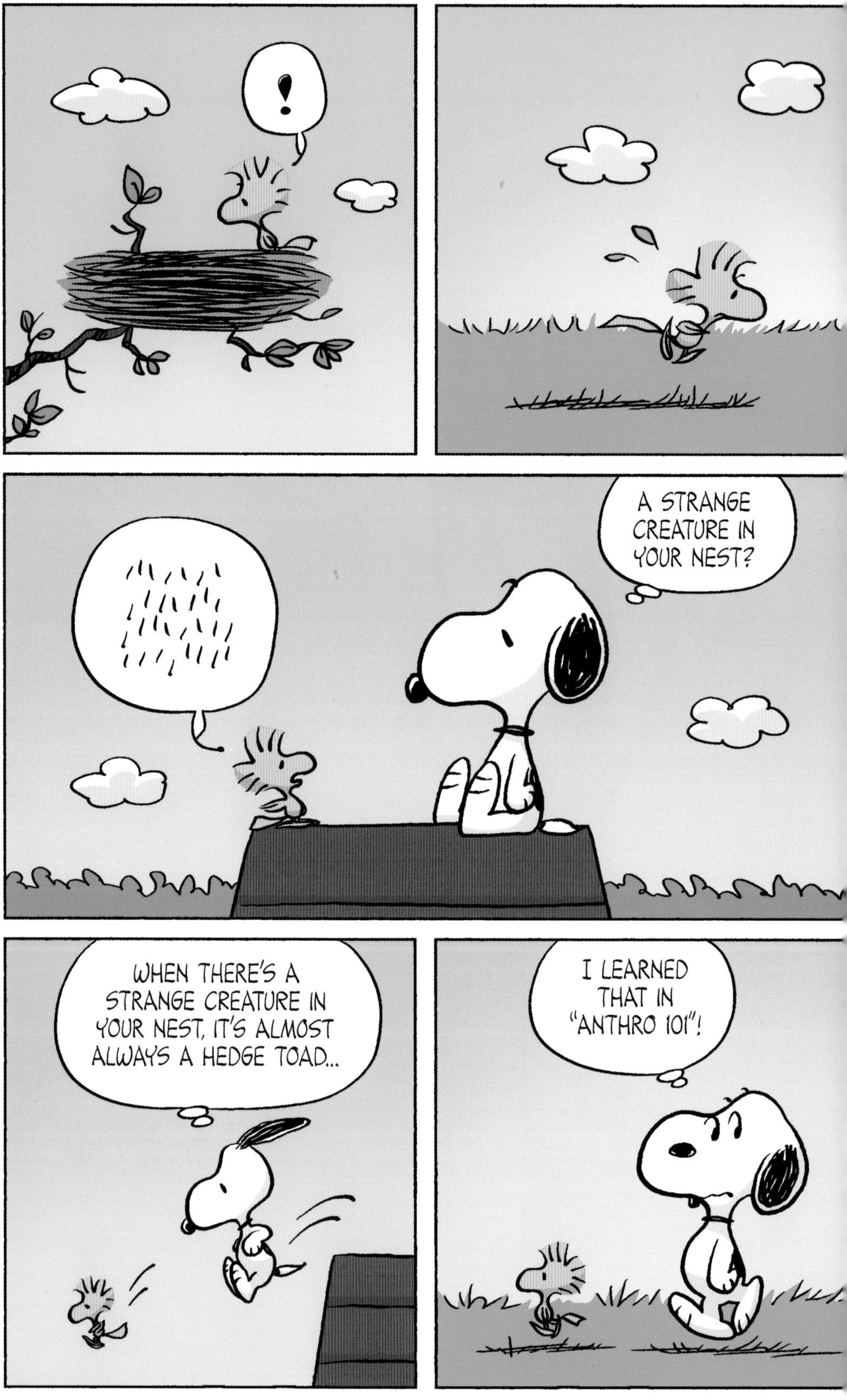
!
A STRANGE CREATURE IN YOUR NEST?
WHEN THERE'S A STRANGE CREATURE IN YOUR NEST, IT'S ALMOST ALWAYS A HEDGE TOAD...
I LEARNED THAT IN "ANTHRO 101"!

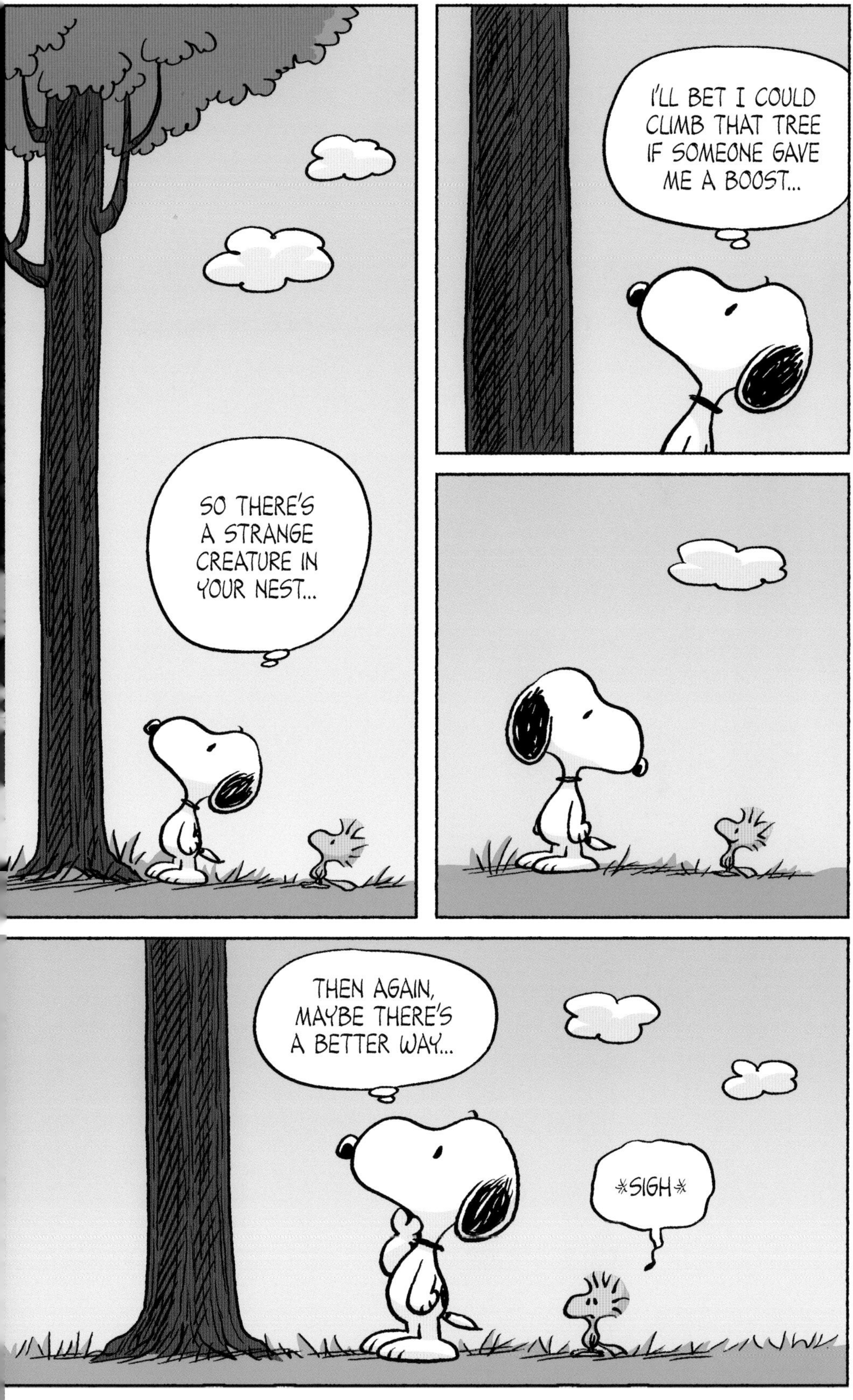
SO THERE'S A STRANGE CREATURE IN YOUR NEST...
I'LL BET I COULD CLIMB THAT TREE IF SOMEONE GAVE ME A BOOST...
THEN AGAIN, MAYBE THERE'S A BETTER WAY...
SIGH

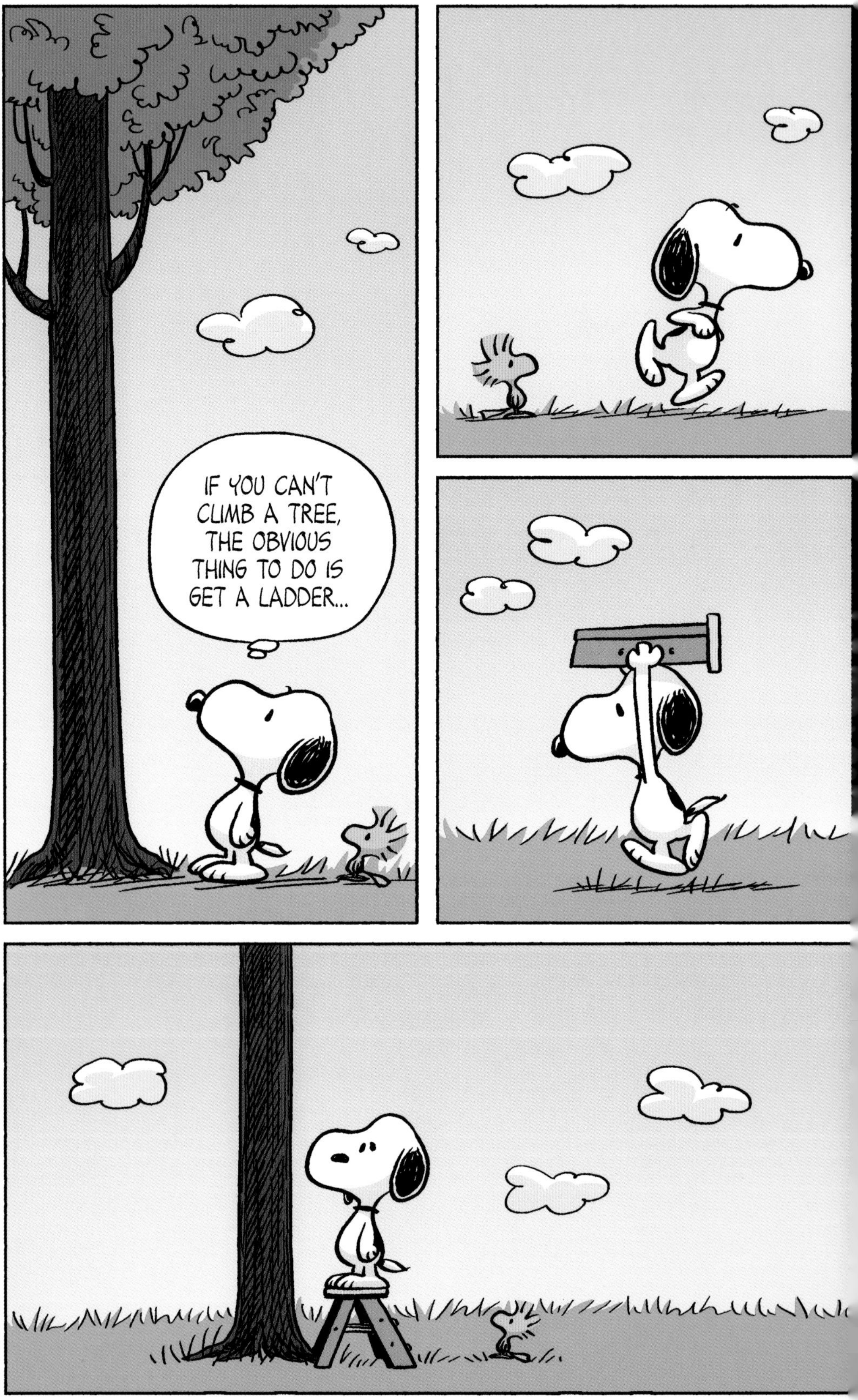

IF YOU CAN'T CLIMB A TREE, THE OBVIOUS THING TO DO IS GET A LADDER...

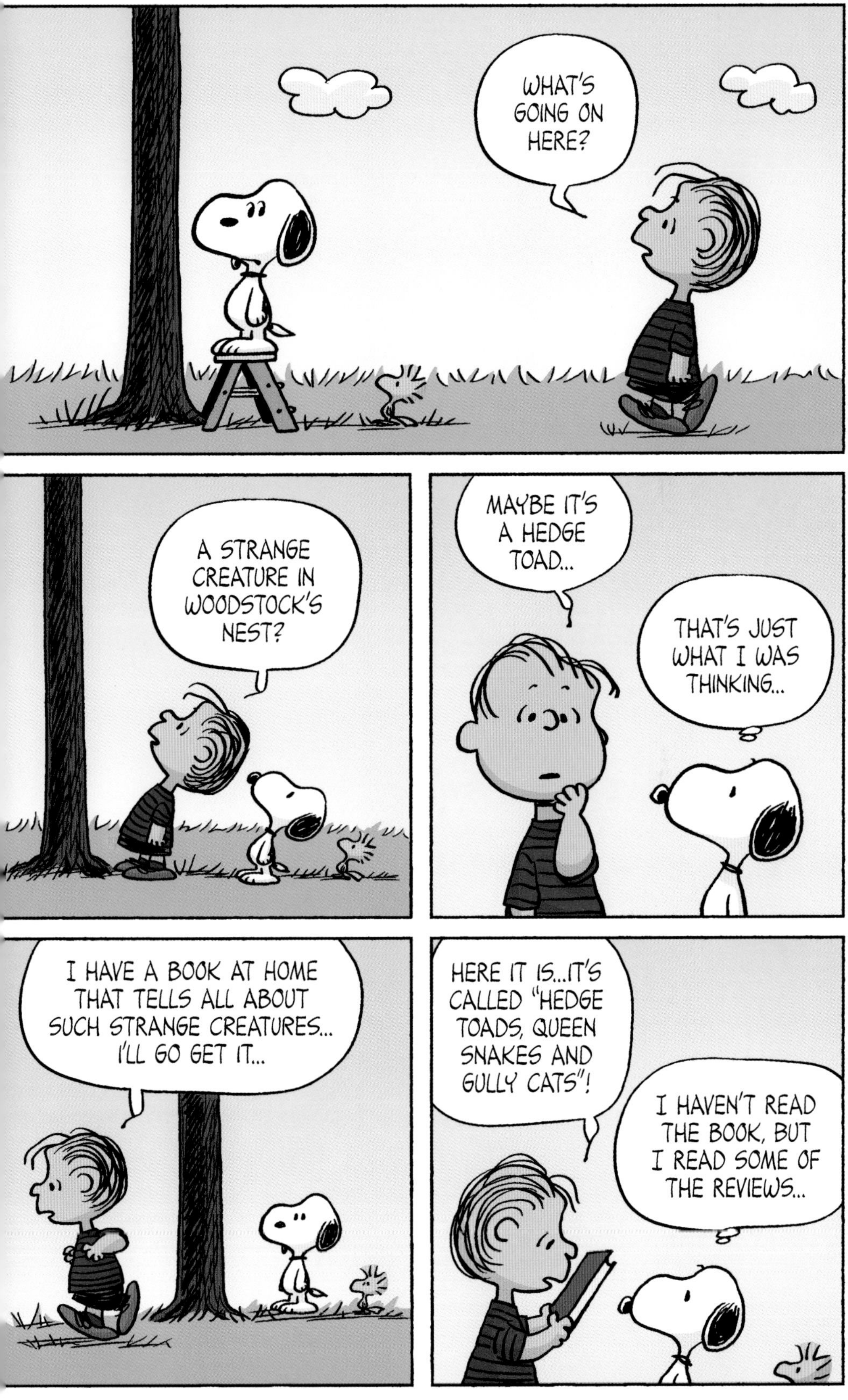
WHAT'S GOING ON HERE?
A STRANGE CREATURE IN WOODSTOCK'S NEST?
MAYBE IT'S A HEDGE TOAD...
THAT'S JUST WHAT I WAS THINKING...
I HAVE A BOOK AT HOME THAT TELLS ALL ABOUT SUCH STRANGE CREATURES... I'LL GO GET IT...
HERE IT IS...IT'S CALLED "HEDGE TOADS, QUEEN SNAKES AND GULLY CATS"!
I HAVEN'T READ THE BOOK, BUT I READ SOME OF THE REVIEWS...

THE ONLY WAY TO FIND OUT WHO'S IN WOODSTOCK'S NEST IS TO CLIMB THIS TREE AND SEE FOR OURSELVES...

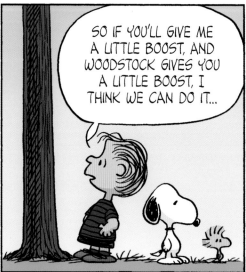

SO IF YOU'LL GIVE ME A LITTLE BOOST, AND WOODSTOCK GIVES YOU A LITTLE BOOST, I THINK WE CAN DO IT...

OKAY... BOOST!

I'M BOOSTING! BUT I'M NOT SURE IF MY BOOSTER IS BOOSTING!

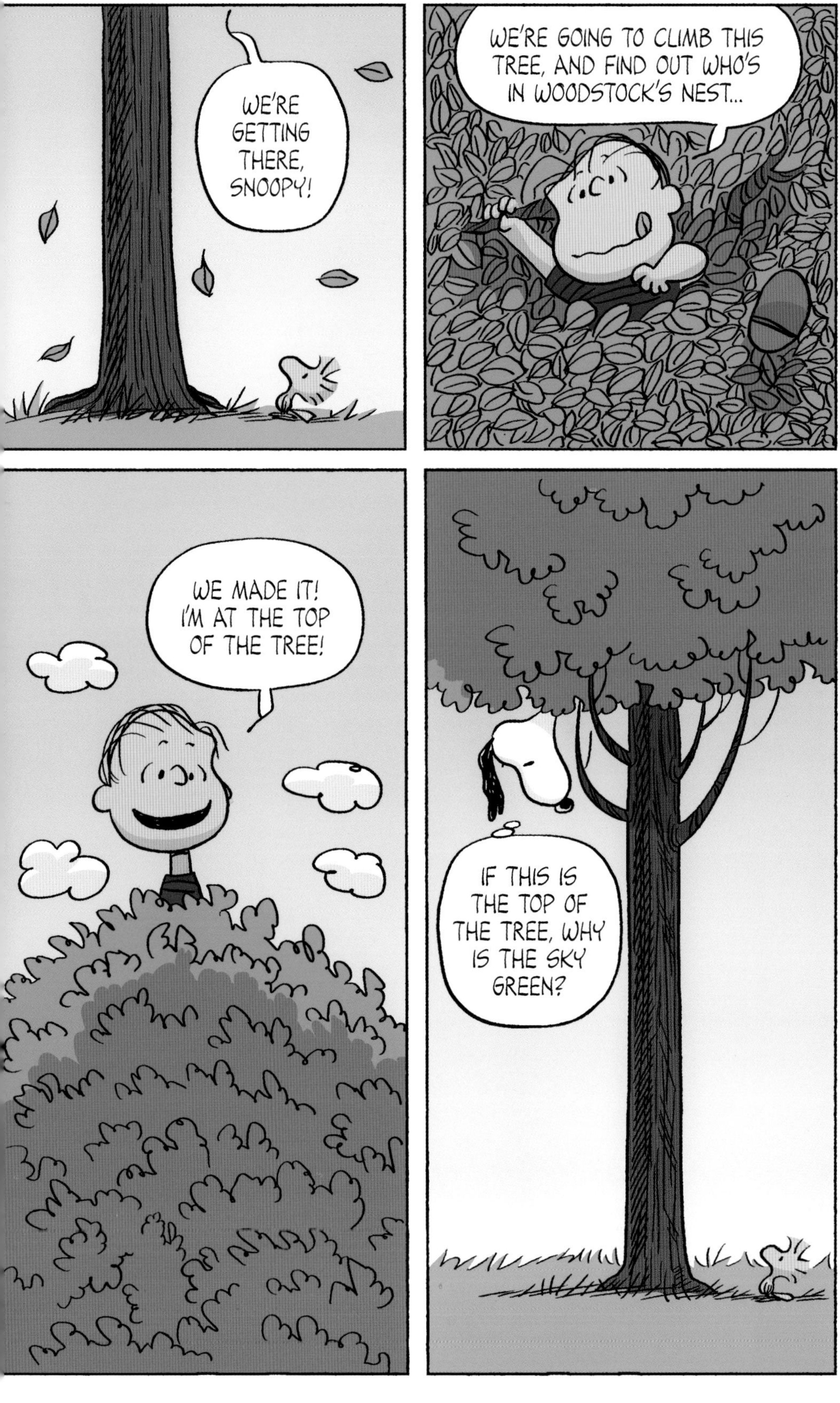
WE'RE GETTING THERE, SNOOPY!
WE'RE GOING TO CLIMB THIS TREE, AND FIND OUT WHO'S IN WOODSTOCK'S NEST...
WE MADE IT! I'M AT THE TOP OF THE TREE!
IF THIS IS THE TOP OF THE TREE, WHY IS THE SKY GREEN?

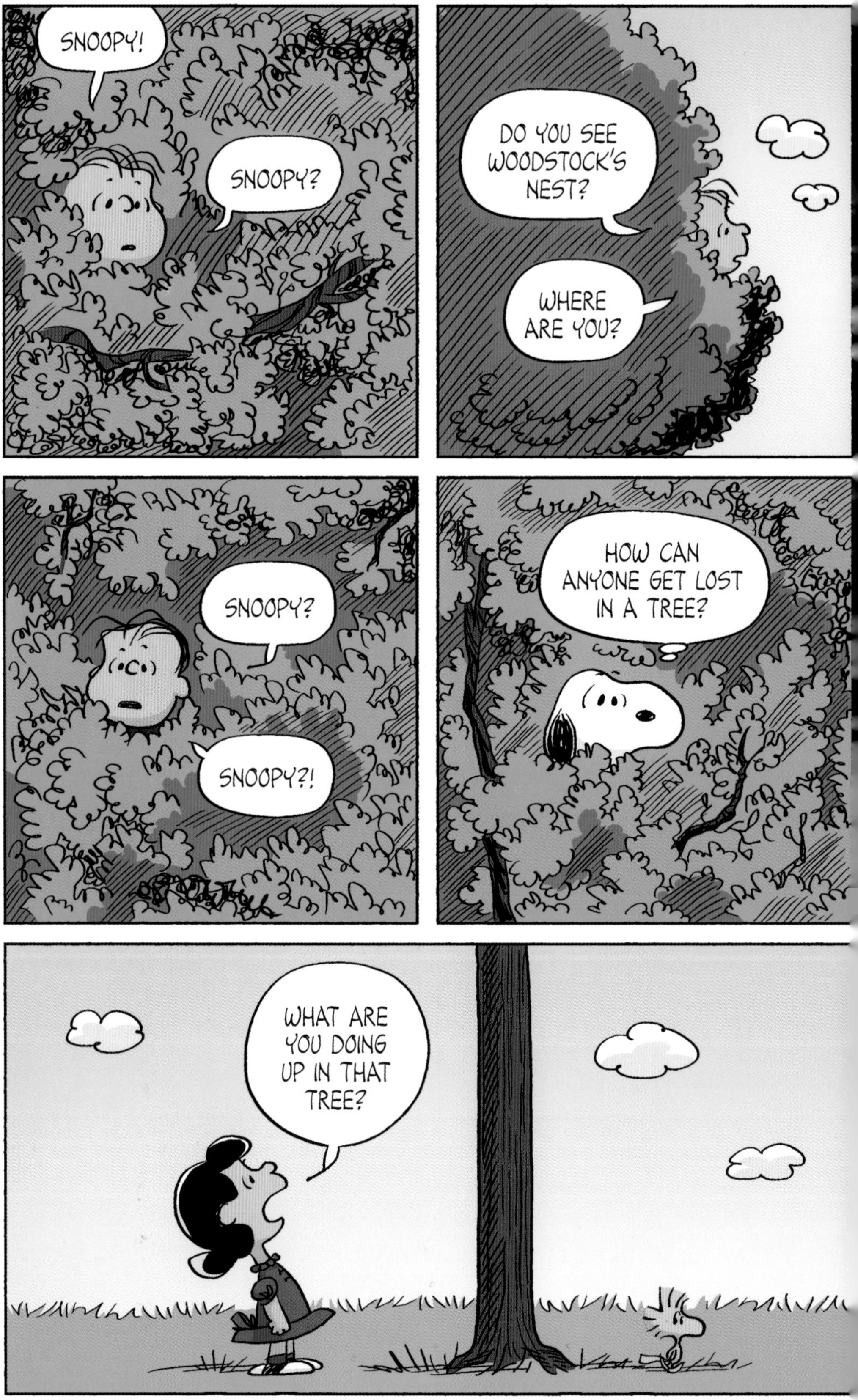
SNOOPY!
SNOOPY?
DO YOU SEE WOODSTOCK'S NEST?
WHERE ARE YOU?
SNOOPY?
SNOOPY?!
HOW CAN ANYONE GET LOST IN A TREE?
WHAT ARE YOU DOING UP IN THAT TREE?

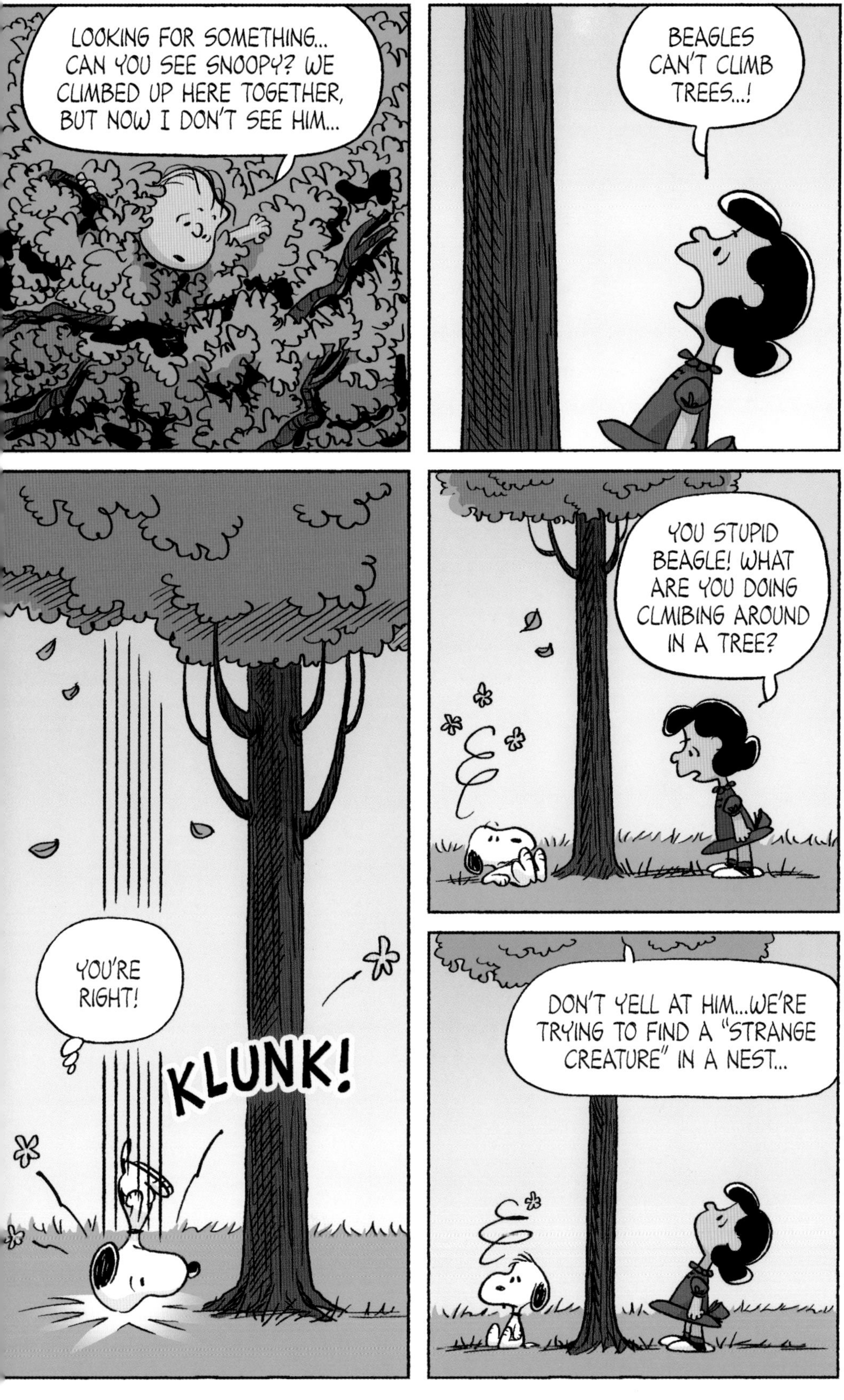
LOOKING FOR SOMETHING... CAN YOU SEE SNOOPY? WE CLIMBED UP HERE TOGETHER, BUT NOW I DON'T SEE HIM...
BEAGLES CAN'T CLIMB TREES...!
YOU'RE RIGHT!
KLUNK!
YOU STUPID BEAGLE! WHAT ARE YOU DOING CLMIBING AROUND IN A TREE?
DON'T YELL AT HIM...WE'RE TRYING TO FIND A "STRANGE CREATURE" IN A NEST...

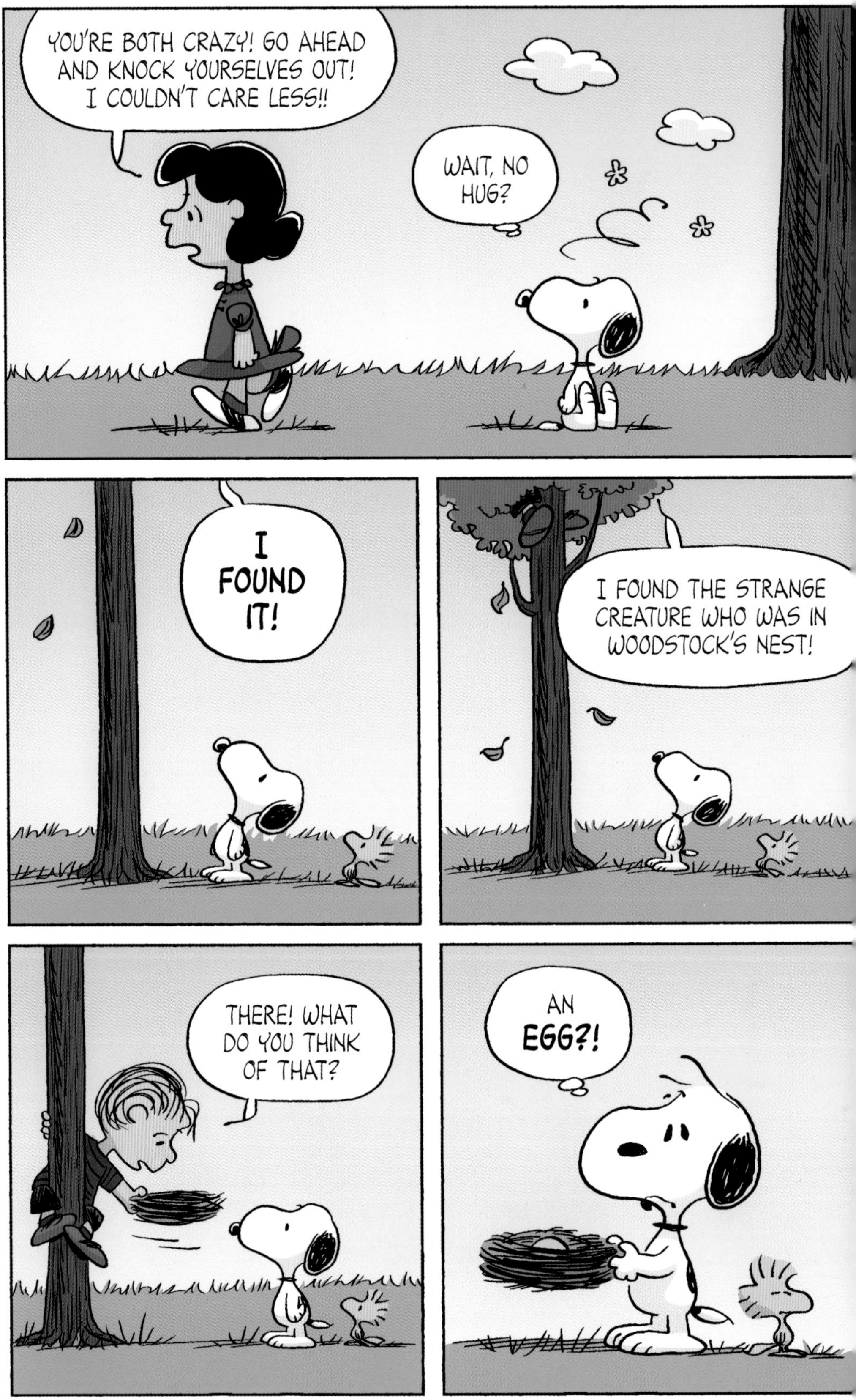
YOU'RE BOTH CRAZY! GO AHEAD AND KNOCK YOURSELVES OUT! I COULDN'T CARE LESS!!
WAIT, NO HUG?
I FOUND IT!
I FOUND THE STRANGE CREATURE WHO WAS IN WOODSTOCK'S NEST!
THERE! WHAT DO YOU THINK OF THAT?
AN EGG?!

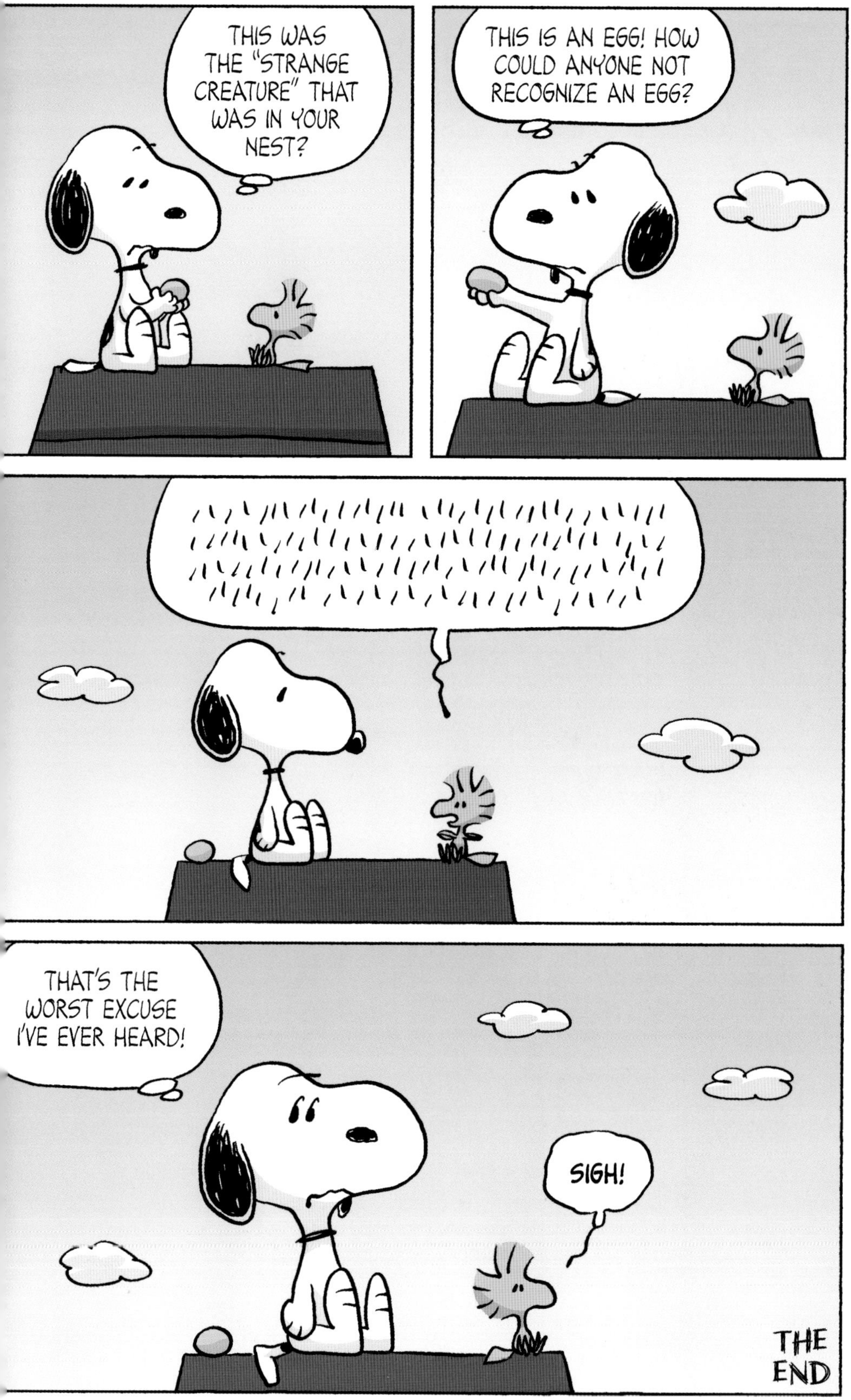
THIS WAS THE "STRANGE CREATURE" THAT WAS IN YOUR NEST?
THIS IS AN EGG! HOW COULD ANYONE NOT RECOGNIZE AN EGG?
THAT'S THE WORST EXCUSE I'VE EVER HEARD!
SIGH!
THE END

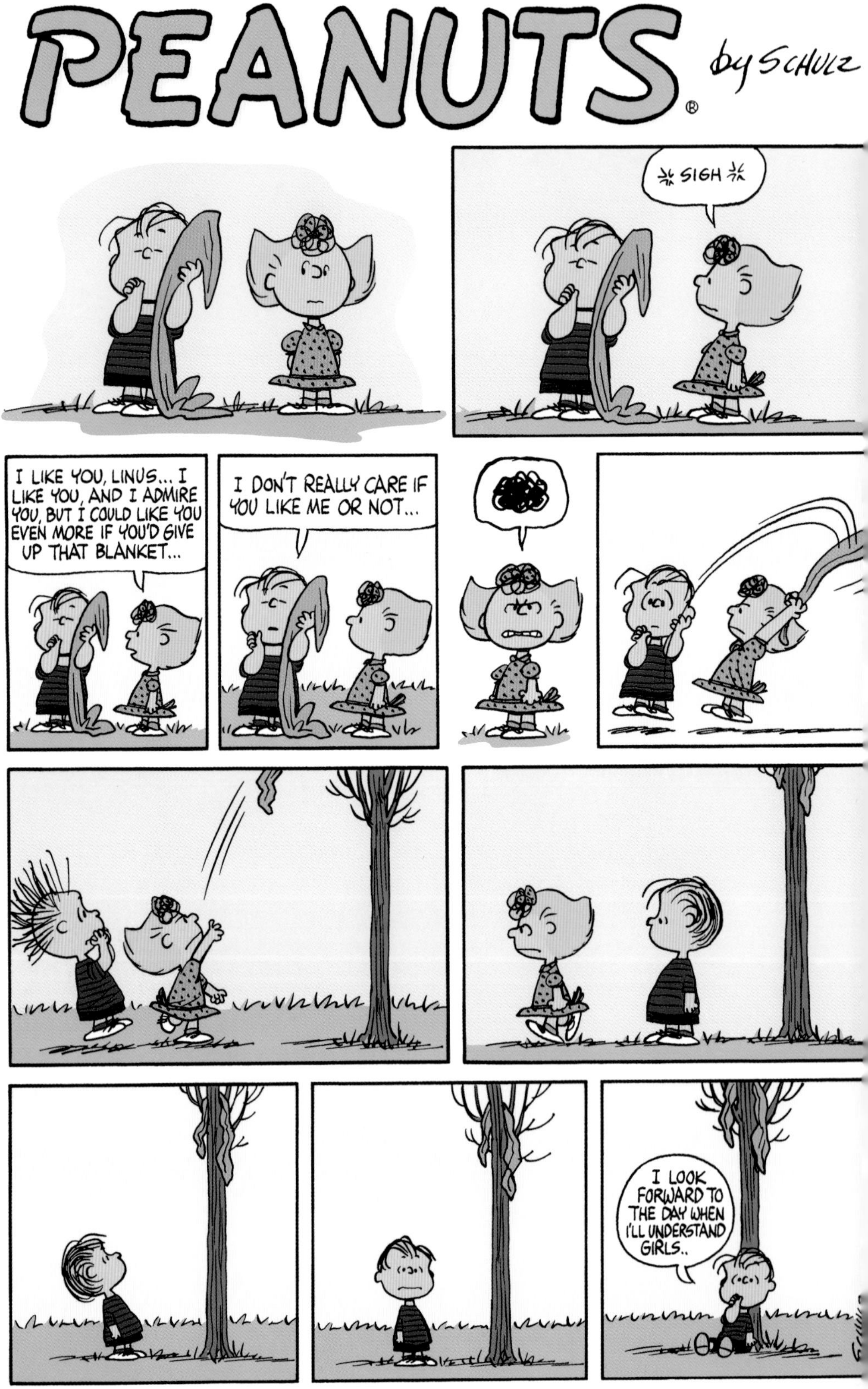
PEANUTS
by SCHULZ
SIGH
I LIKE YOU, LINUS... I LIKE YOU, AND I ADMIRE YOU, BUT I COULD LIKE YOU EVEN MORE IF YOU'D GIVE UP THAT BLANKET...
I DON'T REALLY CARE IF YOU LIKE ME OR NOT...
I LOOK FORWARD TO THE DAY WHEN I'LL UNDERSTAND GIRLS..

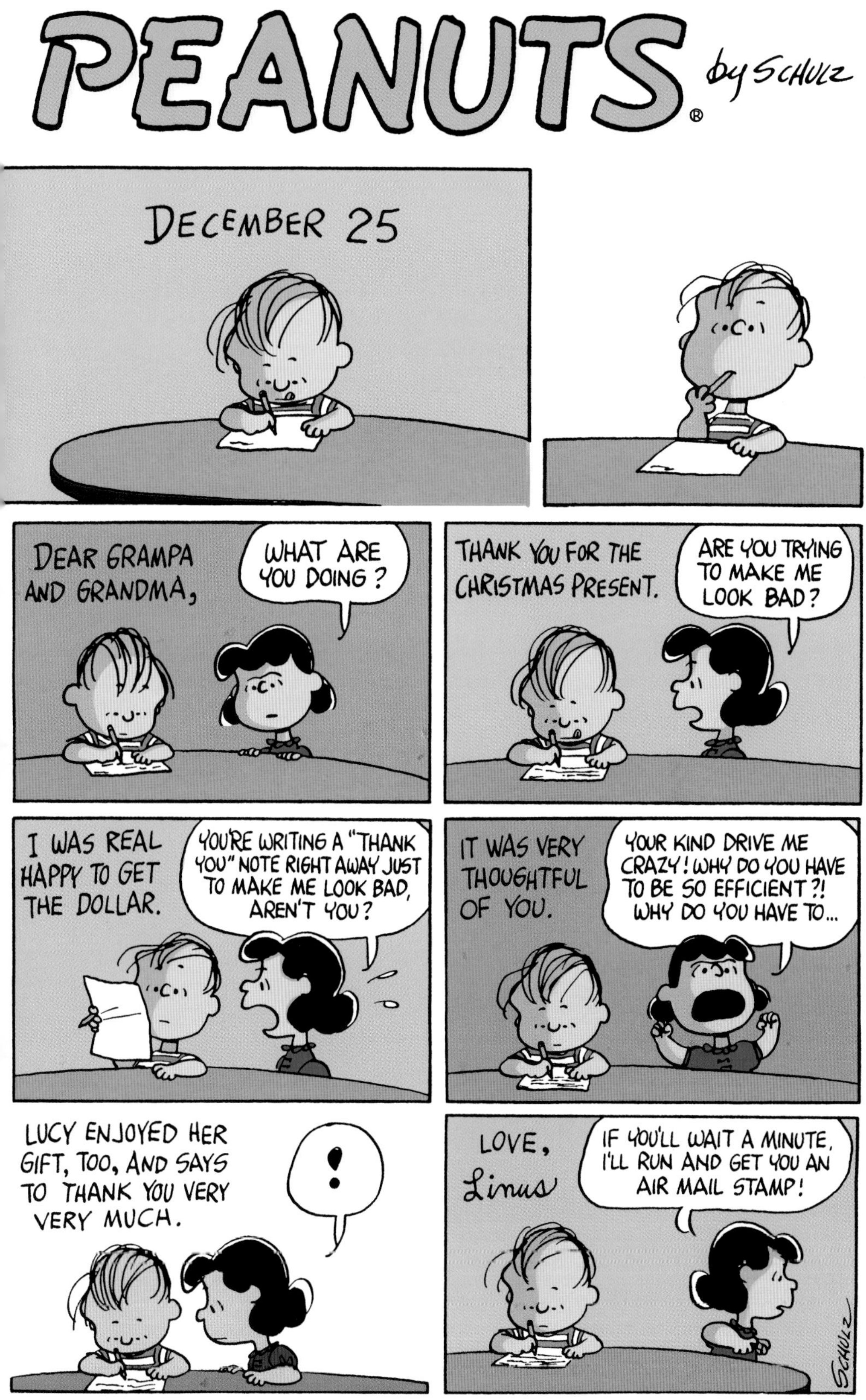
PEANUTS
by SCHULZ
DECEMBER 25
DEAR GRAMPA AND GRANDMA,
WHAT ARE YOU DOING?
THANK YOU FOR THE CHRISTMAS PRESENT.
ARE YOU TRYING TO MAKE ME LOOK BAD?
I WAS REAL HAPPY TO GET THE DOLLAR.
YOU'RE WRITING A "THANK YOU" NOTE RIGHT AWAY JUST TO MAKE ME LOOK BAD, AREN'T YOU?
IT WAS VERY THOUGHTFUL OF YOU.
YOUR KIND DRIVE ME CRAZY! WHY DO YOU HAVE TO BE SO EFFICIENT?! WHY DO YOU HAVE TO...
LUCY ENJOYED HER GIFT, TOO, AND SAYS TO THANK YOU VERY VERY MUCH.
!
LOVE, Linus
IF YOU'LL WAIT A MINUTE, I'LL RUN AND GET YOU AN AIR MAIL STAMP!
SCHULZ

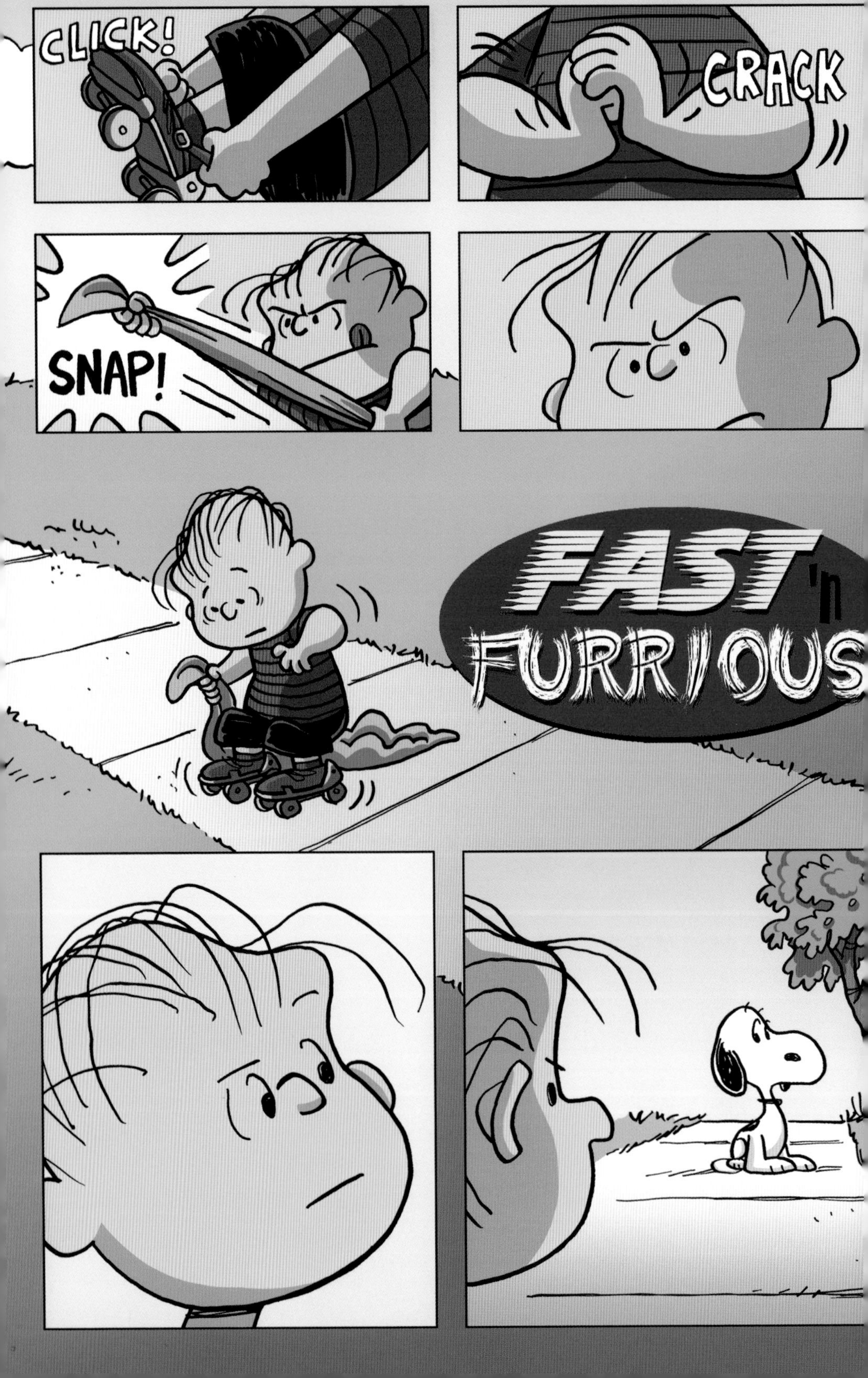
CLICK!
CRACK
SNAP!
FAST 'n FURRIOUS

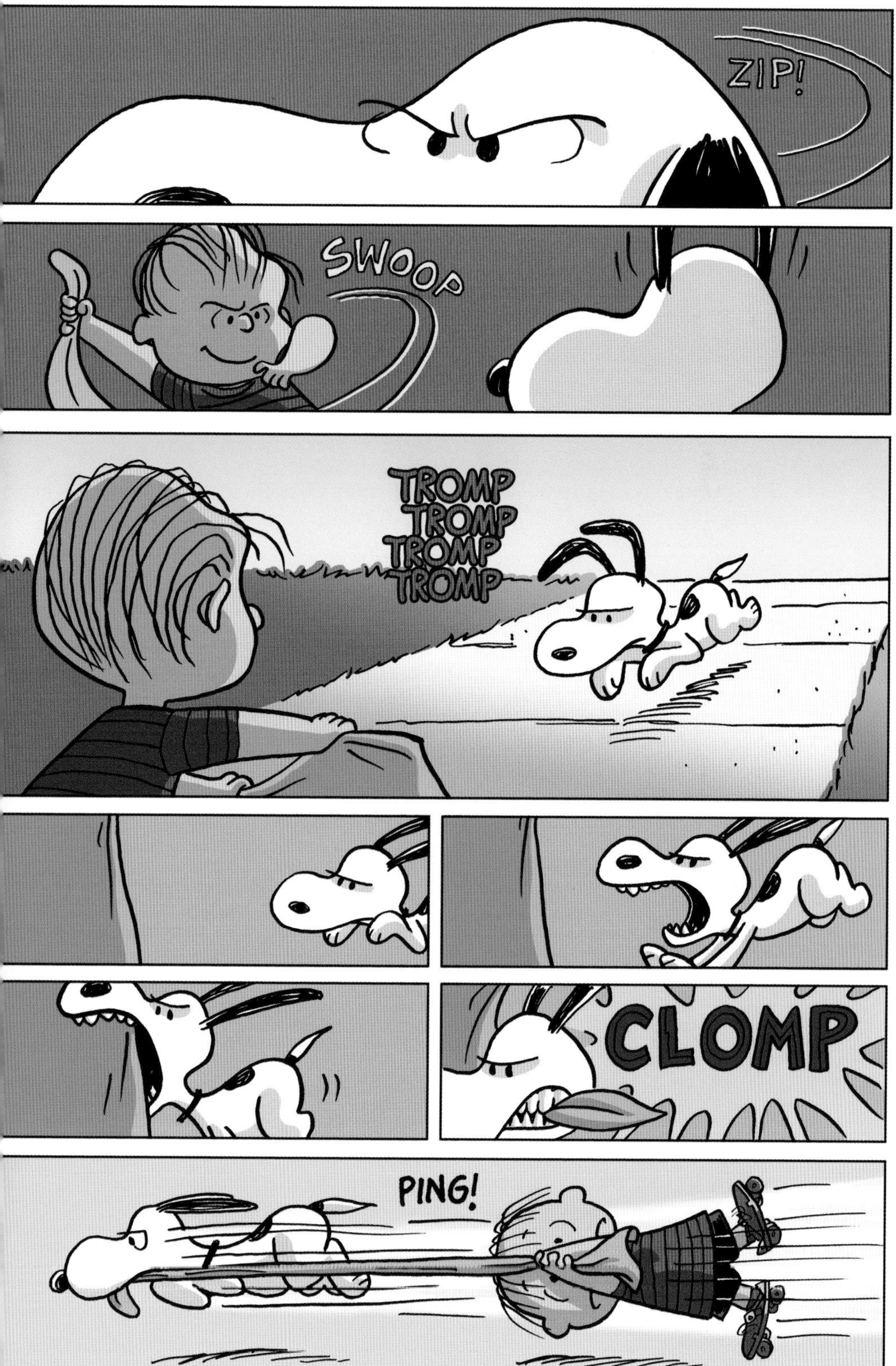
ZIP!
SWOOP
TROMP
TROMP
TROMP
TROMP
CLOMP
PING!

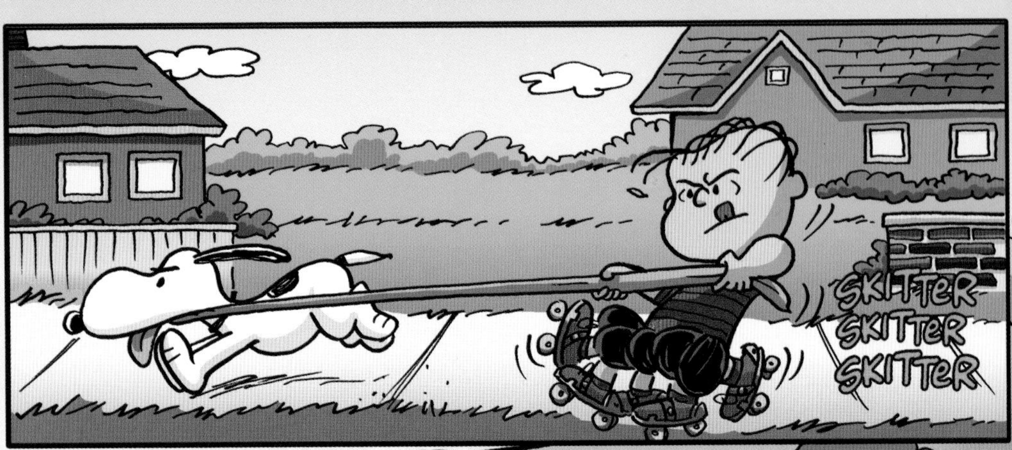
SKITTER
SKITTER
SKITTER
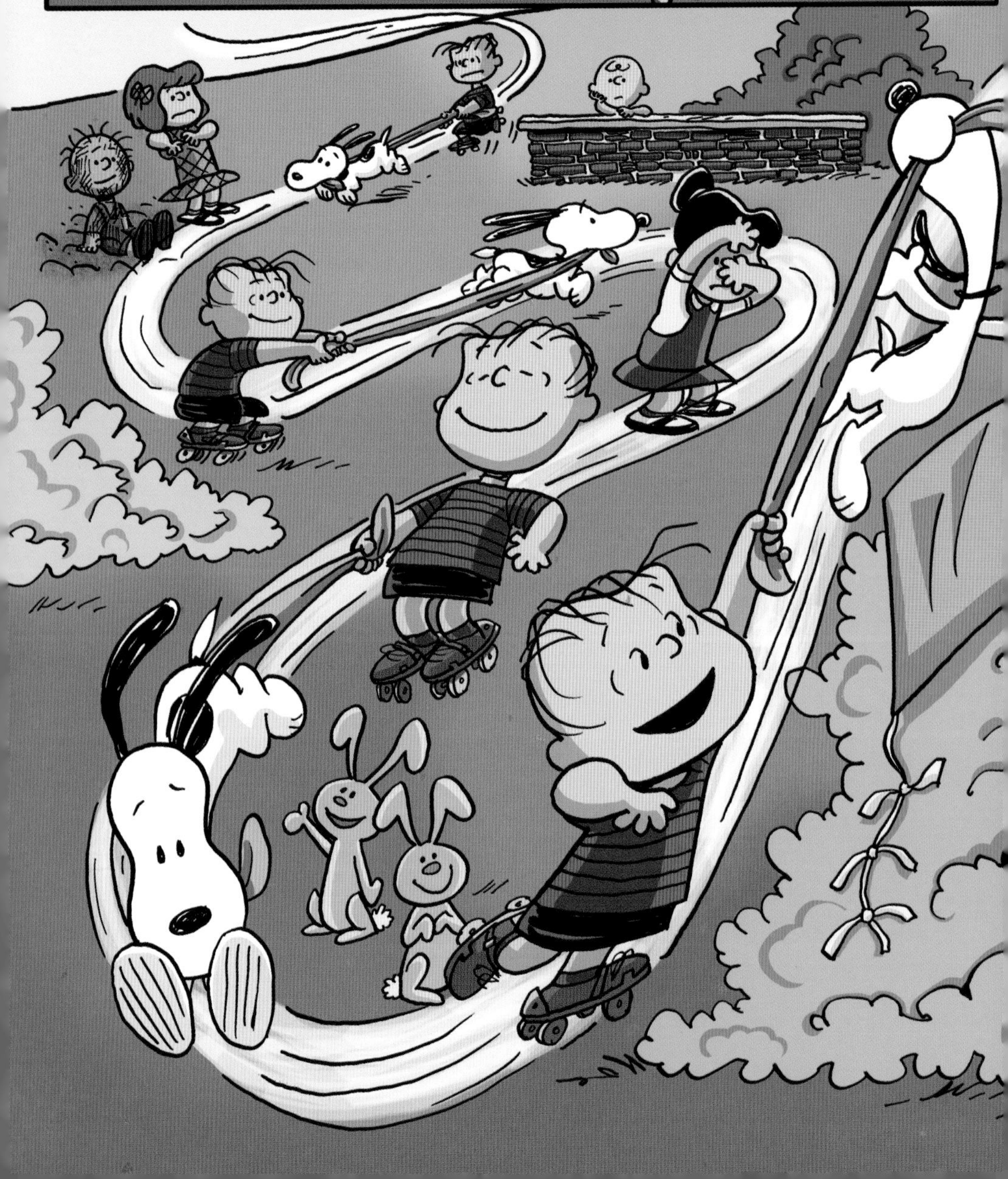

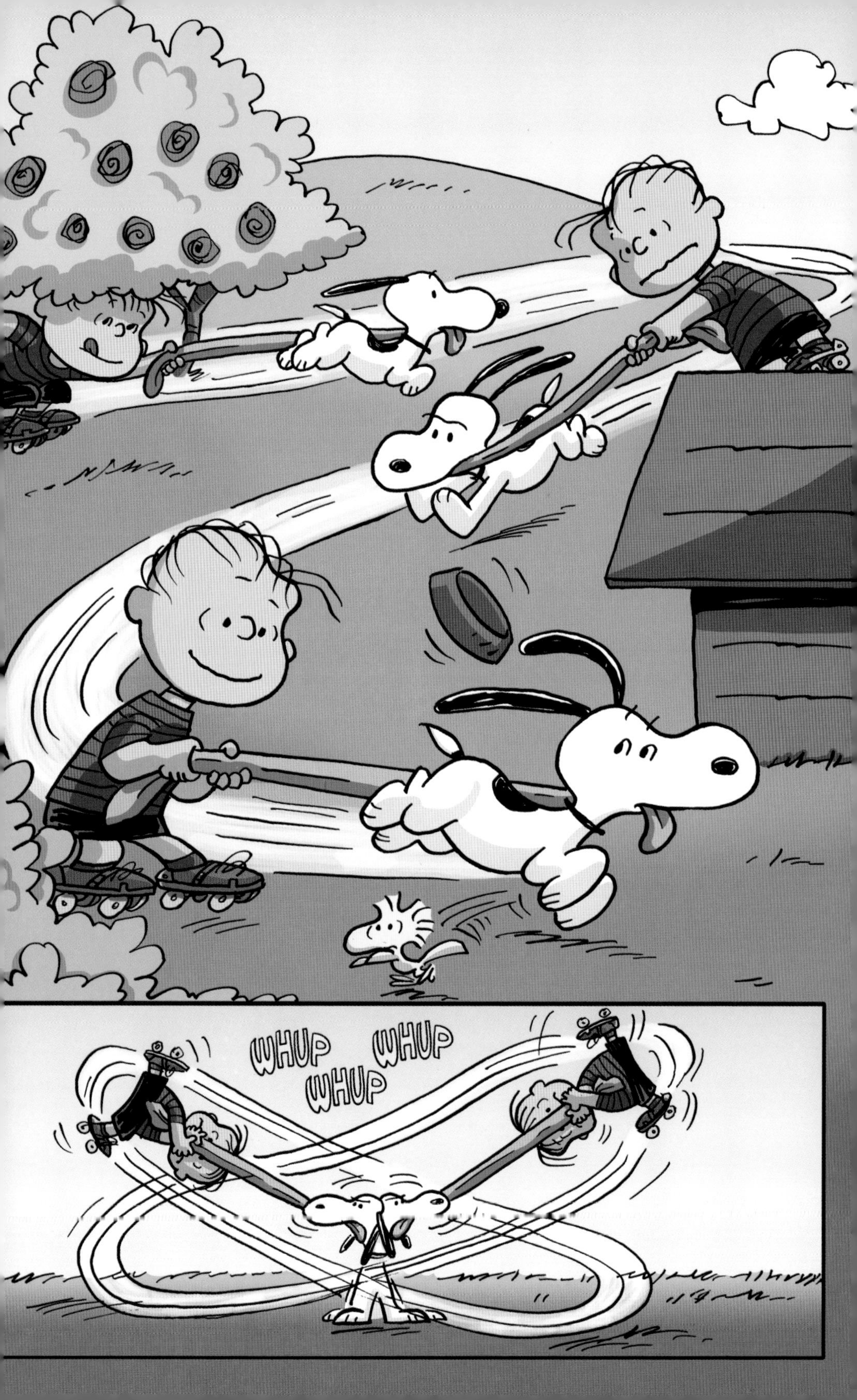
WHUP
WHUP
WHUP

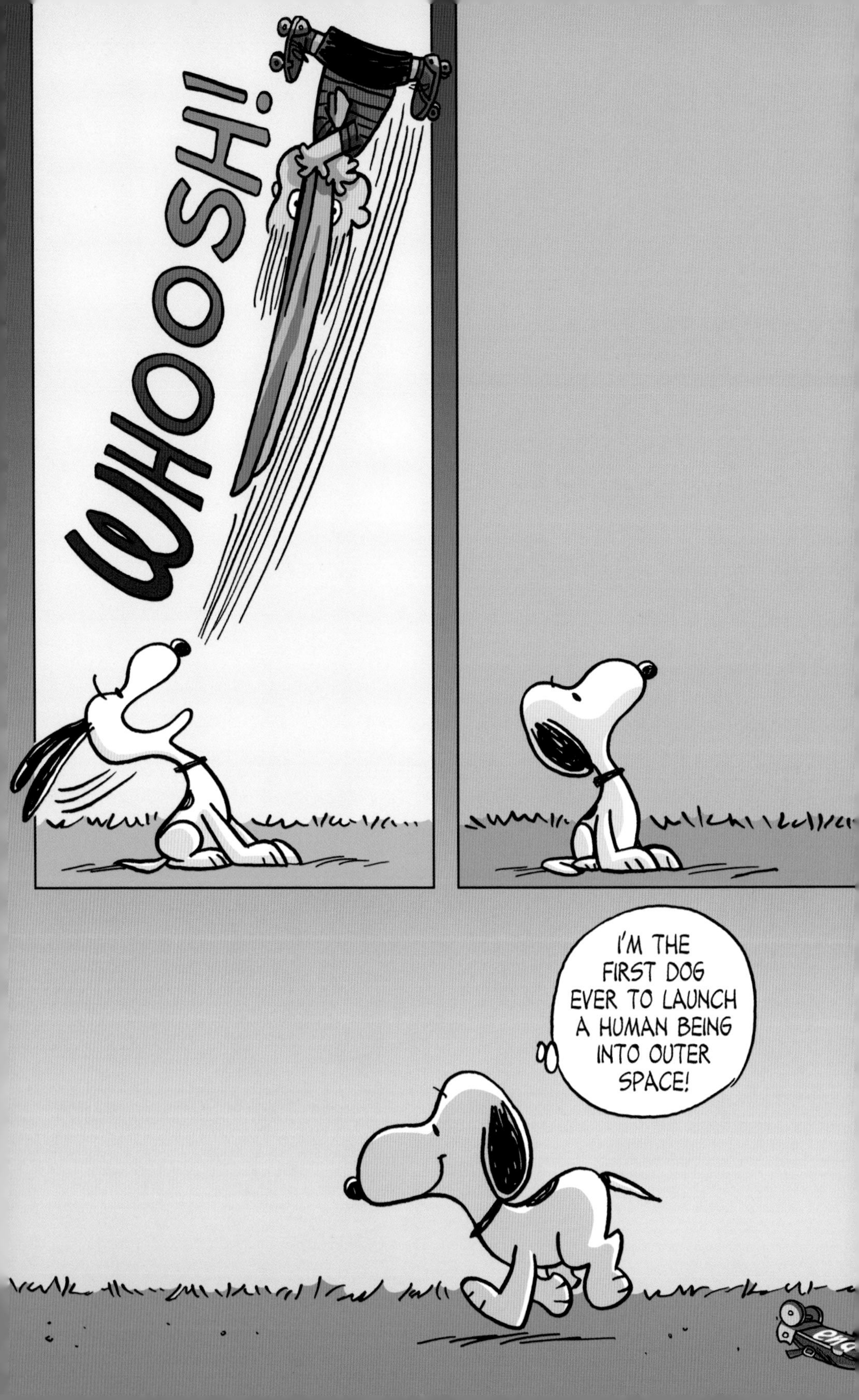
WHOOSH!
I'M THE FIRST DOG EVER TO LAUNCH A HUMAN BEING INTO OUTER SPACE!

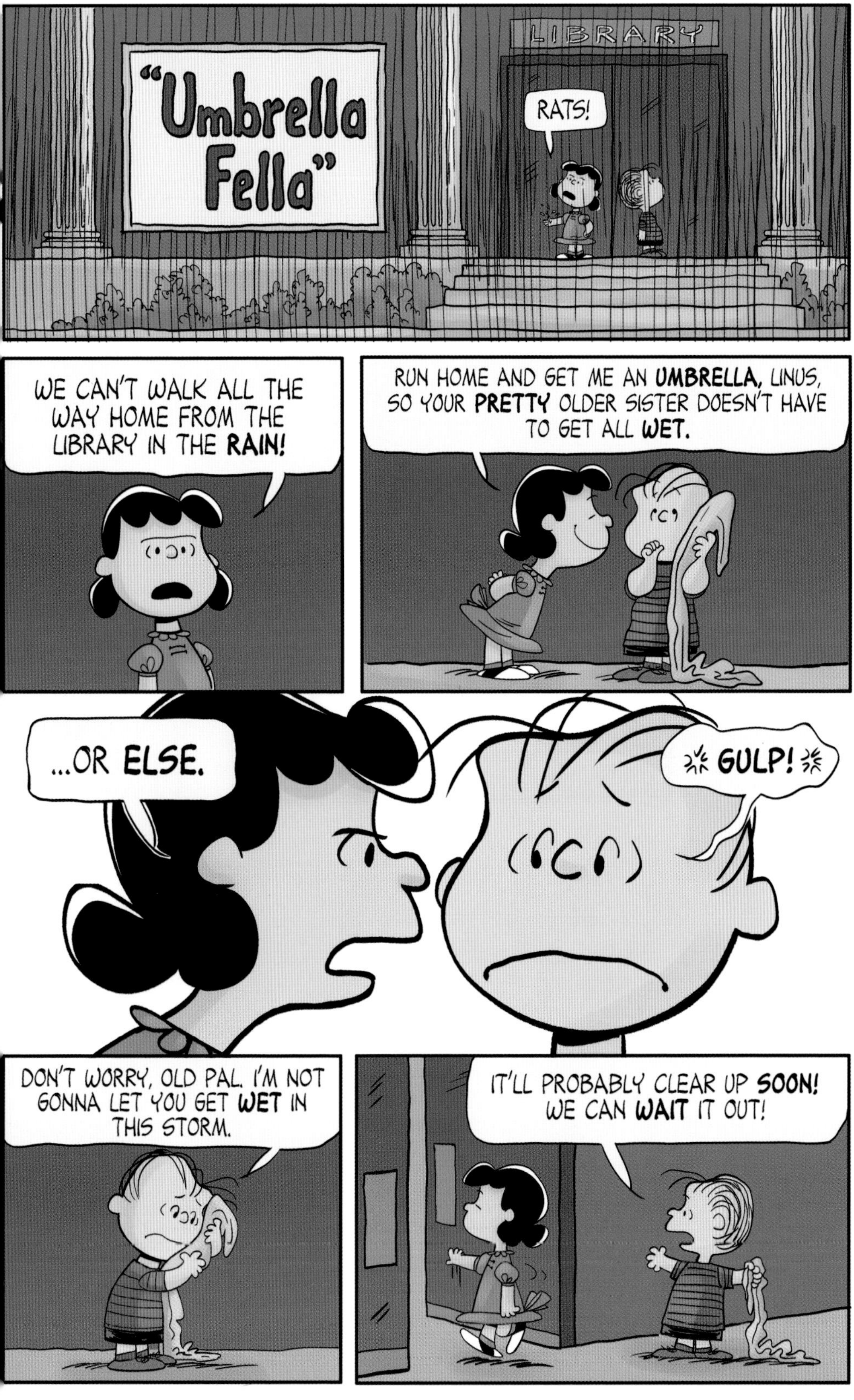

"Umbrella Fella"
LIBRARY
RATS!
WE CAN'T WALK ALL THE WAY HOME FROM THE LIBRARY IN THE RAIN!
RUN HOME AND GET ME AN UMBRELLA, LINUS, SO YOUR PRETTY OLDER SISTER DOESN'T HAVE TO GET ALL WET.
...OR ELSE.
GULP!
DON'T WORRY, OLD PAL. I'M NOT GONNA LET YOU GET WET IN THIS STORM.
IT'LL PROBABLY CLEAR UP SOON! WE CAN WAIT IT OUT!

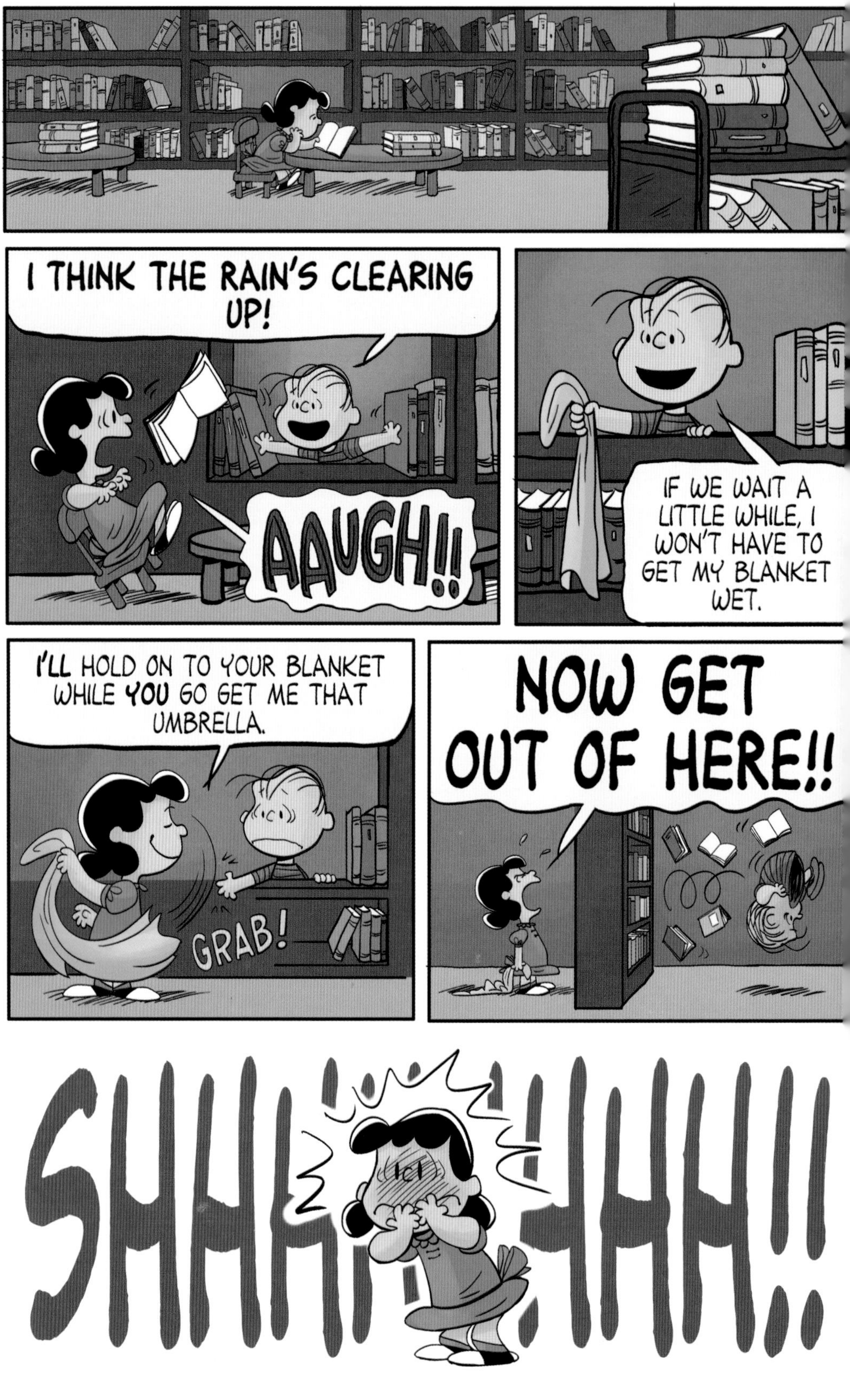
I THINK THE RAIN'S CLEARING UP!
AAUGH!!
IF WE WAIT A LITTLE WHILE, I WON'T HAVE TO GET MY BLANKET WET.
I'LL HOLD ON TO YOUR BLANKET WHILE YOU GO GET ME THAT UMBRELLA.
GRAB!
NOW GET OUT OF HERE!!
SHHHHHHH!!

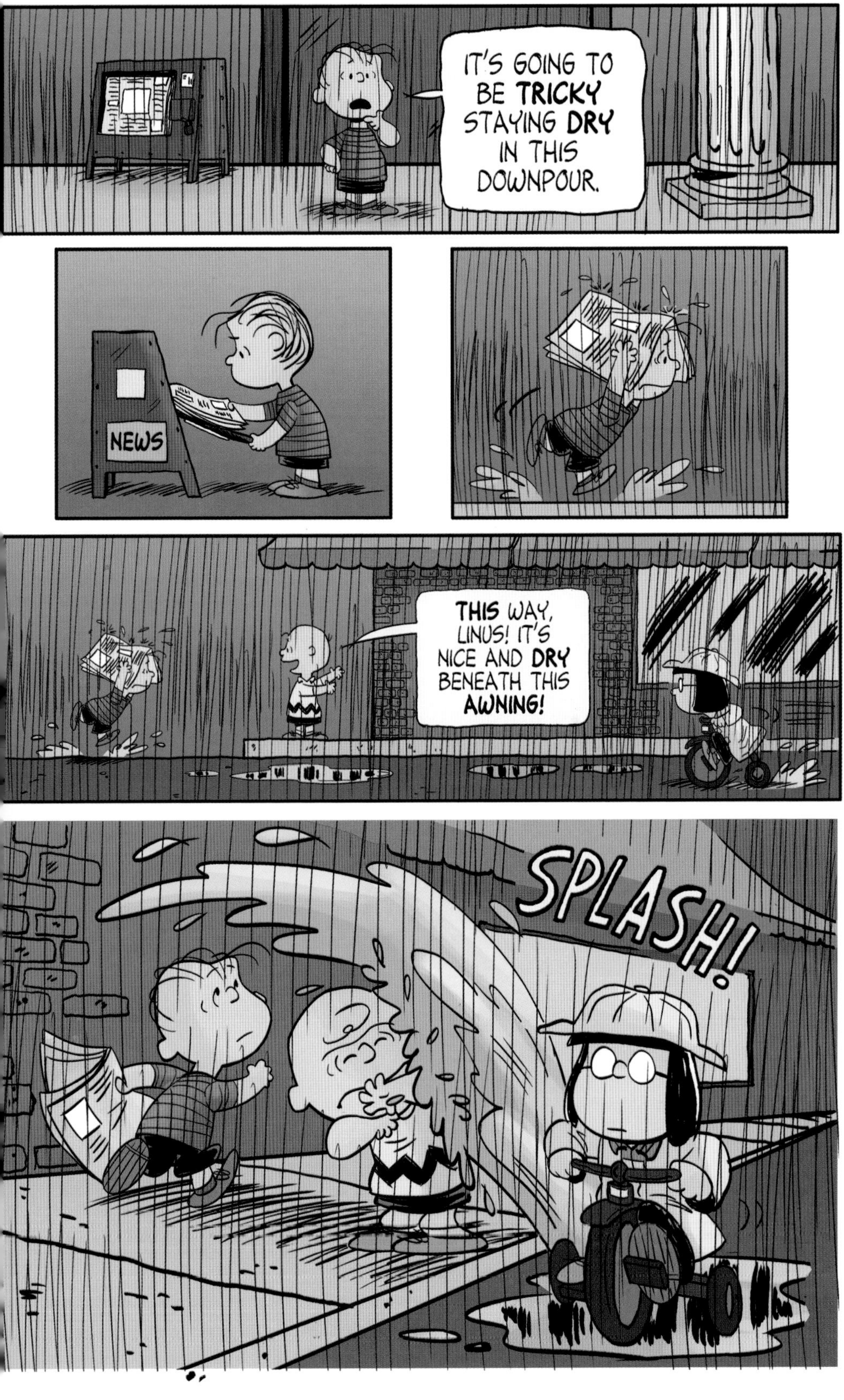
IT'S GOING TO BE **TRICKY** STAYING **DRY** IN THIS DOWNPOUR.
NEWS
THIS WAY, LINUS! IT'S NICE AND **DRY** BENEATH THIS **AWNING!**
SPLASH!

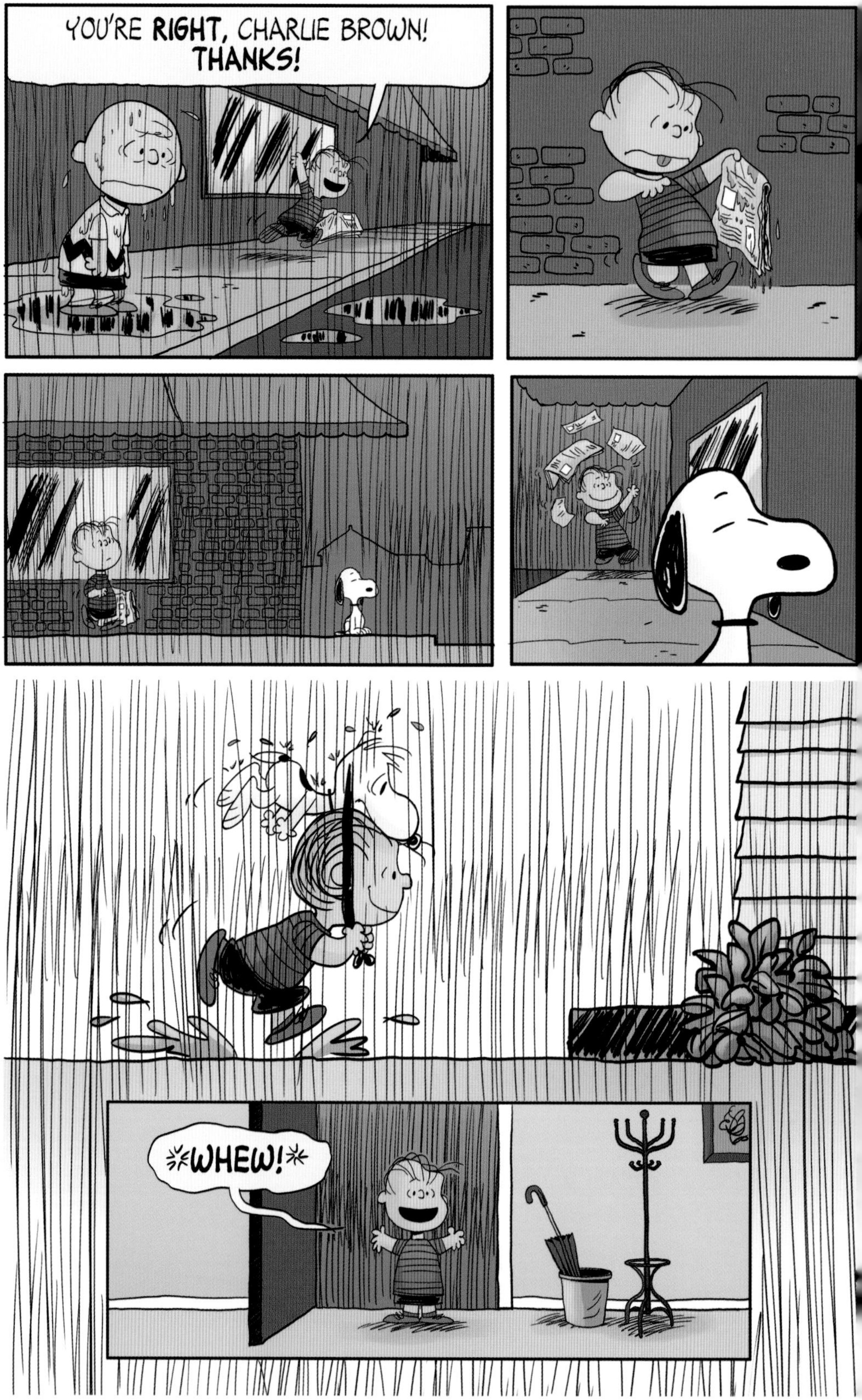
YOU'RE RIGHT, CHARLIE BROWN! THANKS!
WHEW!

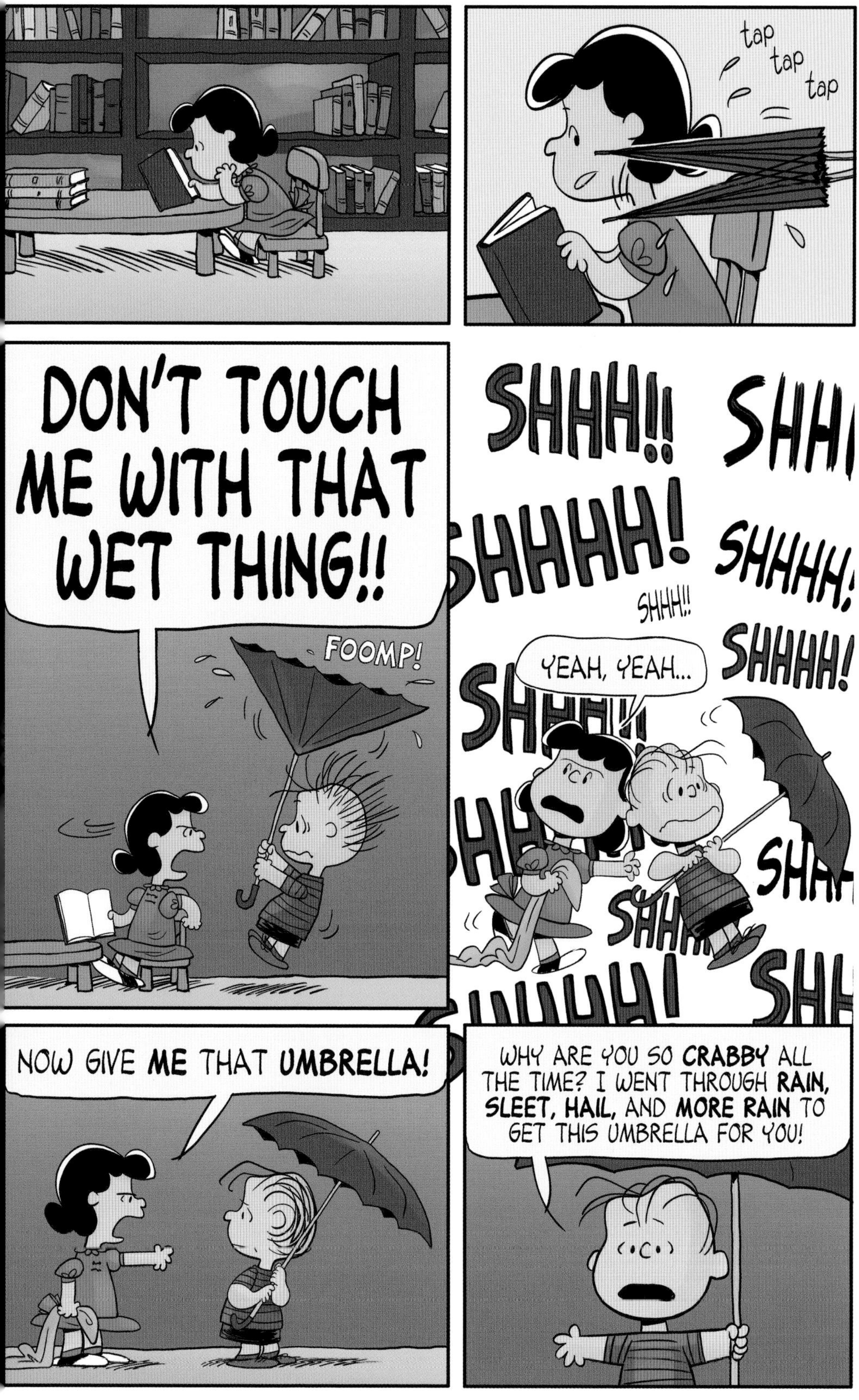

tap tap tap
DON'T TOUCH ME WITH THAT WET THING!!
FOOMP!
SHHH!!
SHHHH!
SHHHH!
SHHH!!
YEAH, YEAH...
SHHHH!
NOW GIVE ME THAT UMBRELLA!
WHY ARE YOU SO CRABBY ALL THE TIME? I WENT THROUGH RAIN, SLEET, HAIL, AND MORE RAIN TO GET THIS UMBRELLA FOR YOU!

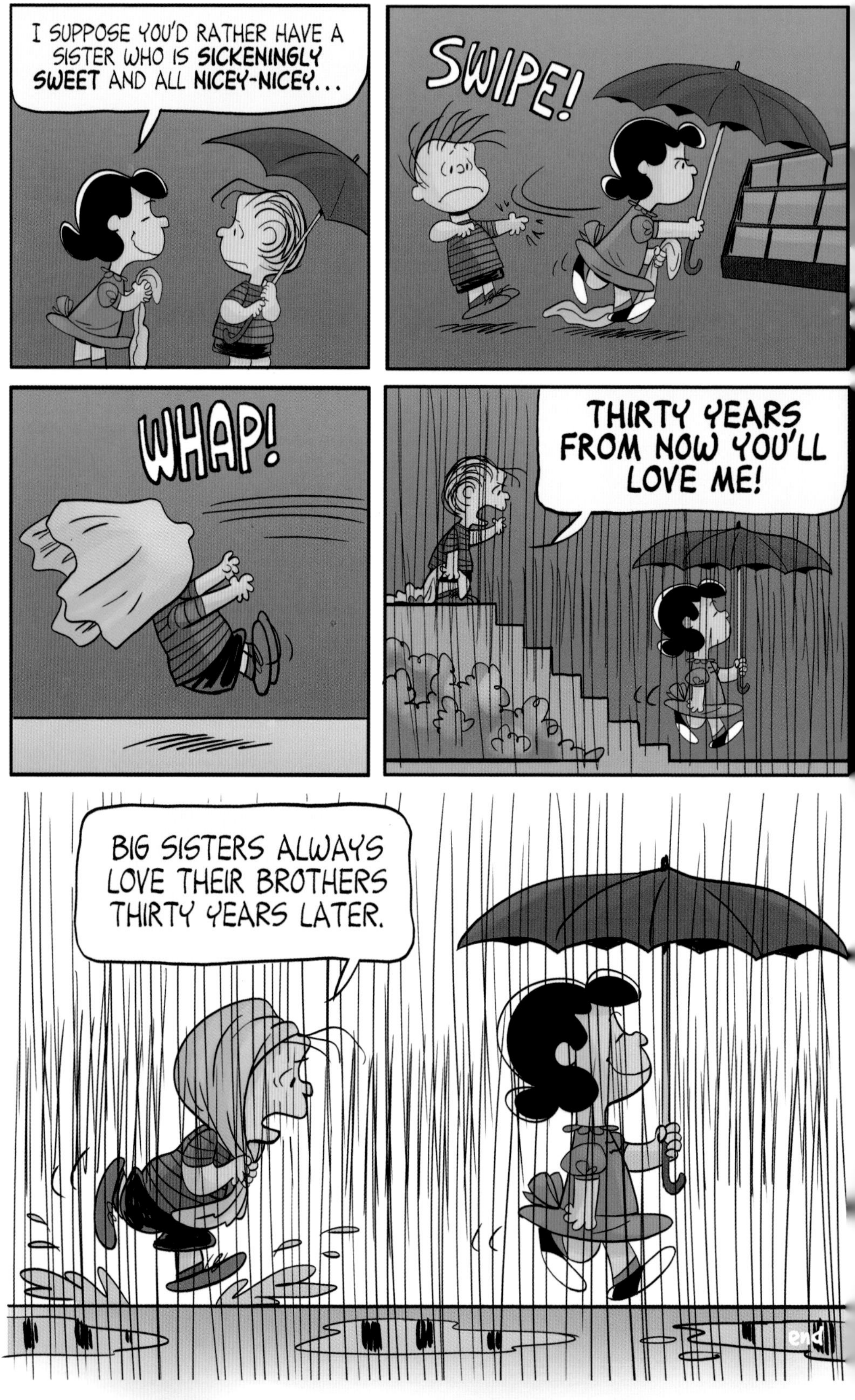
I SUPPOSE YOU'D RATHER HAVE A SISTER WHO IS SICKENINGLY SWEET AND ALL NICEY-NICEY...
SWIPE!
WHAP!
THIRTY YEARS FROM NOW YOU'LL LOVE ME!
BIG SISTERS ALWAYS LOVE THEIR BROTHERS THIRTY YEARS LATER.
end

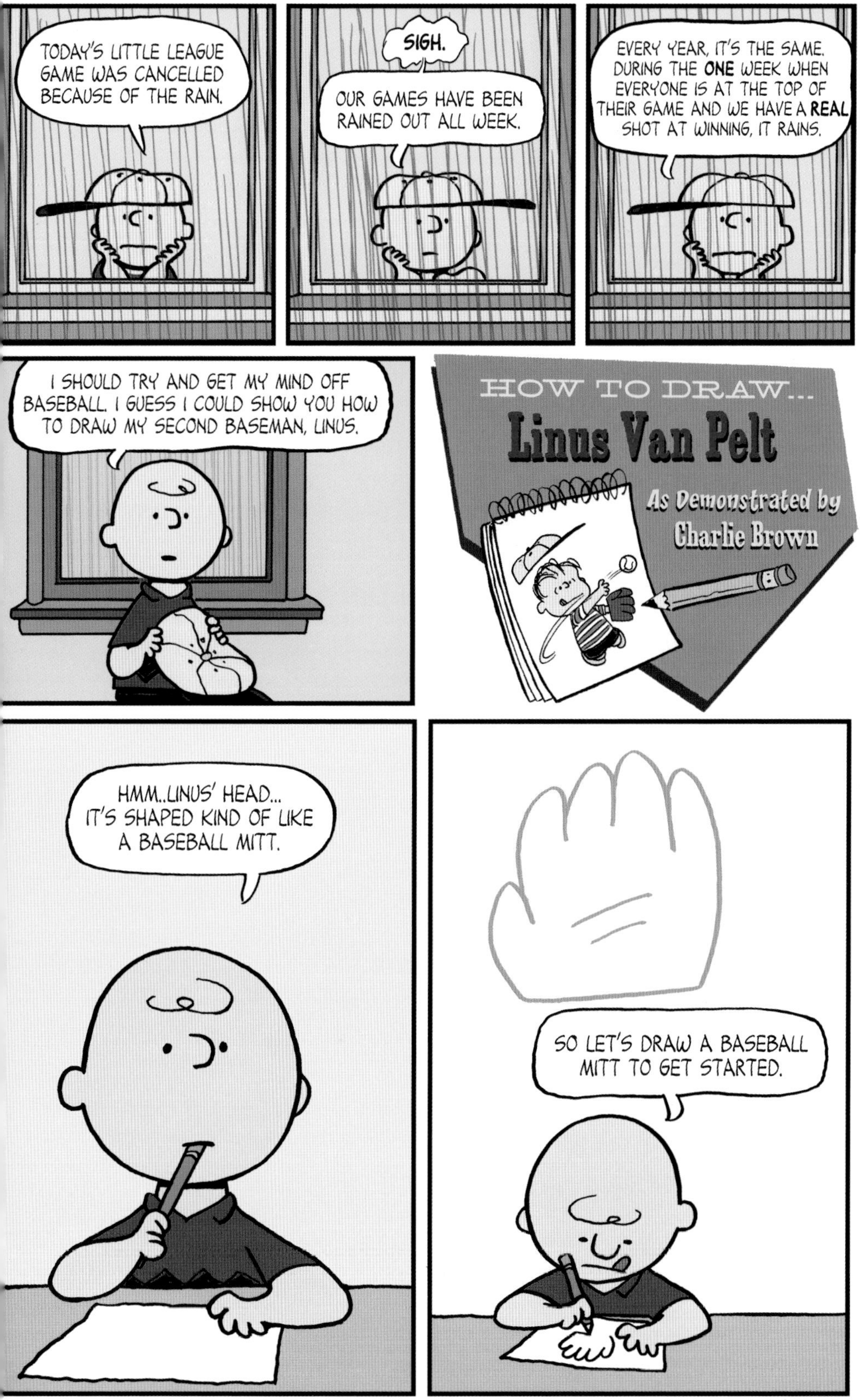
TODAY'S LITTLE LEAGUE GAME WAS CANCELLED BECAUSE OF THE RAIN.
SIGH.
OUR GAMES HAVE BEEN RAINED OUT ALL WEEK.
EVERY YEAR, IT'S THE SAME. DURING THE ONE WEEK WHEN EVERYONE IS AT THE TOP OF THEIR GAME AND WE HAVE A REAL SHOT AT WINNING, IT RAINS.
I SHOULD TRY AND GET MY MIND OFF BASEBALL. I GUESS I COULD SHOW YOU HOW TO DRAW MY SECOND BASEMAN, LINUS.
HOW TO DRAW...
Linus Van Pelt
As Demonstrated by Charlie Brown
HMM..LINUS' HEAD... IT'S SHAPED KIND OF LIKE A BASEBALL MITT.
SO LET'S DRAW A BASEBALL MITT TO GET STARTED.

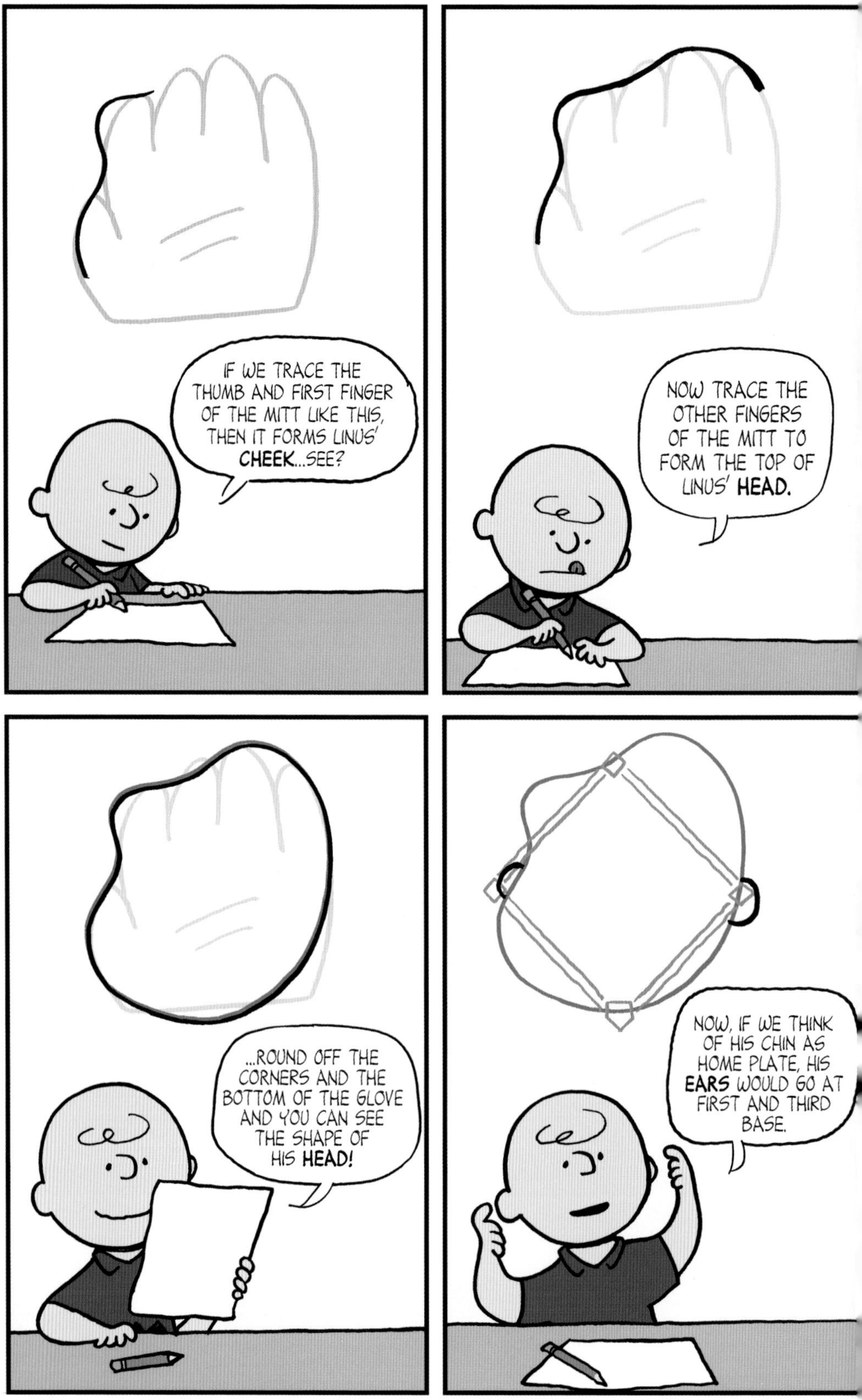
IF WE TRACE THE THUMB AND FIRST FINGER OF THE MITT LIKE THIS, THEN IT FORMS LINUS' **CHEEK**...SEE?
NOW TRACE THE OTHER FINGERS OF THE MITT TO FORM THE TOP OF LINUS' **HEAD.**
...ROUND OFF THE CORNERS AND THE BOTTOM OF THE GLOVE AND YOU CAN SEE THE SHAPE OF HIS **HEAD!**
NOW, IF WE THINK OF HIS CHIN AS HOME PLATE, HIS **EARS** WOULD GO AT FIRST AND THIRD BASE.

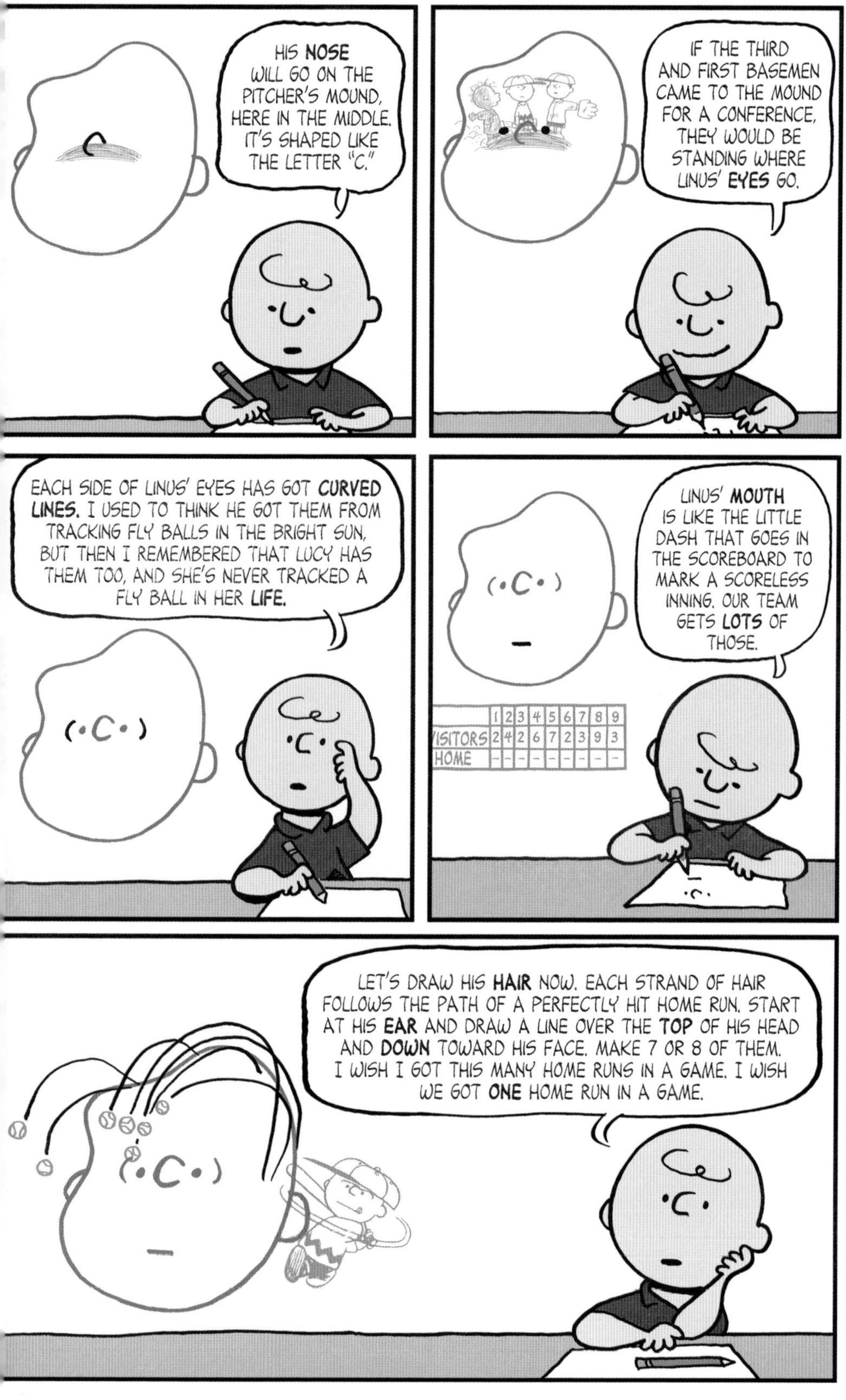
HIS **NOSE** WILL GO ON THE PITCHER'S MOUND, HERE IN THE MIDDLE. IT'S SHAPED LIKE THE LETTER "C."
IF THE THIRD AND FIRST BASEMEN CAME TO THE MOUND FOR A CONFERENCE, THEY WOULD BE STANDING WHERE LINUS' **EYES** GO.
EACH SIDE OF LINUS' EYES HAS GOT **CURVED LINES.** I USED TO THINK HE GOT THEM FROM TRACKING FLY BALLS IN THE BRIGHT SUN, BUT THEN I REMEMBERED THAT LUCY HAS THEM TOO, AND SHE'S NEVER TRACKED A FLY BALL IN HER **LIFE.**
LINUS' **MOUTH** IS LIKE THE LITTLE DASH THAT GOES IN THE SCOREBOARD TO MARK A SCORELESS INNING. OUR TEAM GETS **LOTS** OF THOSE.
1 2 3 4 5 6 7 8 9
VISITORS 2 4 2 6 7 2 3 9 3
HOME - - - - - - - - -
LET'S DRAW HIS **HAIR** NOW. EACH STRAND OF HAIR FOLLOWS THE PATH OF A PERFECTLY HIT HOME RUN. START AT HIS **EAR** AND DRAW A LINE OVER THE **TOP** OF HIS HEAD AND **DOWN** TOWARD HIS FACE. MAKE 7 OR 8 OF THEM. I WISH I GOT THIS MANY HOME RUNS IN A GAME. I WISH WE GOT **ONE** HOME RUN IN A GAME.

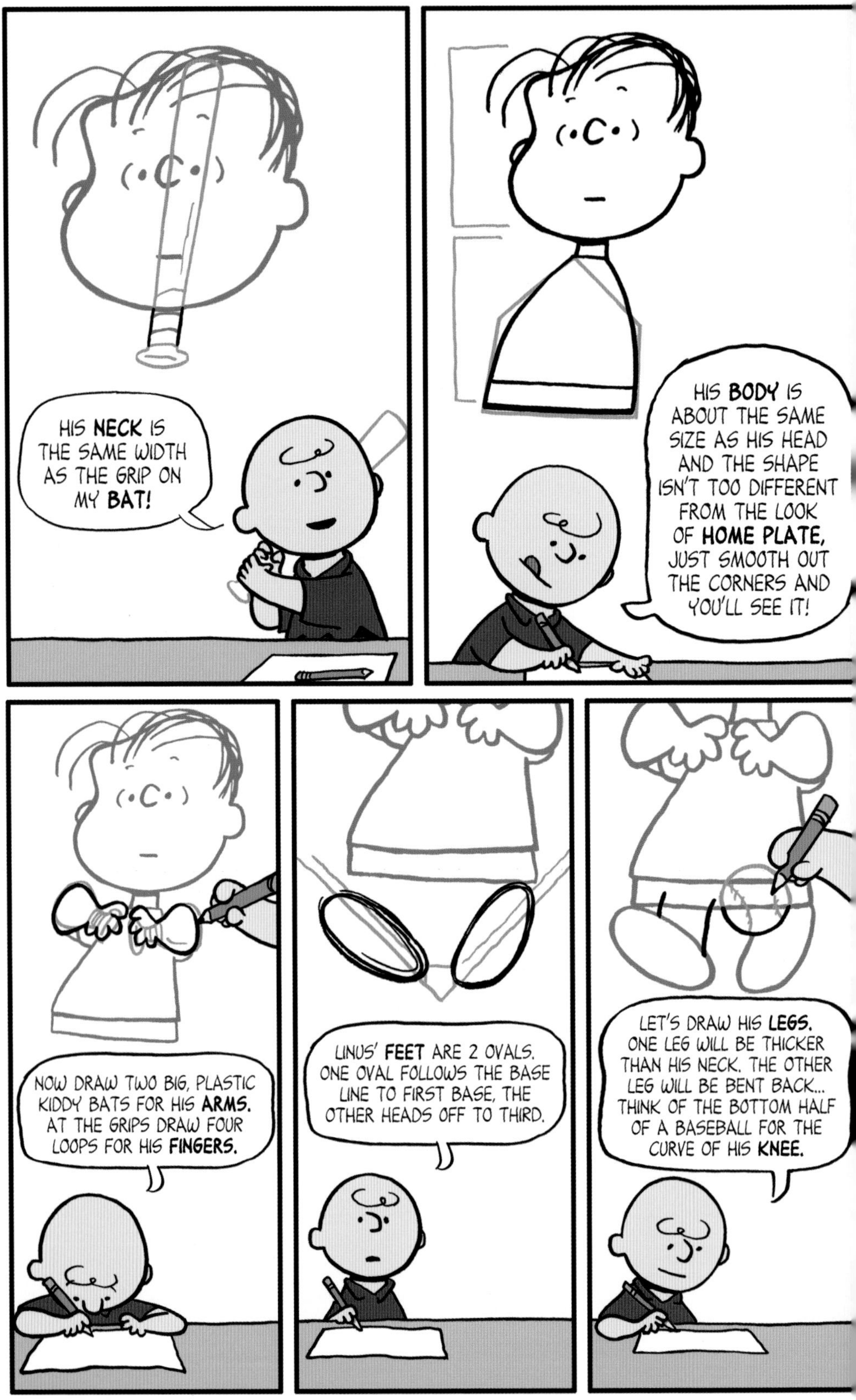
HIS **NECK** IS THE SAME WIDTH AS THE GRIP ON MY **BAT!**
HIS **BODY** IS ABOUT THE SAME SIZE AS HIS HEAD AND THE SHAPE ISN'T TOO DIFFERENT FROM THE LOOK OF **HOME PLATE,** JUST SMOOTH OUT THE CORNERS AND YOU'LL SEE IT!
NOW DRAW TWO BIG, PLASTIC KIDDY BATS FOR HIS **ARMS.** AT THE GRIPS DRAW FOUR LOOPS FOR HIS **FINGERS.**
LINUS' **FEET** ARE 2 OVALS. ONE OVAL FOLLOWS THE BASE LINE TO FIRST BASE, THE OTHER HEADS OFF TO THIRD.
LET'S DRAW HIS **LEGS.** ONE LEG WILL BE THICKER THAN HIS NECK. THE OTHER LEG WILL BE BENT BACK... THINK OF THE BOTTOM HALF OF A BASEBALL FOR THE CURVE OF HIS **KNEE.**

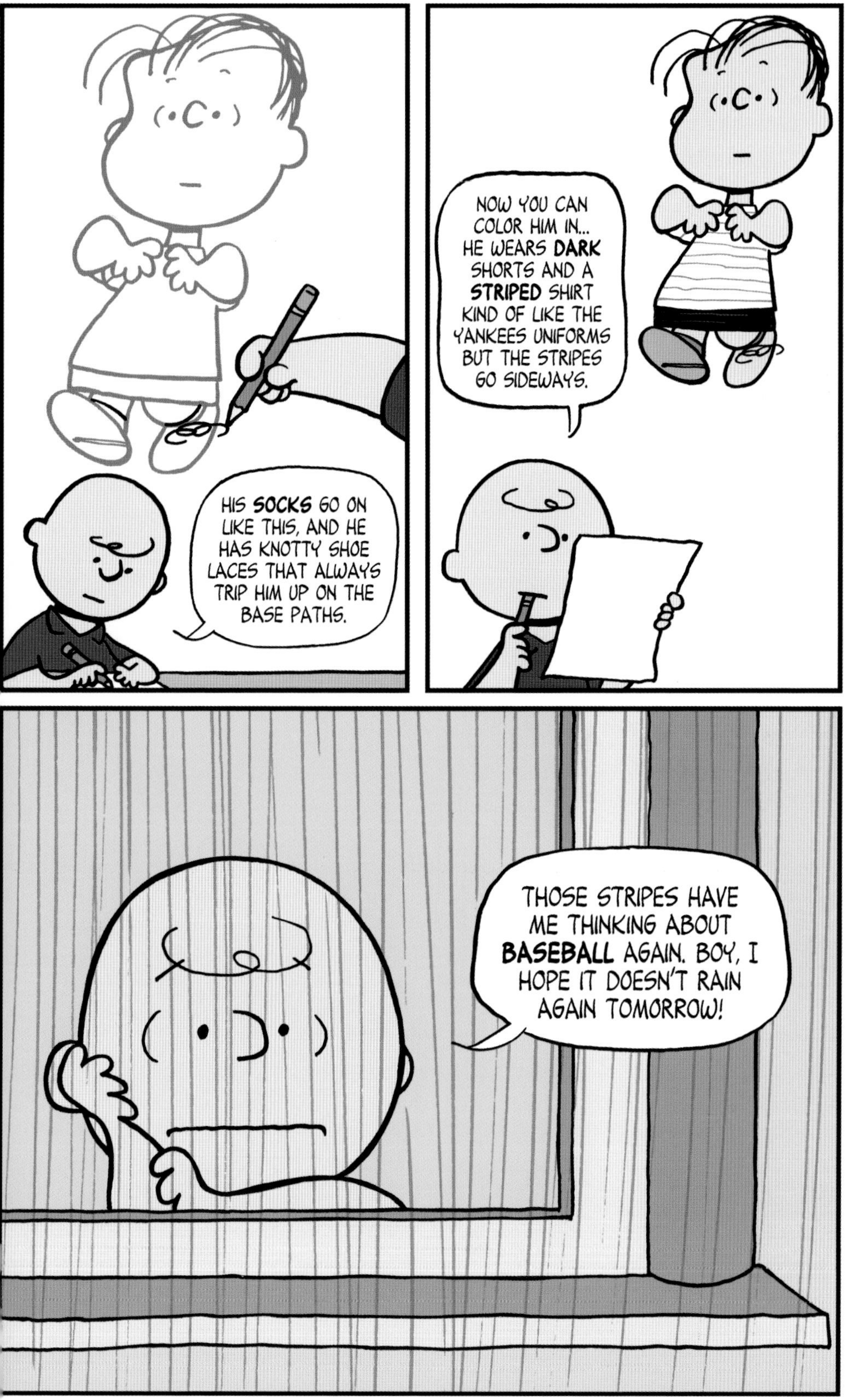
HIS **SOCKS** GO ON LIKE THIS, AND HE HAS KNOTTY SHOE LACES THAT ALWAYS TRIP HIM UP ON THE BASE PATHS.
NOW YOU CAN COLOR HIM IN... HE WEARS **DARK** SHORTS AND A **STRIPED** SHIRT KIND OF LIKE THE YANKEES UNIFORMS BUT THE STRIPES GO SIDEWAYS.
THOSE STRIPES HAVE ME THINKING ABOUT **BASEBALL** AGAIN. BOY, I HOPE IT DOESN'T RAIN AGAIN TOMORROW!

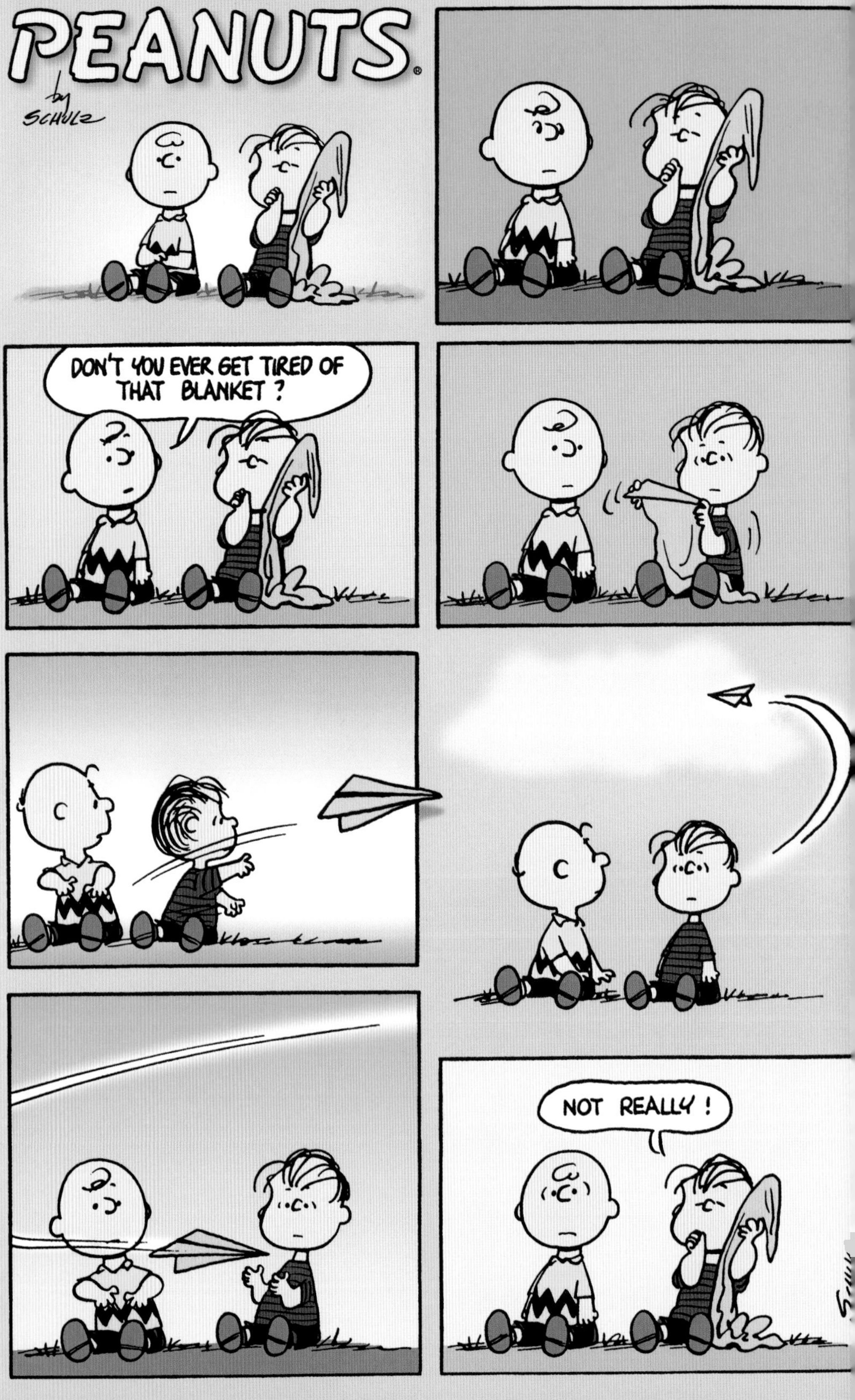
PEANUTS
by SCHULZ
DON'T YOU EVER GET TIRED OF THAT BLANKET ?
NOT REALLY !

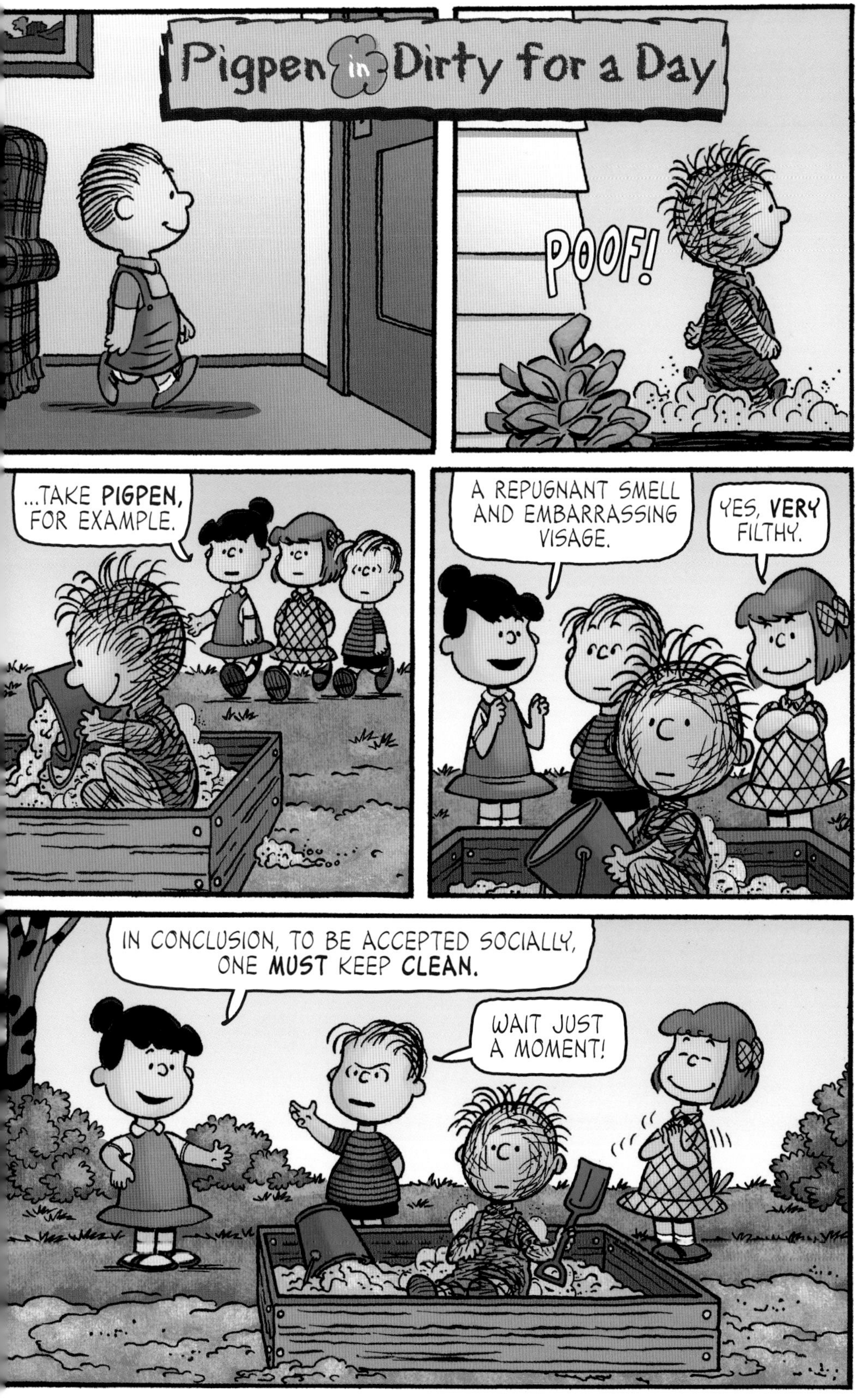
Pigpen in Dirty for a Day
POOF!
...TAKE PIGPEN, FOR EXAMPLE.
A REPUGNANT SMELL AND EMBARRASSING VISAGE.
YES, VERY FILTHY.
IN CONCLUSION, TO BE ACCEPTED SOCIALLY, ONE MUST KEEP CLEAN.
WAIT JUST A MOMENT!

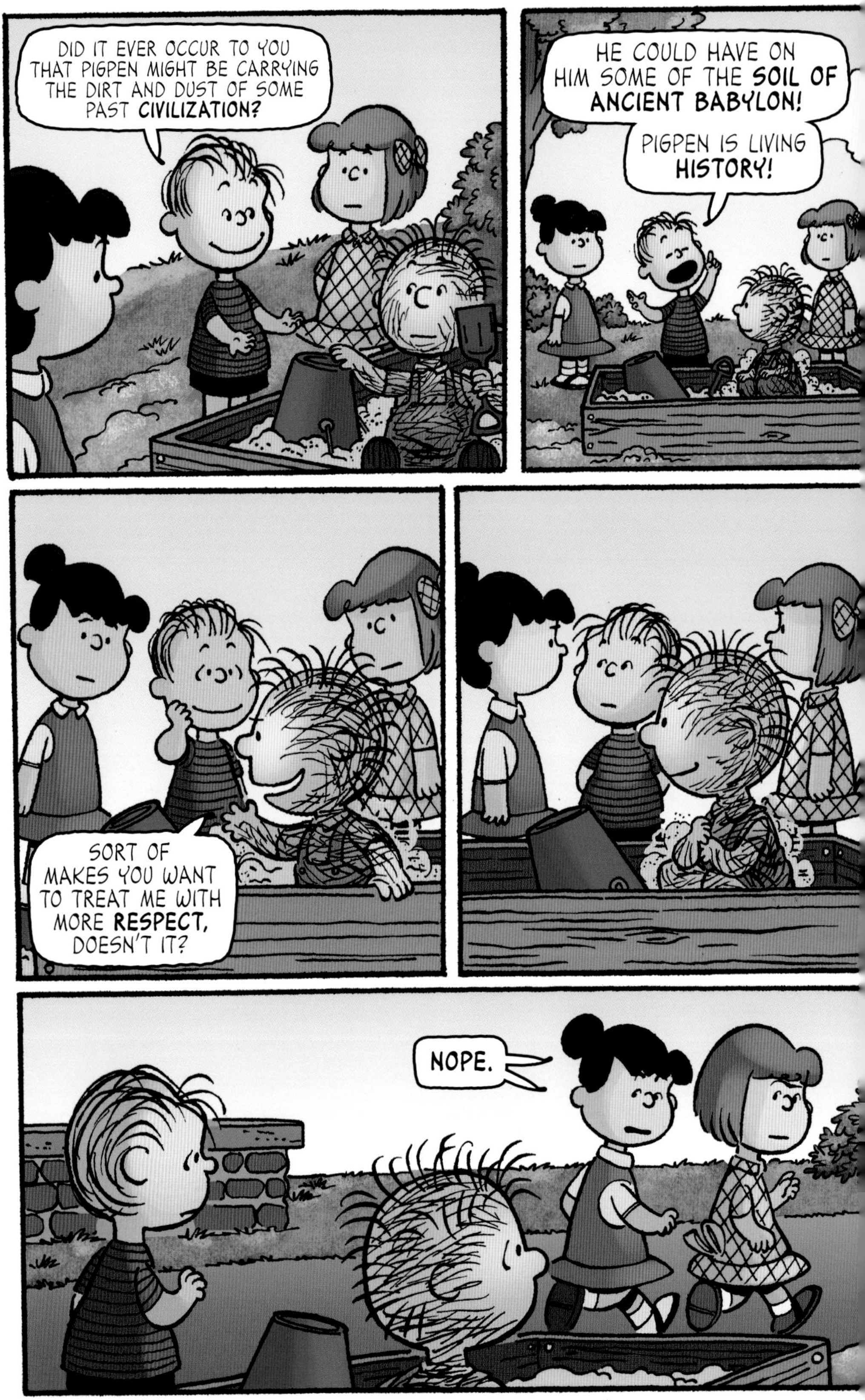
DID IT EVER OCCUR TO YOU THAT PIGPEN MIGHT BE CARRYING THE DIRT AND DUST OF SOME PAST CIVILIZATION?
HE COULD HAVE ON HIM SOME OF THE SOIL OF ANCIENT BABYLON!
PIGPEN IS LIVING HISTORY!
SORT OF MAKES YOU WANT TO TREAT ME WITH MORE RESPECT, DOESN'T IT?
NOPE.

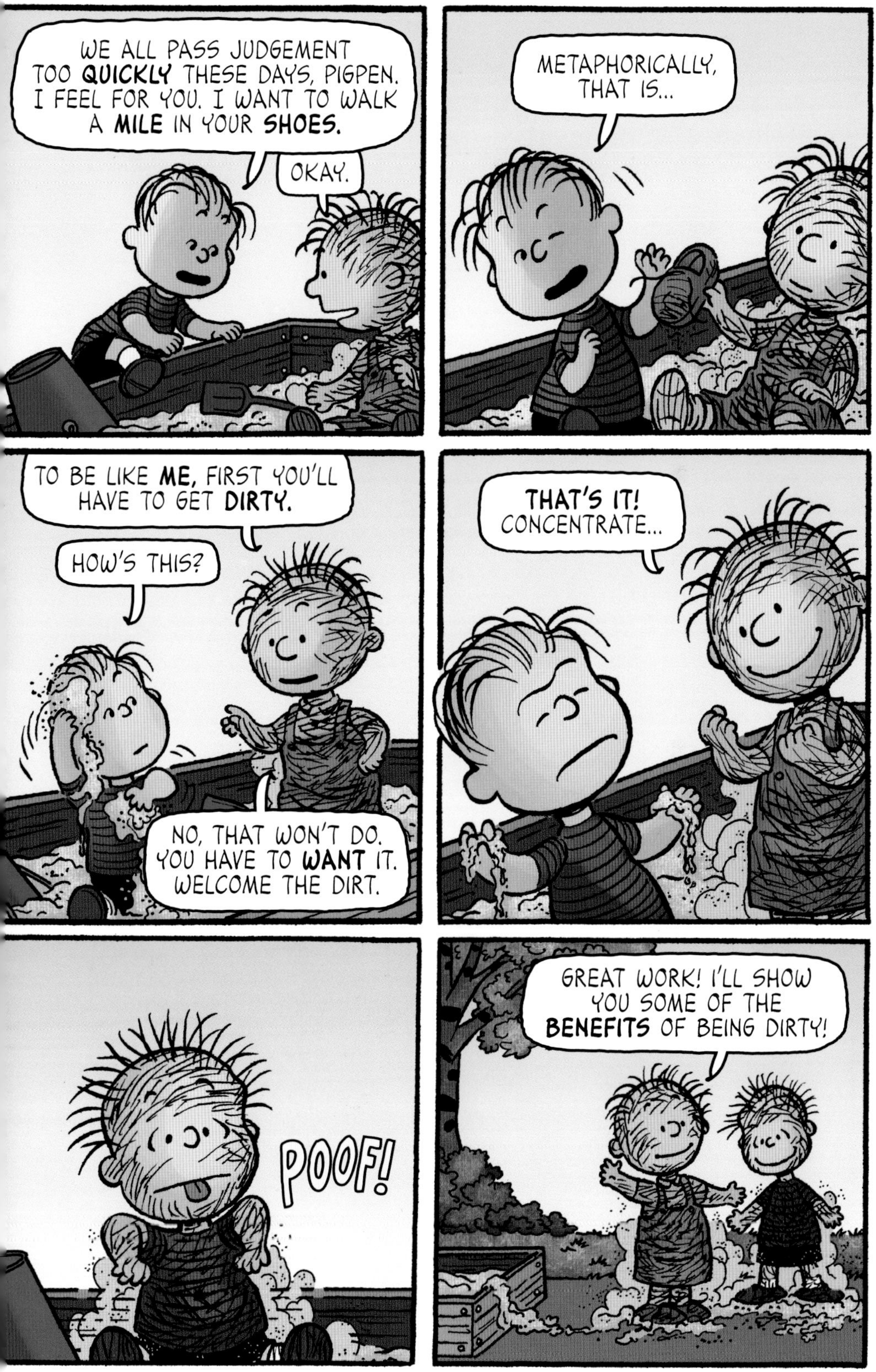
WE ALL PASS JUDGEMENT TOO QUICKLY THESE DAYS, PIGPEN. I FEEL FOR YOU. I WANT TO WALK A MILE IN YOUR SHOES.
OKAY.
METAPHORICALLY, THAT IS...
TO BE LIKE ME, FIRST YOU'LL HAVE TO GET DIRTY.
HOW'S THIS?
NO, THAT WON'T DO. YOU HAVE TO WANT IT. WELCOME THE DIRT.
THAT'S IT! CONCENTRATE...
POOF!
GREAT WORK! I'LL SHOW YOU SOME OF THE BENEFITS OF BEING DIRTY!

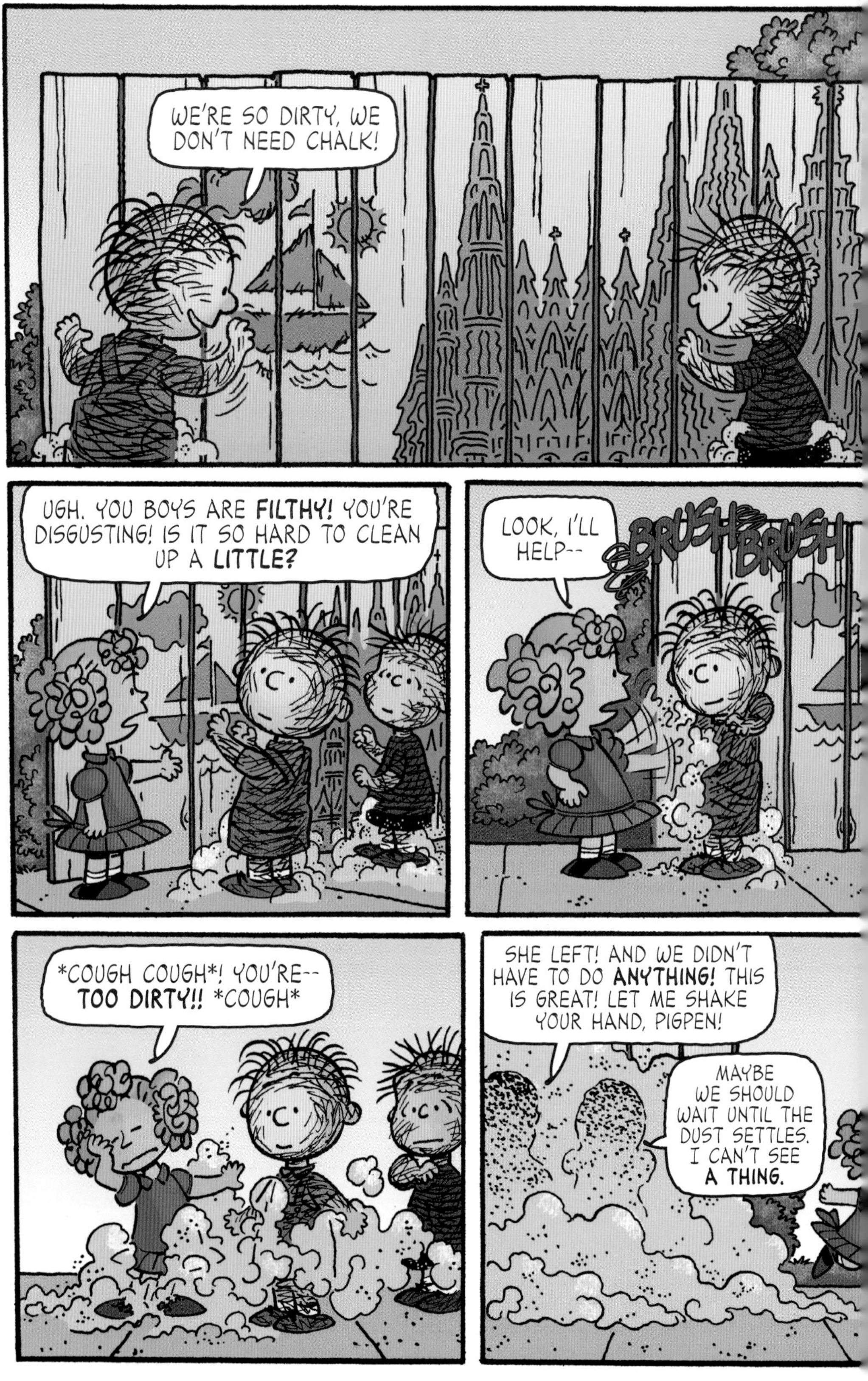
WE'RE SO DIRTY, WE DON'T NEED CHALK!
UGH. YOU BOYS ARE FILTHY! YOU'RE DISGUSTING! IS IT SO HARD TO CLEAN UP A LITTLE?
LOOK, I'LL HELP--
BRUSH BRUSH
COUGH COUGH! YOU'RE-- TOO DIRTY!! *COUGH*
SHE LEFT! AND WE DIDN'T HAVE TO DO ANYTHING! THIS IS GREAT! LET ME SHAKE YOUR HAND, PIGPEN!
MAYBE WE SHOULD WAIT UNTIL THE DUST SETTLES. I CAN'T SEE A THING.

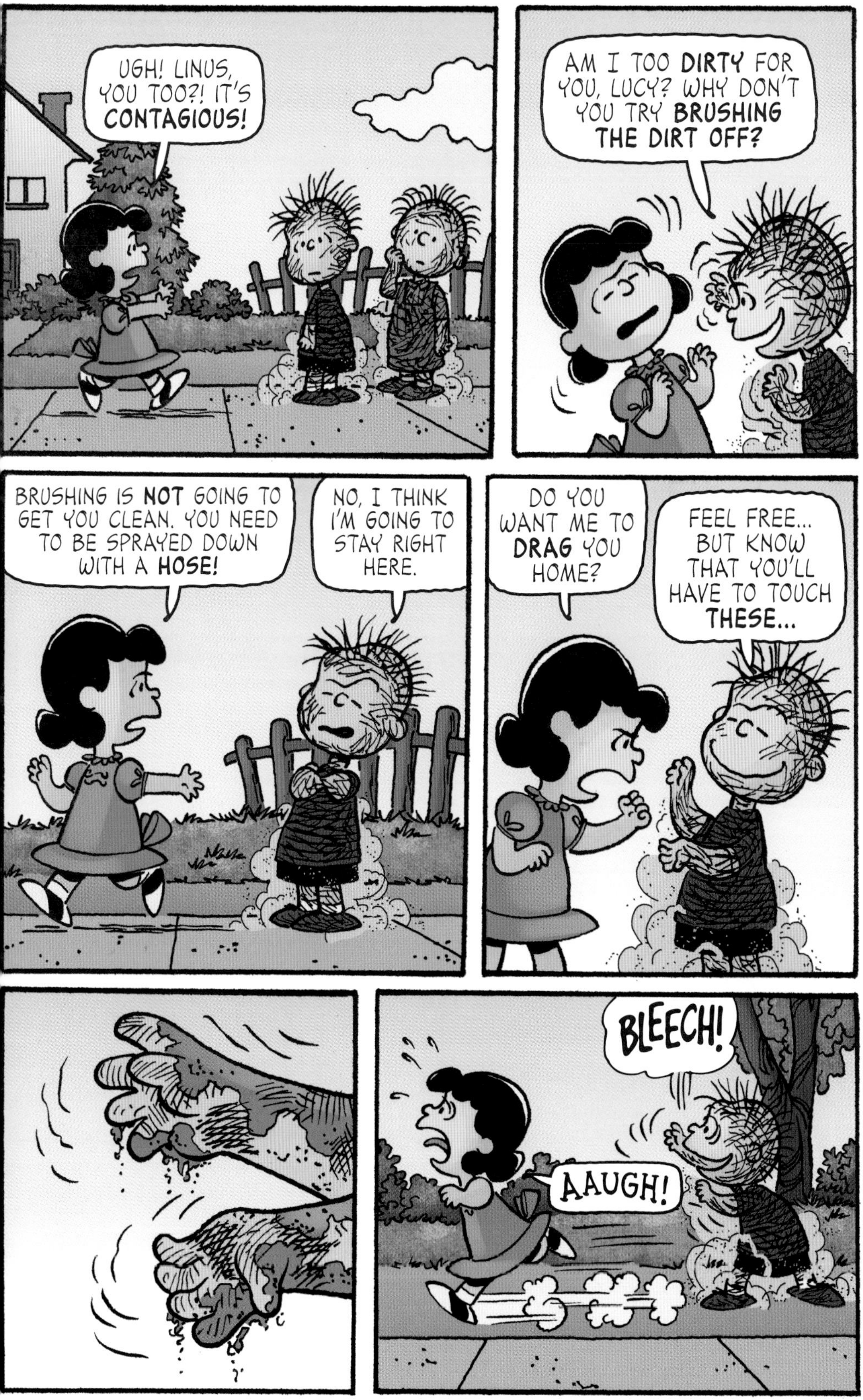
UGH! LINUS, YOU TOO?! IT'S CONTAGIOUS!
AM I TOO DIRTY FOR YOU, LUCY? WHY DON'T YOU TRY BRUSHING THE DIRT OFF?
BRUSHING IS NOT GOING TO GET YOU CLEAN. YOU NEED TO BE SPRAYED DOWN WITH A HOSE!
NO, I THINK I'M GOING TO STAY RIGHT HERE.
DO YOU WANT ME TO DRAG YOU HOME?
FEEL FREE... BUT KNOW THAT YOU'LL HAVE TO TOUCH THESE...
BLEECH!
AAUGH!

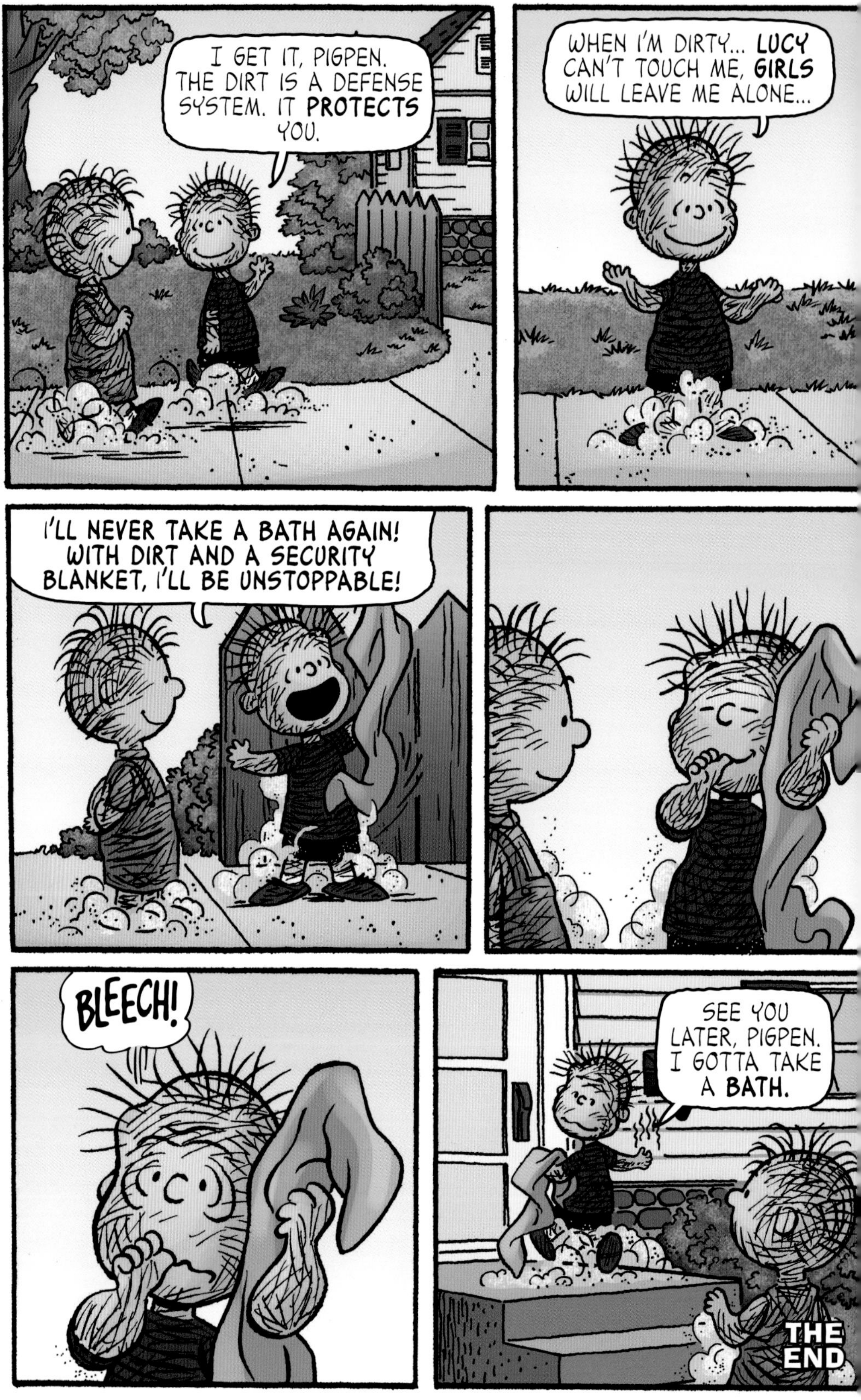
I GET IT, PIGPEN. THE DIRT IS A DEFENSE SYSTEM. IT **PROTECTS** YOU.
WHEN I'M DIRTY... **LUCY** CAN'T TOUCH ME, **GIRLS** WILL LEAVE ME ALONE...
I'LL NEVER TAKE A BATH AGAIN! WITH DIRT AND A SECURITY BLANKET, I'LL BE UNSTOPPABLE!
BLEECH!
SEE YOU LATER, PIGPEN. I GOTTA TAKE A **BATH.**
THE END

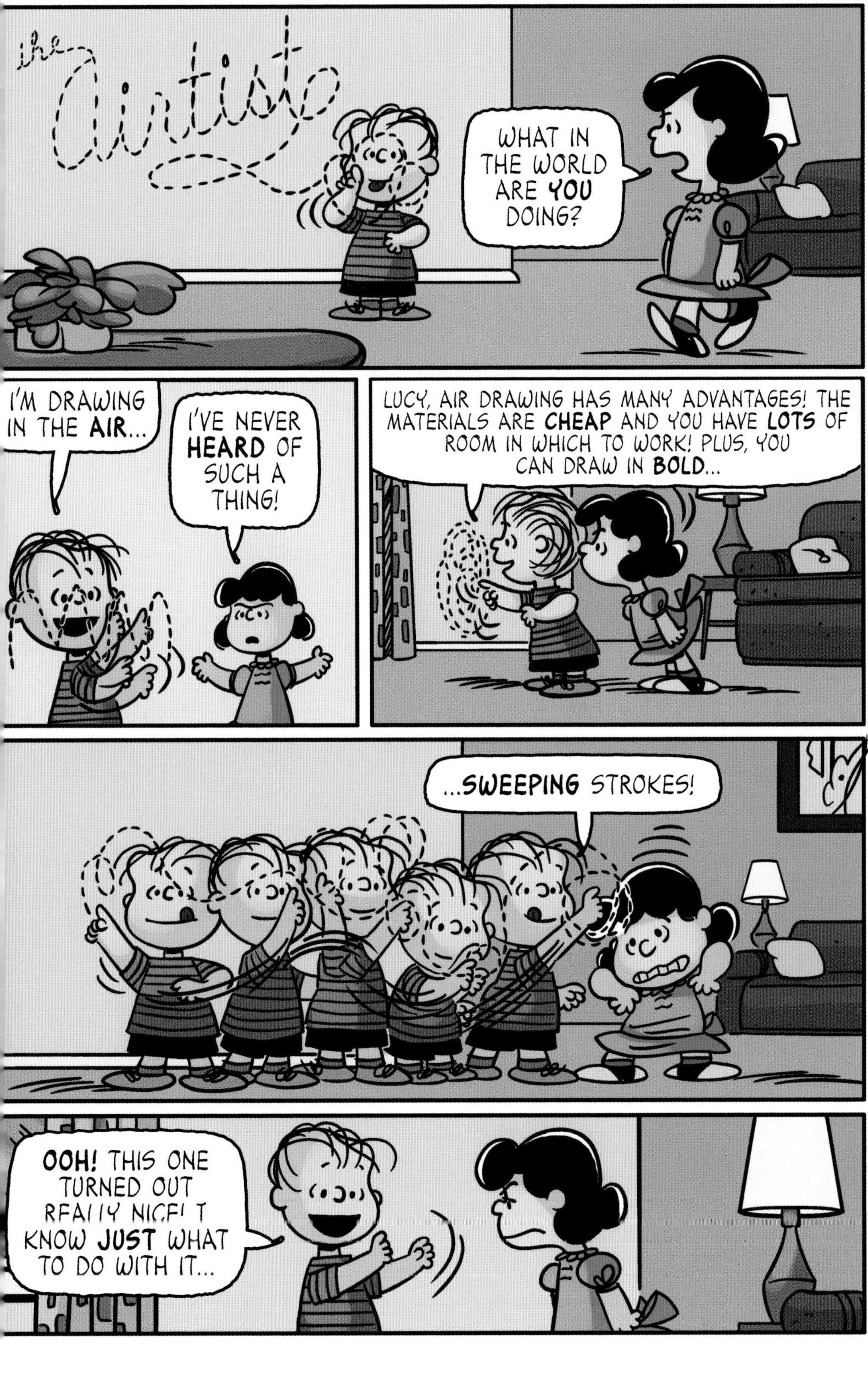
the Artist
WHAT IN THE WORLD ARE **YOU** DOING?
I'M DRAWING IN THE **AIR**...
I'VE NEVER **HEARD** OF SUCH A THING!
LUCY, AIR DRAWING HAS MANY ADVANTAGES! THE MATERIALS ARE **CHEAP** AND YOU HAVE **LOTS** OF ROOM IN WHICH TO WORK! PLUS, YOU CAN DRAW IN **BOLD**...
...**SWEEPING** STROKES!
OOH! THIS ONE TURNED OUT REALLY NICE! I KNOW **JUST** WHAT TO DO WITH IT...

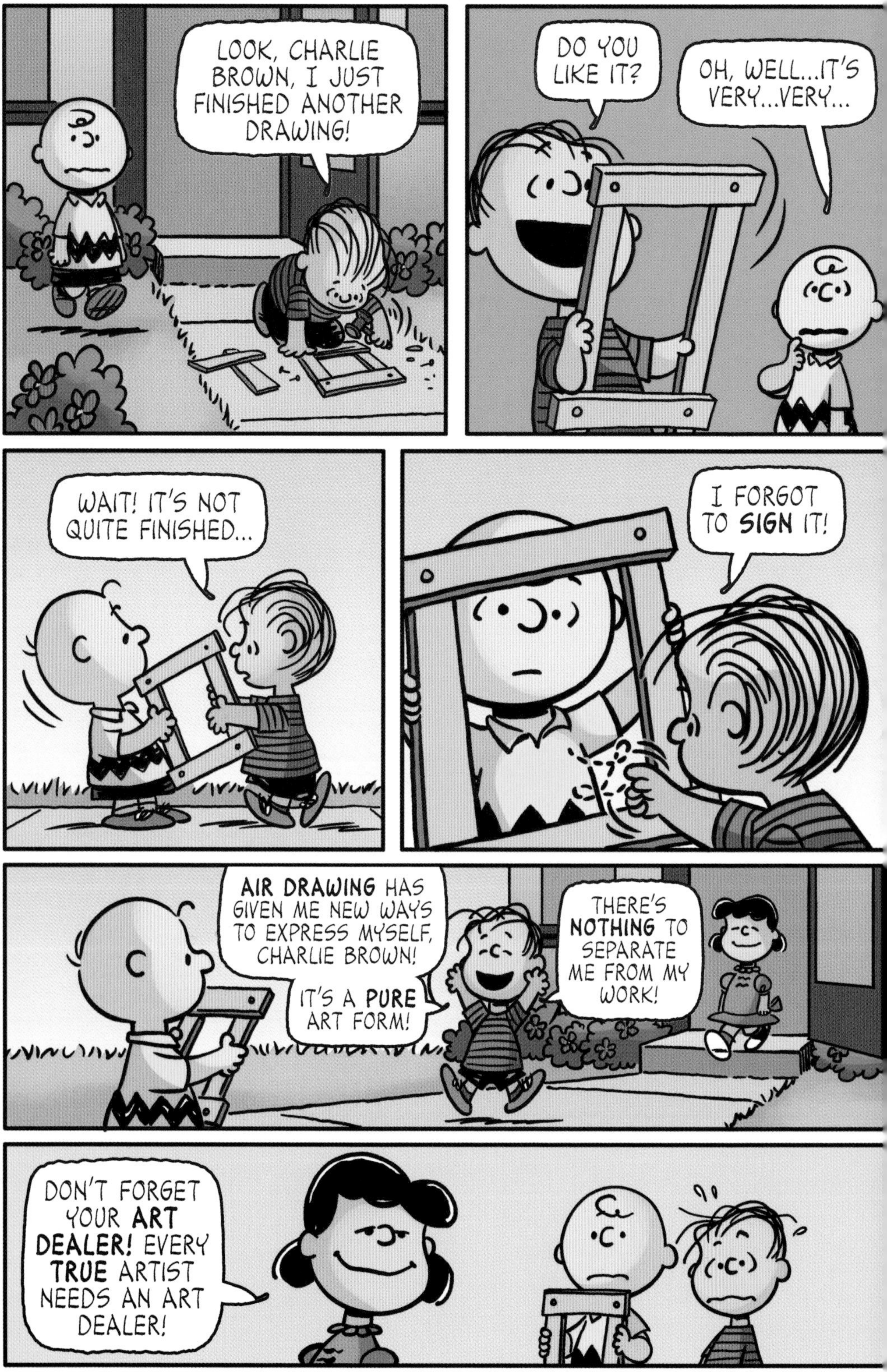
LOOK, CHARLIE BROWN, I JUST FINISHED ANOTHER DRAWING!
DO YOU LIKE IT?
OH, WELL...IT'S VERY...VERY...
WAIT! IT'S NOT QUITE FINISHED...
I FORGOT TO **SIGN** IT!
AIR DRAWING HAS GIVEN ME NEW WAYS TO EXPRESS MYSELF, CHARLIE BROWN!
IT'S A **PURE** ART FORM!
THERE'S **NOTHING** TO SEPARATE ME FROM MY WORK!
DON'T FORGET YOUR **ART DEALER!** EVERY **TRUE** ARTIST NEEDS AN ART DEALER!

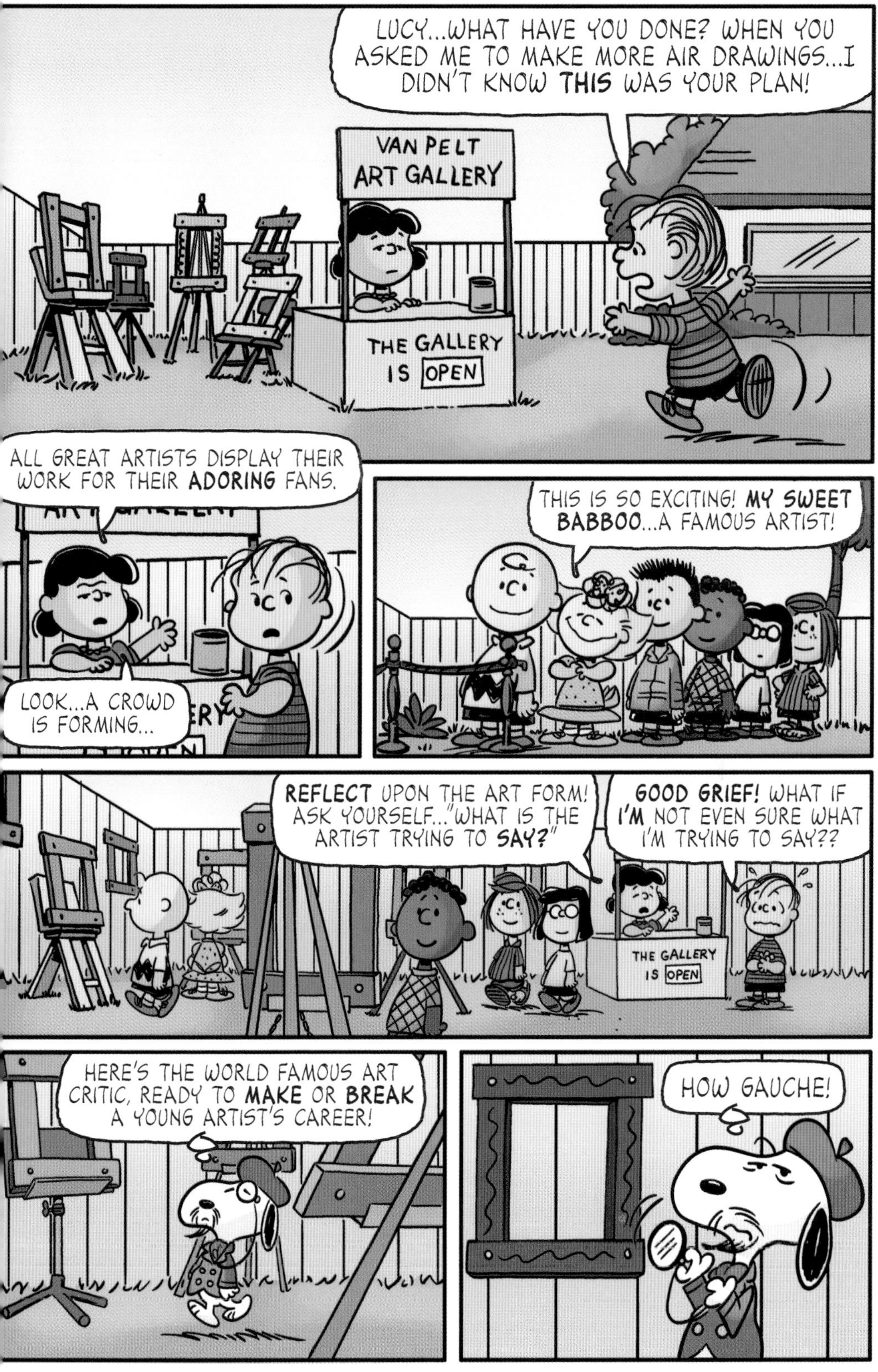

LUCY...WHAT HAVE YOU DONE? WHEN YOU ASKED ME TO MAKE MORE AIR DRAWINGS...I DIDN'T KNOW THIS WAS YOUR PLAN!
VAN PELT ART GALLERY
THE GALLERY IS OPEN
ALL GREAT ARTISTS DISPLAY THEIR WORK FOR THEIR ADORING FANS.
LOOK...A CROWD IS FORMING...
THIS IS SO EXCITING! MY SWEET BABBOO...A FAMOUS ARTIST!
REFLECT UPON THE ART FORM! ASK YOURSELF..."WHAT IS THE ARTIST TRYING TO SAY?"
GOOD GRIEF! WHAT IF I'M NOT EVEN SURE WHAT I'M TRYING TO SAY??
THE GALLERY IS OPEN
HERE'S THE WORLD FAMOUS ART CRITIC, READY TO MAKE OR BREAK A YOUNG ARTIST'S CAREER!
HOW GAUCHE!

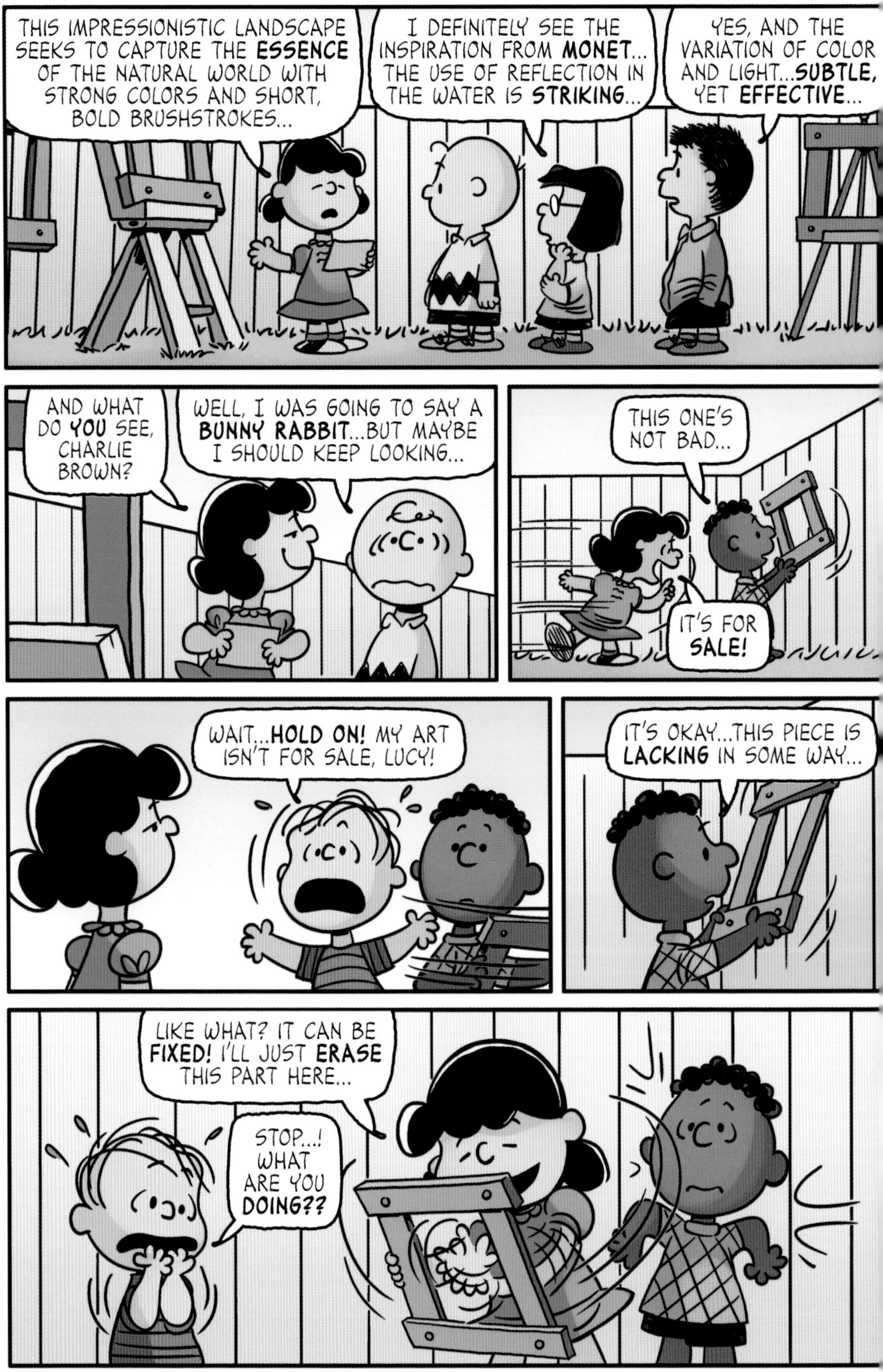

THIS IMPRESSIONISTIC LANDSCAPE SEEKS TO CAPTURE THE **ESSENCE** OF THE NATURAL WORLD WITH STRONG COLORS AND SHORT, BOLD BRUSHSTROKES...
I DEFINITELY SEE THE INSPIRATION FROM **MONET**... THE USE OF REFLECTION IN THE WATER IS **STRIKING**...
YES, AND THE VARIATION OF COLOR AND LIGHT...**SUBTLE**, YET **EFFECTIVE**...
AND WHAT DO **YOU** SEE, CHARLIE BROWN?
WELL, I WAS GOING TO SAY A **BUNNY RABBIT**...BUT MAYBE I SHOULD KEEP LOOKING...
THIS ONE'S NOT BAD...
IT'S FOR **SALE!**
WAIT...**HOLD ON!** MY ART ISN'T FOR SALE, LUCY!
IT'S OKAY...THIS PIECE IS **LACKING** IN SOME WAY...
LIKE WHAT? IT CAN BE **FIXED!** I'LL JUST **ERASE** THIS PART HERE...
STOP...! WHAT ARE YOU **DOING??**

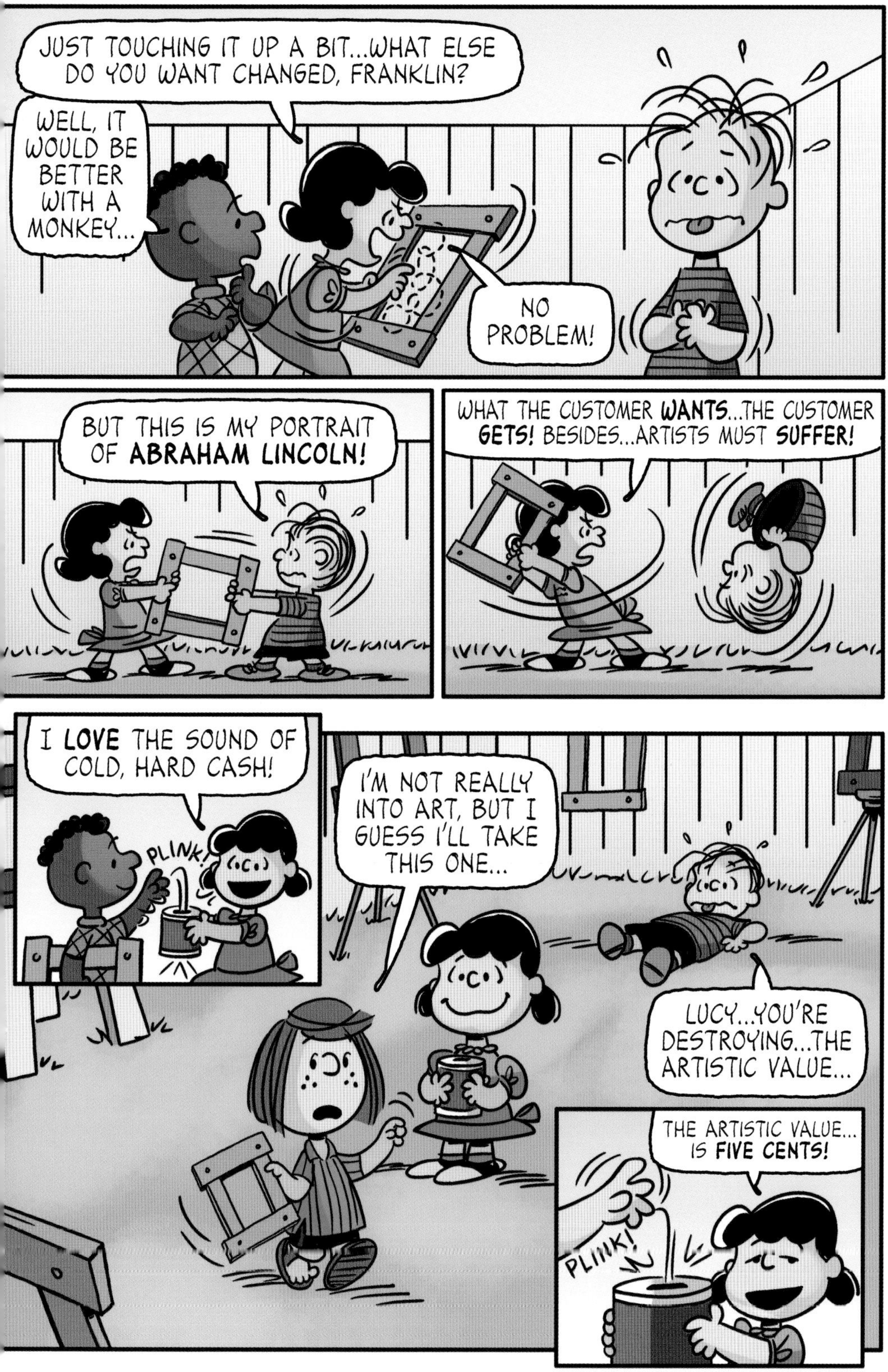
JUST TOUCHING IT UP A BIT...WHAT ELSE DO YOU WANT CHANGED, FRANKLIN?
WELL, IT WOULD BE BETTER WITH A MONKEY...
NO PROBLEM!
BUT THIS IS MY PORTRAIT OF **ABRAHAM LINCOLN!**
WHAT THE CUSTOMER **WANTS**...THE CUSTOMER **GETS!** BESIDES...ARTISTS MUST **SUFFER!**
I **LOVE** THE SOUND OF COLD, HARD CASH!
PLINK!
I'M NOT REALLY INTO ART, BUT I GUESS I'LL TAKE THIS ONE...
LUCY...YOU'RE DESTROYING...THE ARTISTIC VALUE...
THE ARTISTIC VALUE... IS **FIVE CENTS!**
PLINK!

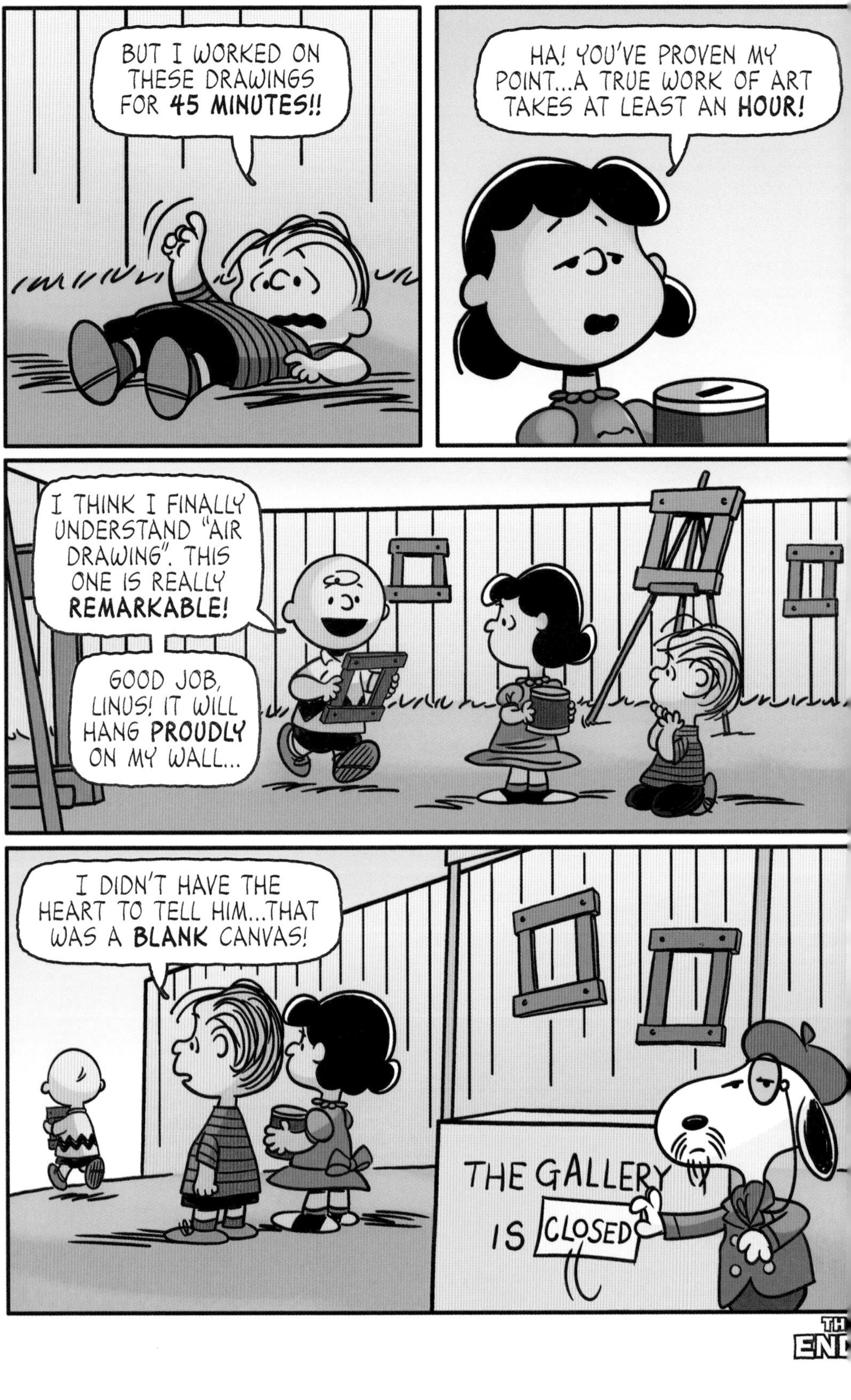
BUT I WORKED ON THESE DRAWINGS FOR **45 MINUTES!!**
HA! YOU'VE PROVEN MY POINT...A TRUE WORK OF ART TAKES AT LEAST AN **HOUR!**
I THINK I FINALLY UNDERSTAND "AIR DRAWING". THIS ONE IS REALLY **REMARKABLE!**
GOOD JOB, LINUS! IT WILL HANG **PROUDLY** ON MY WALL...
I DIDN'T HAVE THE HEART TO TELL HIM...THAT WAS A **BLANK** CANVAS!
THE GALLERY IS CLOSED

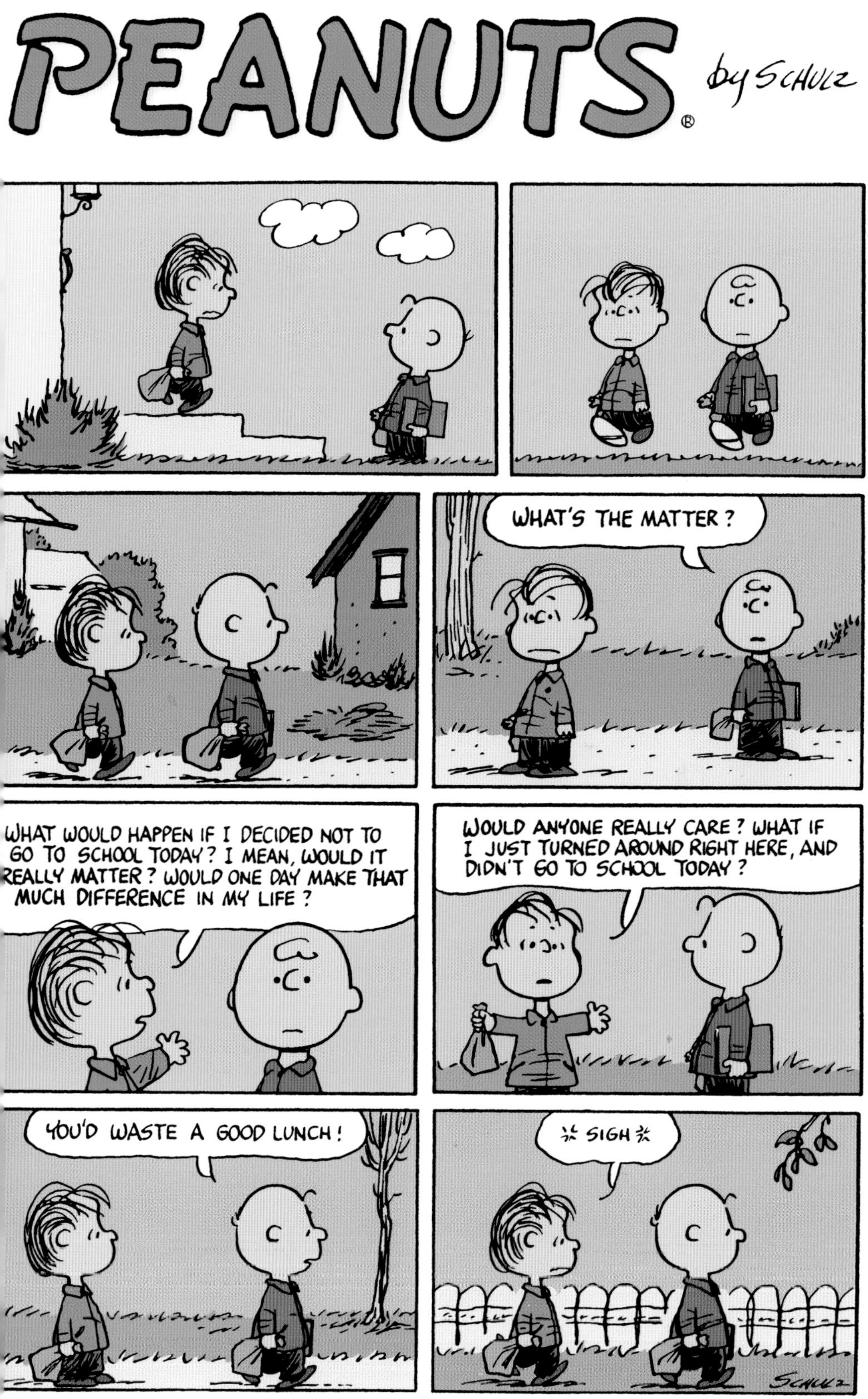
PEANUTS
by SCHULZ
WHAT'S THE MATTER ?
WHAT WOULD HAPPEN IF I DECIDED NOT TO GO TO SCHOOL TODAY? I MEAN, WOULD IT REALLY MATTER? WOULD ONE DAY MAKE THAT MUCH DIFFERENCE IN MY LIFE?
WOULD ANYONE REALLY CARE? WHAT IF I JUST TURNED AROUND RIGHT HERE, AND DIDN'T GO TO SCHOOL TODAY?
YOU'D WASTE A GOOD LUNCH!
SIGH
SCHULZ

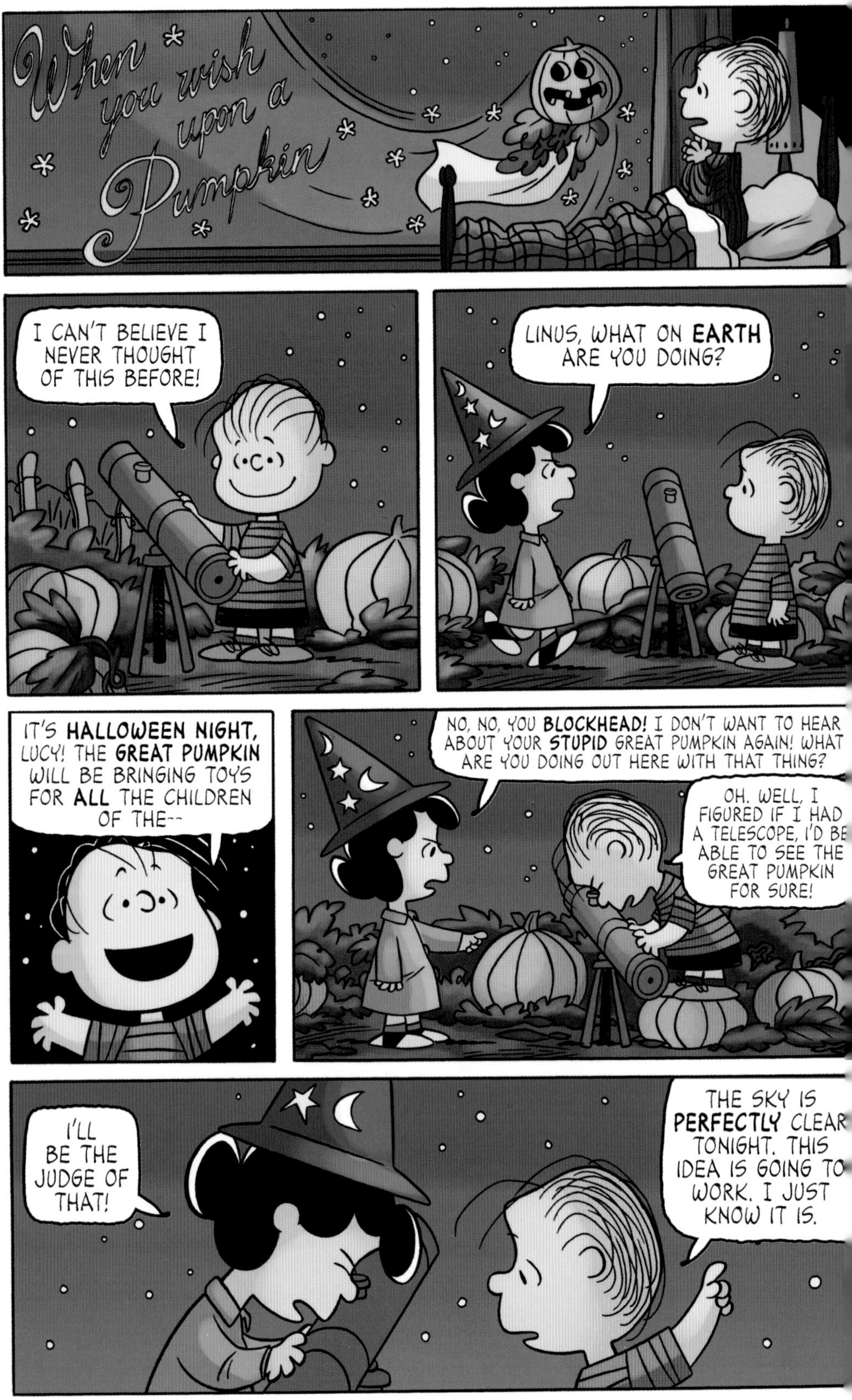
When you wish upon a Pumpkin
I CAN'T BELIEVE I NEVER THOUGHT OF THIS BEFORE!
LINUS, WHAT ON EARTH ARE YOU DOING?
IT'S HALLOWEEN NIGHT, LUCY! THE GREAT PUMPKIN WILL BE BRINGING TOYS FOR ALL THE CHILDREN OF THE--
NO, NO, YOU BLOCKHEAD! I DON'T WANT TO HEAR ABOUT YOUR STUPID GREAT PUMPKIN AGAIN! WHAT ARE YOU DOING OUT HERE WITH THAT THING?
OH. WELL, I FIGURED IF I HAD A TELESCOPE, I'D BE ABLE TO SEE THE GREAT PUMPKIN FOR SURE!
I'LL BE THE JUDGE OF THAT!
THE SKY IS PERFECTLY CLEAR TONIGHT. THIS IDEA IS GOING TO WORK. I JUST KNOW IT IS.

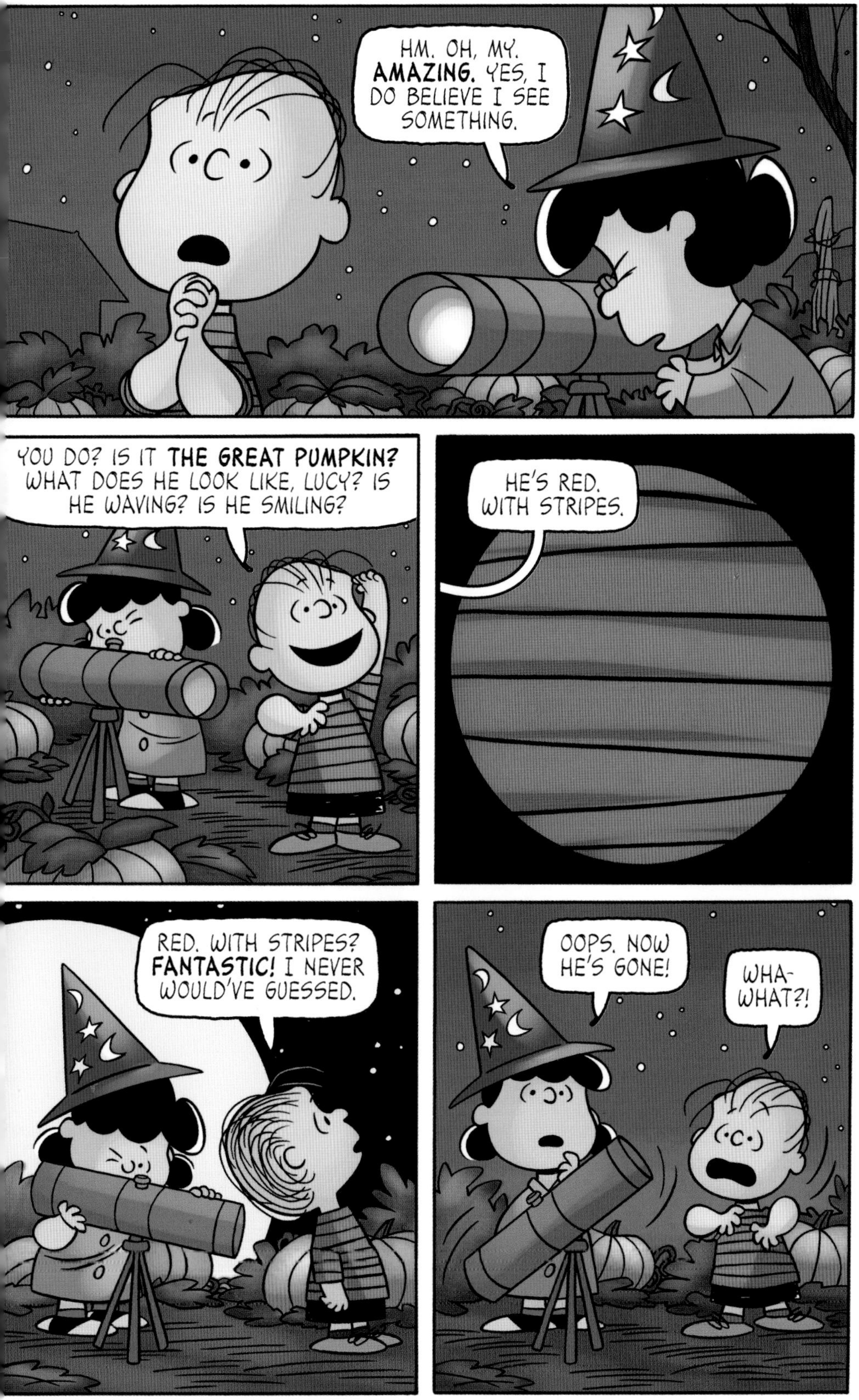

HM. OH, MY. **AMAZING.** YES, I DO BELIEVE I SEE SOMETHING.
YOU DO? IS IT **THE GREAT PUMPKIN?** WHAT DOES HE LOOK LIKE, LUCY? IS HE WAVING? IS HE SMILING?
HE'S RED. WITH STRIPES.
RED. WITH STRIPES? **FANTASTIC!** I NEVER WOULD'VE GUESSED.
OOPS. NOW HE'S GONE!
WHA-WHAT?!

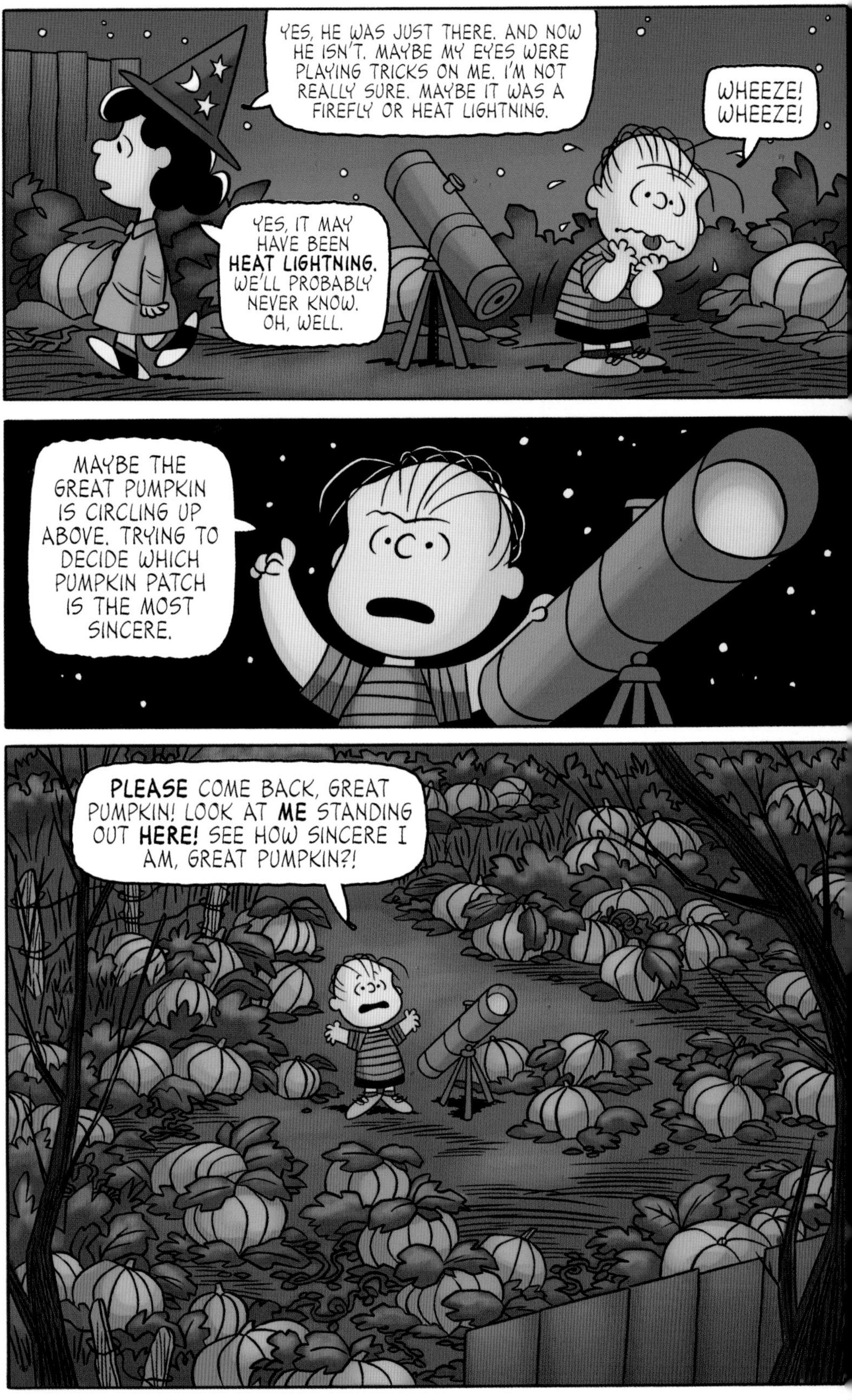

YES, HE WAS JUST THERE. AND NOW HE ISN'T. MAYBE MY EYES WERE PLAYING TRICKS ON ME. I'M NOT REALLY SURE. MAYBE IT WAS A FIREFLY OR HEAT LIGHTNING.
WHEEZE! WHEEZE!
YES, IT MAY HAVE BEEN **HEAT LIGHTNING.** WE'LL PROBABLY NEVER KNOW. OH, WELL.
MAYBE THE GREAT PUMPKIN IS CIRCLING UP ABOVE. TRYING TO DECIDE WHICH PUMPKIN PATCH IS THE MOST SINCERE.
PLEASE COME BACK, GREAT PUMPKIN! LOOK AT **ME** STANDING OUT **HERE!** SEE HOW SINCERE I AM, GREAT PUMPKIN?!

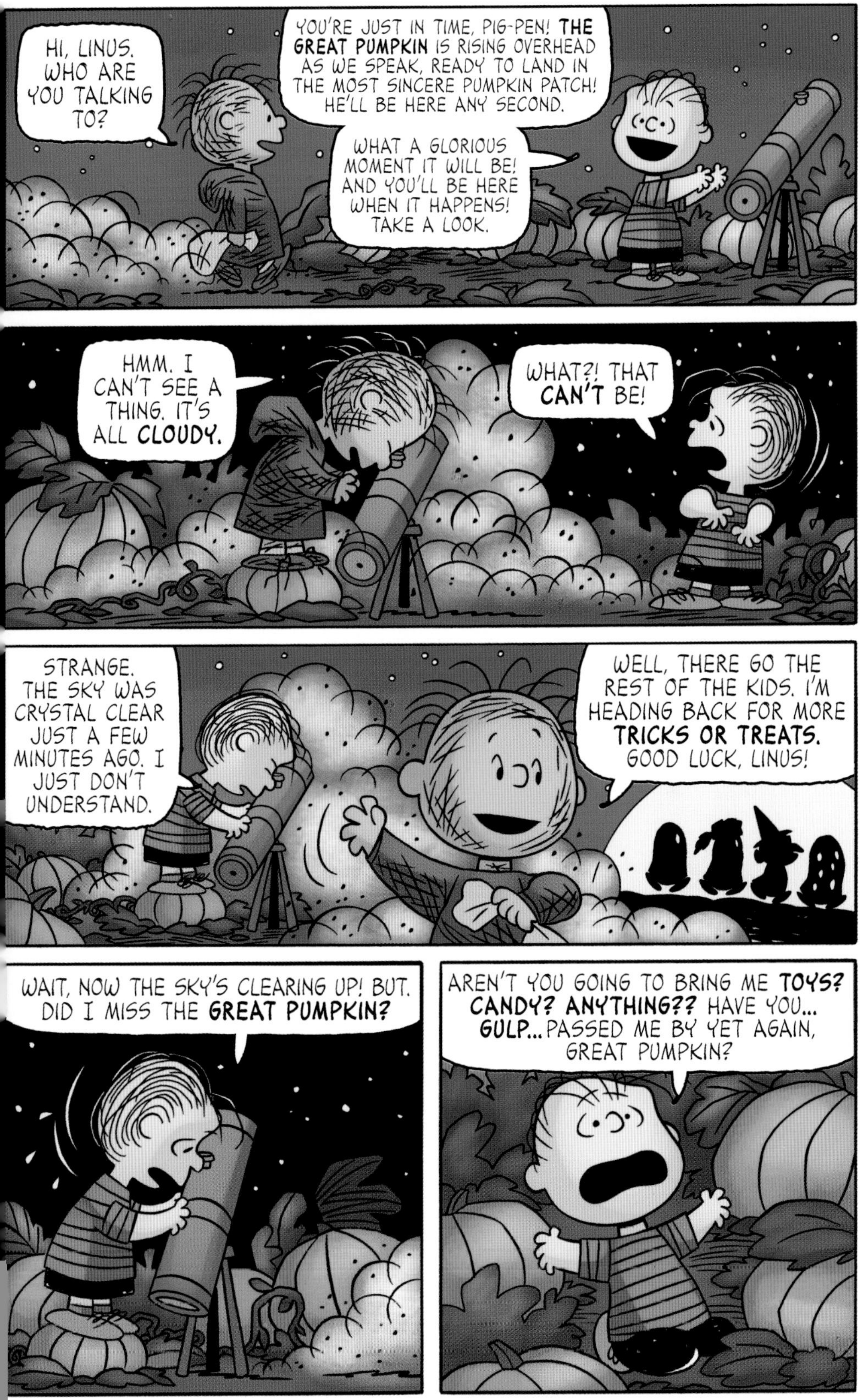
HI, LINUS. WHO ARE YOU TALKING TO?
YOU'RE JUST IN TIME, PIG-PEN! THE GREAT PUMPKIN IS RISING OVERHEAD AS WE SPEAK, READY TO LAND IN THE MOST SINCERE PUMPKIN PATCH! HE'LL BE HERE ANY SECOND.
WHAT A GLORIOUS MOMENT IT WILL BE! AND YOU'LL BE HERE WHEN IT HAPPENS! TAKE A LOOK.
HMM. I CAN'T SEE A THING. IT'S ALL CLOUDY.
WHAT?! THAT CAN'T BE!
STRANGE. THE SKY WAS CRYSTAL CLEAR JUST A FEW MINUTES AGO. I JUST DON'T UNDERSTAND.
WELL, THERE GO THE REST OF THE KIDS. I'M HEADING BACK FOR MORE TRICKS OR TREATS. GOOD LUCK, LINUS!
WAIT, NOW THE SKY'S CLEARING UP! BUT. DID I MISS THE GREAT PUMPKIN?
AREN'T YOU GOING TO BRING ME TOYS? CANDY? ANYTHING?? HAVE YOU... GULP... PASSED ME BY YET AGAIN, GREAT PUMPKIN?

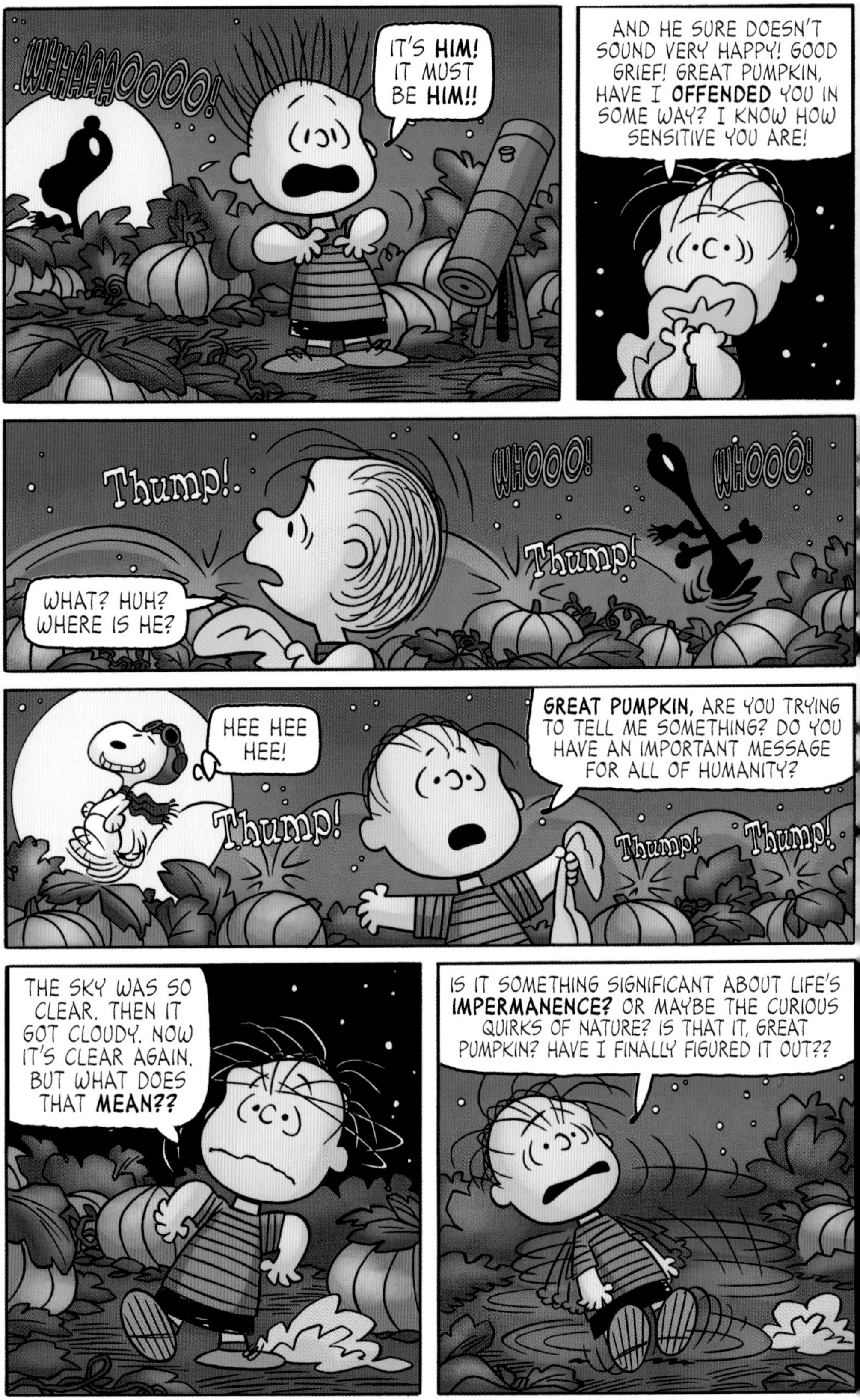
WHHAAAOOOOO!
IT'S HIM! IT MUST BE HIM!!
AND HE SURE DOESN'T SOUND VERY HAPPY! GOOD GRIEF! GREAT PUMPKIN, HAVE I OFFENDED YOU IN SOME WAY? I KNOW HOW SENSITIVE YOU ARE!
Thump!
WHOOO!
WHOOO!
Thump!
WHAT? HUH? WHERE IS HE?
HEE HEE HEE!
GREAT PUMPKIN, ARE YOU TRYING TO TELL ME SOMETHING? DO YOU HAVE AN IMPORTANT MESSAGE FOR ALL OF HUMANITY?
Thump!
Thump!
Thump!
THE SKY WAS SO CLEAR. THEN IT GOT CLOUDY. NOW IT'S CLEAR AGAIN. BUT WHAT DOES THAT MEAN??
IS IT SOMETHING SIGNIFICANT ABOUT LIFE'S IMPERMANENCE? OR MAYBE THE CURIOUS QUIRKS OF NATURE? IS THAT IT, GREAT PUMPKIN? HAVE I FINALLY FIGURED IT OUT??

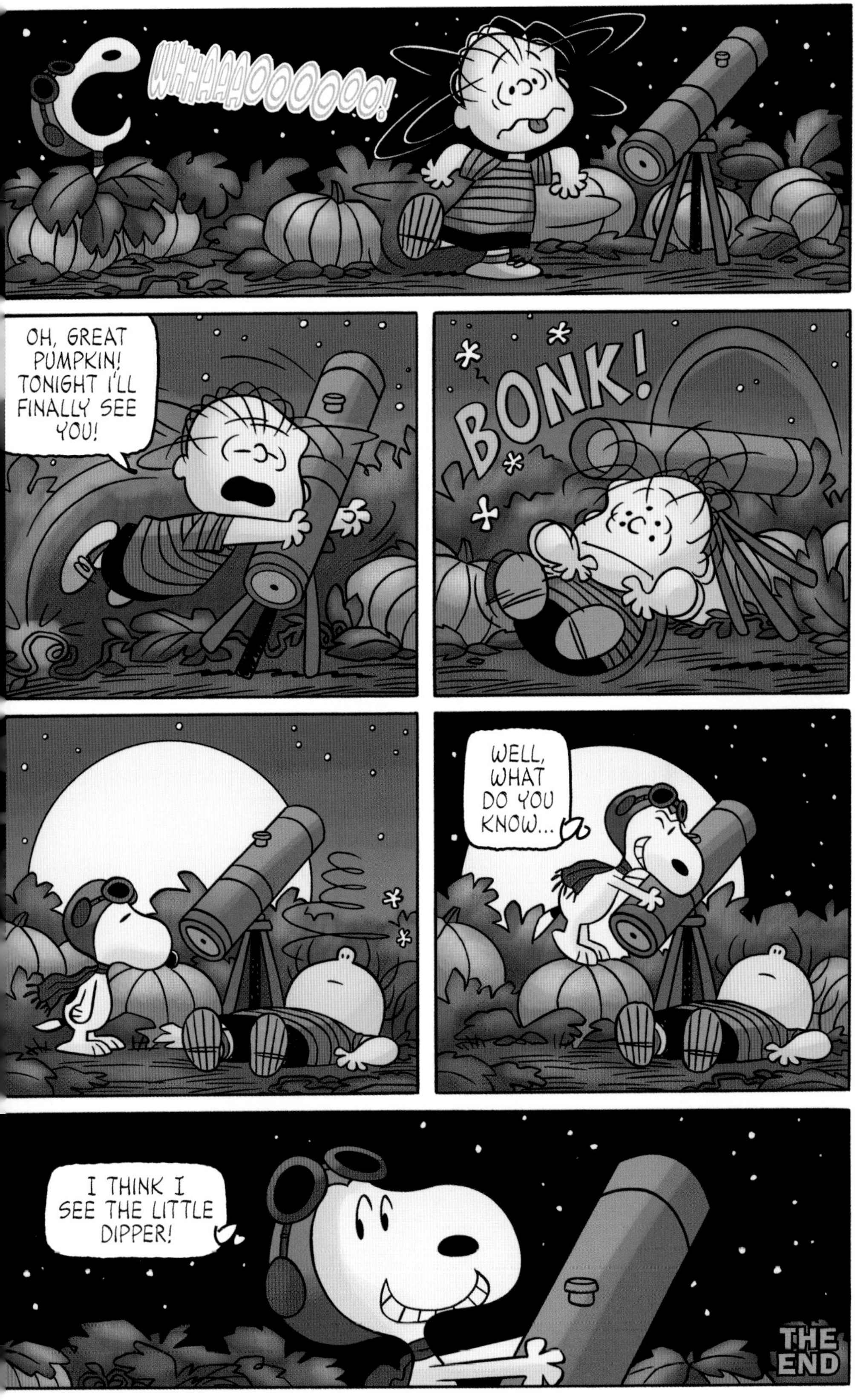
WHHAAAOOOOOO!
OH, GREAT PUMPKIN! TONIGHT I'LL FINALLY SEE YOU!
BONK!
WELL, WHAT DO YOU KNOW...
I THINK I SEE THE LITTLE DIPPER!
THE END

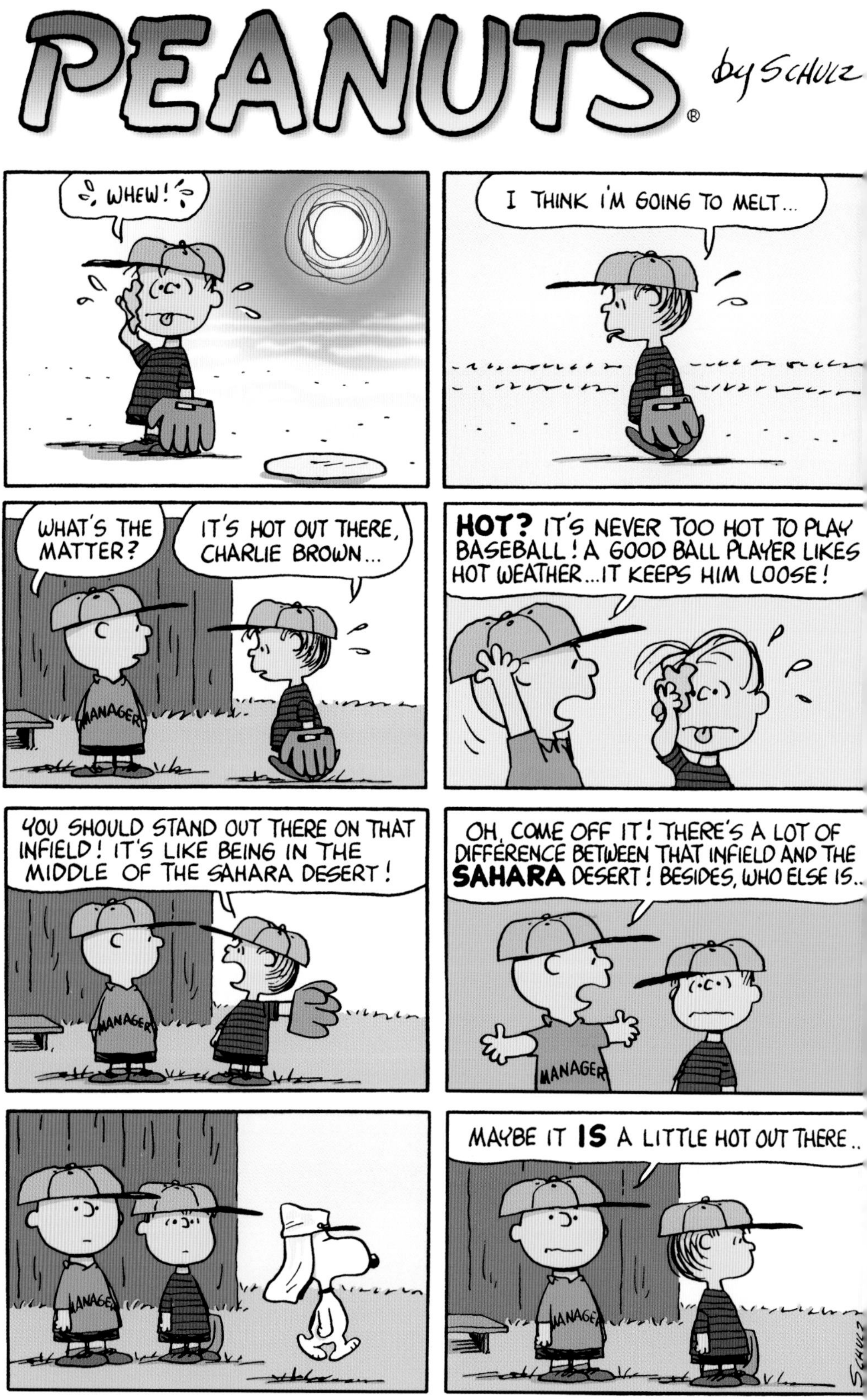
PEANUTS by SCHULZ
WHEW!
I THINK I'M GOING TO MELT...
WHAT'S THE MATTER?
IT'S HOT OUT THERE, CHARLIE BROWN...
MANAGER
HOT? IT'S NEVER TOO HOT TO PLAY BASEBALL! A GOOD BALL PLAYER LIKES HOT WEATHER...IT KEEPS HIM LOOSE!
YOU SHOULD STAND OUT THERE ON THAT INFIELD! IT'S LIKE BEING IN THE MIDDLE OF THE SAHARA DESERT!
MANAGER
OH, COME OFF IT! THERE'S A LOT OF DIFFERENCE BETWEEN THAT INFIELD AND THE SAHARA DESERT! BESIDES, WHO ELSE IS...
MANAGER
MANAGER
MAYBE IT IS A LITTLE HOT OUT THERE...
MANAGER
SCHULZ

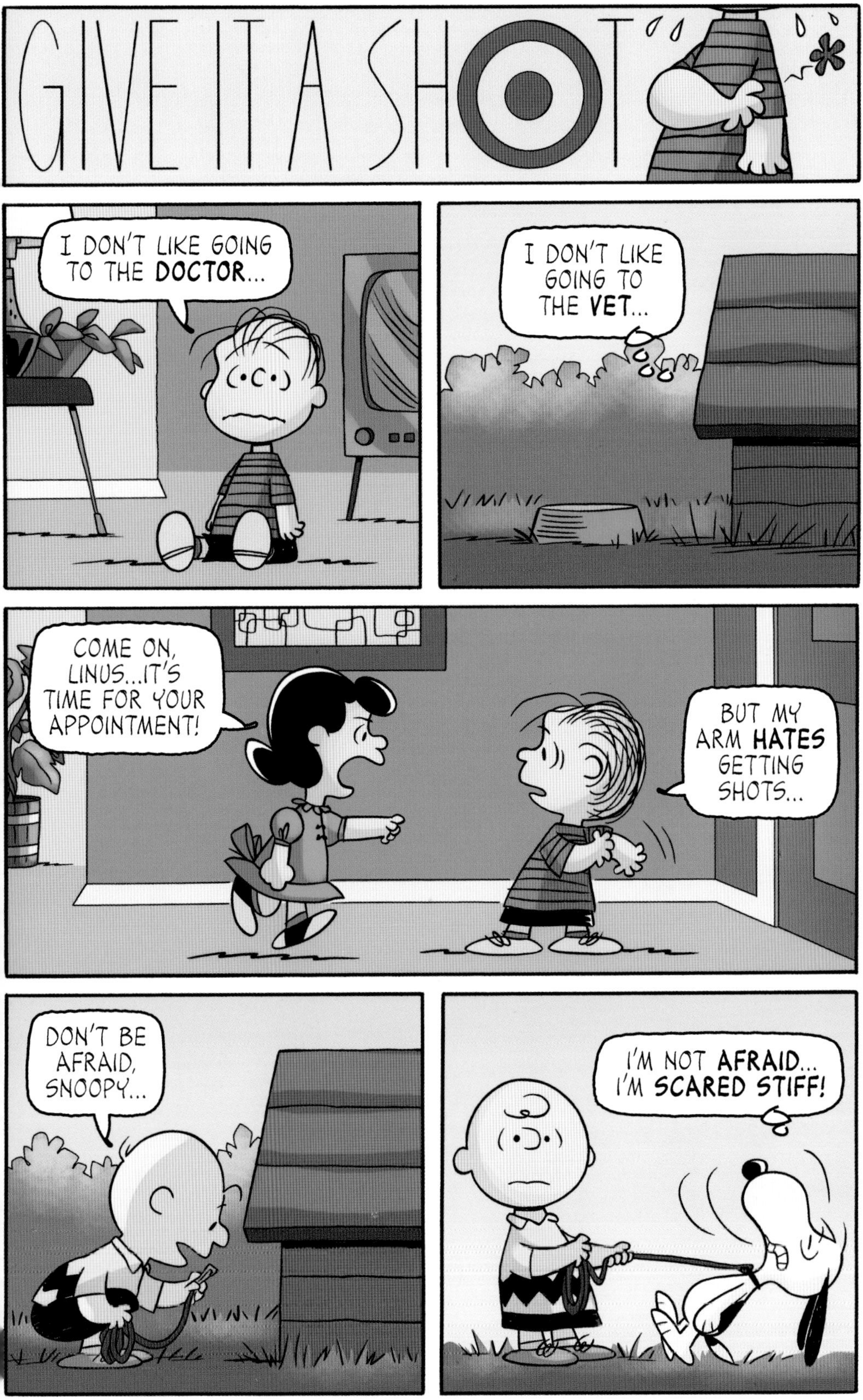
GIVE IT A SHOT
I DON'T LIKE GOING TO THE DOCTOR...
I DON'T LIKE GOING TO THE VET...
COME ON, LINUS...IT'S TIME FOR YOUR APPOINTMENT!
BUT MY ARM HATES GETTING SHOTS...
DON'T BE AFRAID, SNOOPY...
I'M NOT AFRAID... I'M SCARED STIFF!

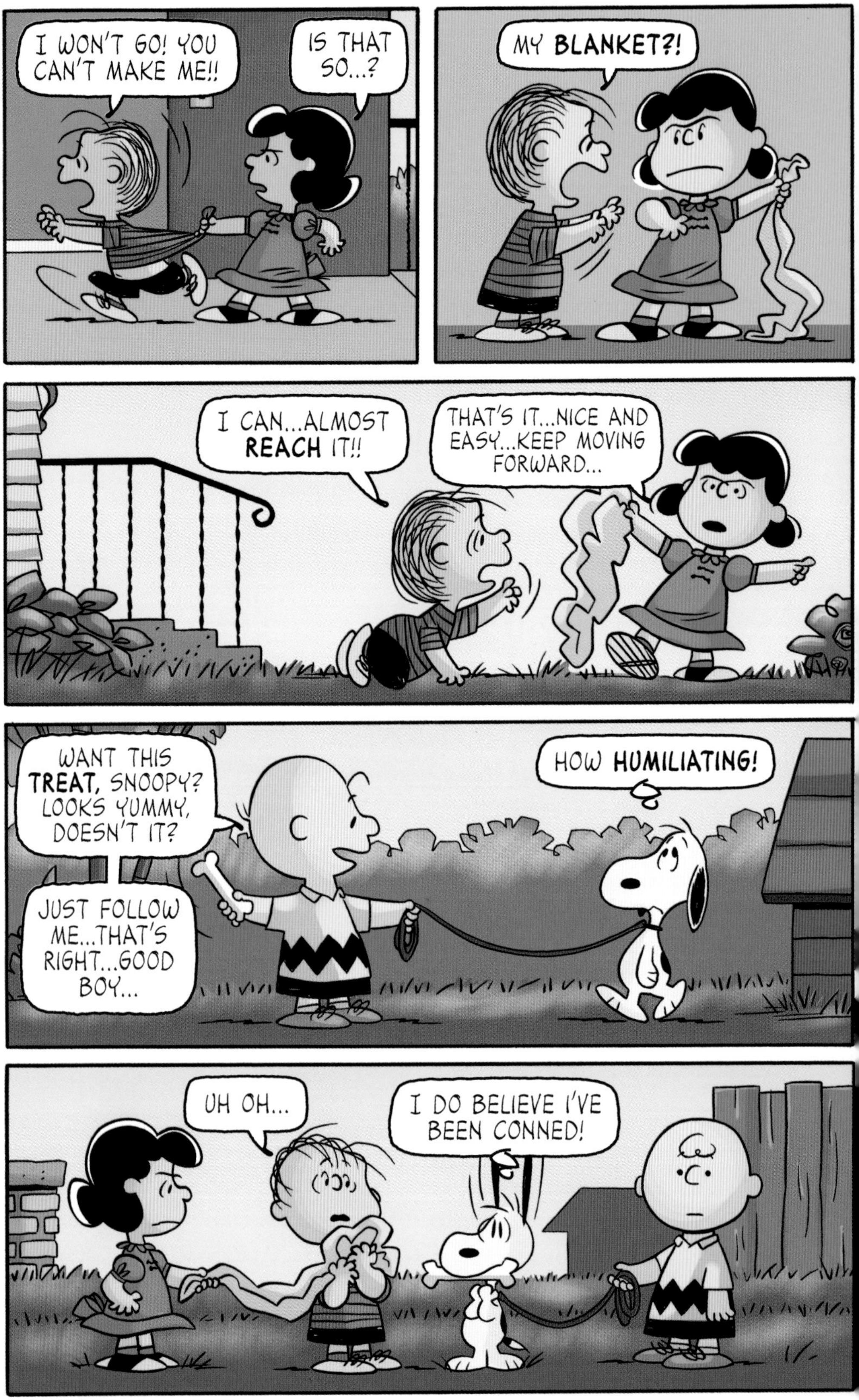

I WON'T GO! YOU CAN'T MAKE ME!!
IS THAT SO...?
MY **BLANKET?!**
I CAN...ALMOST **REACH** IT!!
THAT'S IT...NICE AND EASY...KEEP MOVING FORWARD...
WANT THIS **TREAT,** SNOOPY? LOOKS YUMMY, DOESN'T IT?
JUST FOLLOW ME...THAT'S RIGHT...GOOD BOY...
HOW **HUMILIATING!**
UH OH...
I DO BELIEVE I'VE BEEN CONNED!

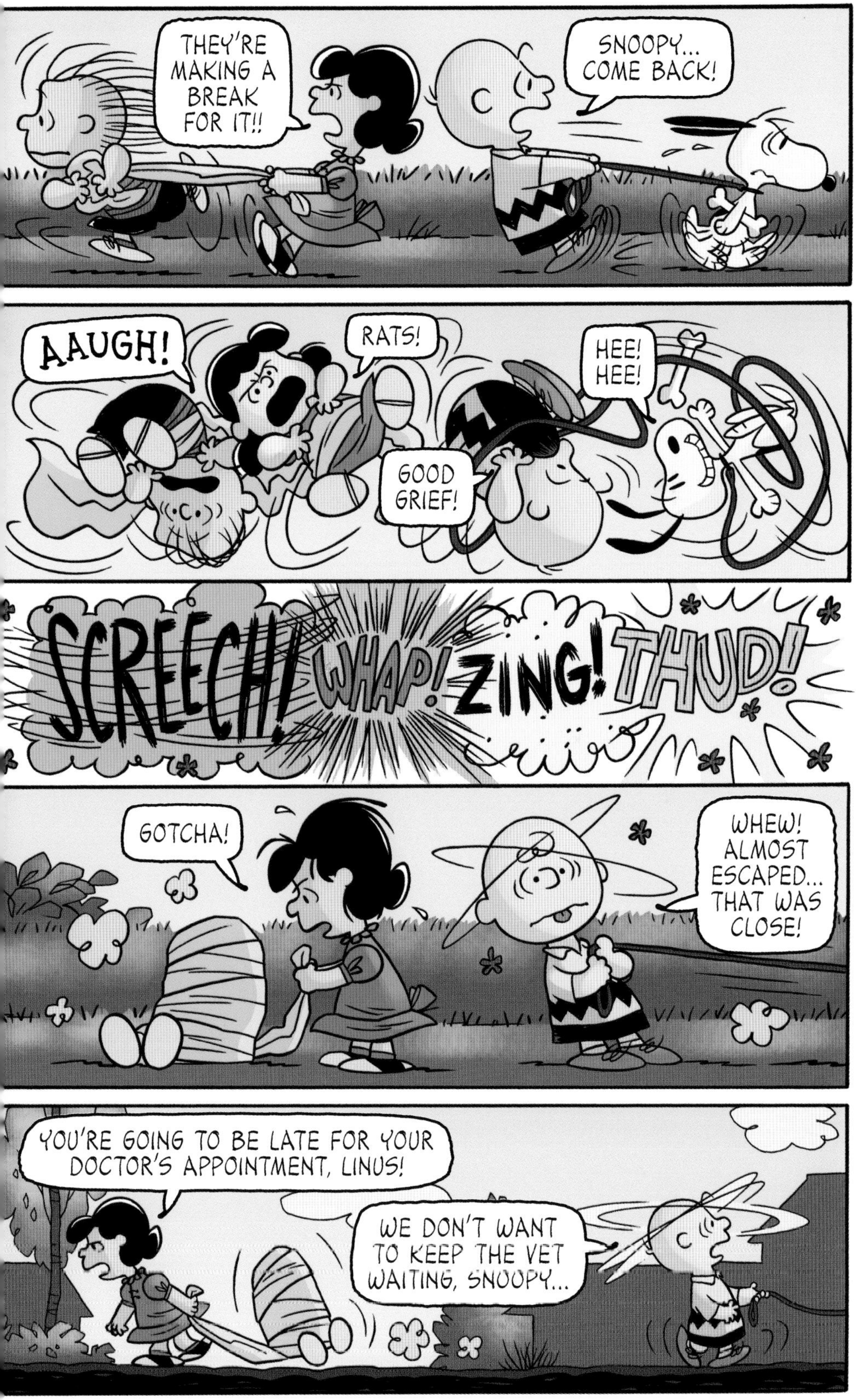
THEY'RE MAKING A BREAK FOR IT!!
SNOOPY... COME BACK!
AAUGH!
RATS!
HEE! HEE!
GOOD GRIEF!
SCREECH!
WHAP!
ZING!
THUD!
GOTCHA!
WHEW! ALMOST ESCAPED... THAT WAS CLOSE!
YOU'RE GOING TO BE LATE FOR YOUR DOCTOR'S APPOINTMENT, LINUS!
WE DON'T WANT TO KEEP THE VET WAITING, SNOOPY...

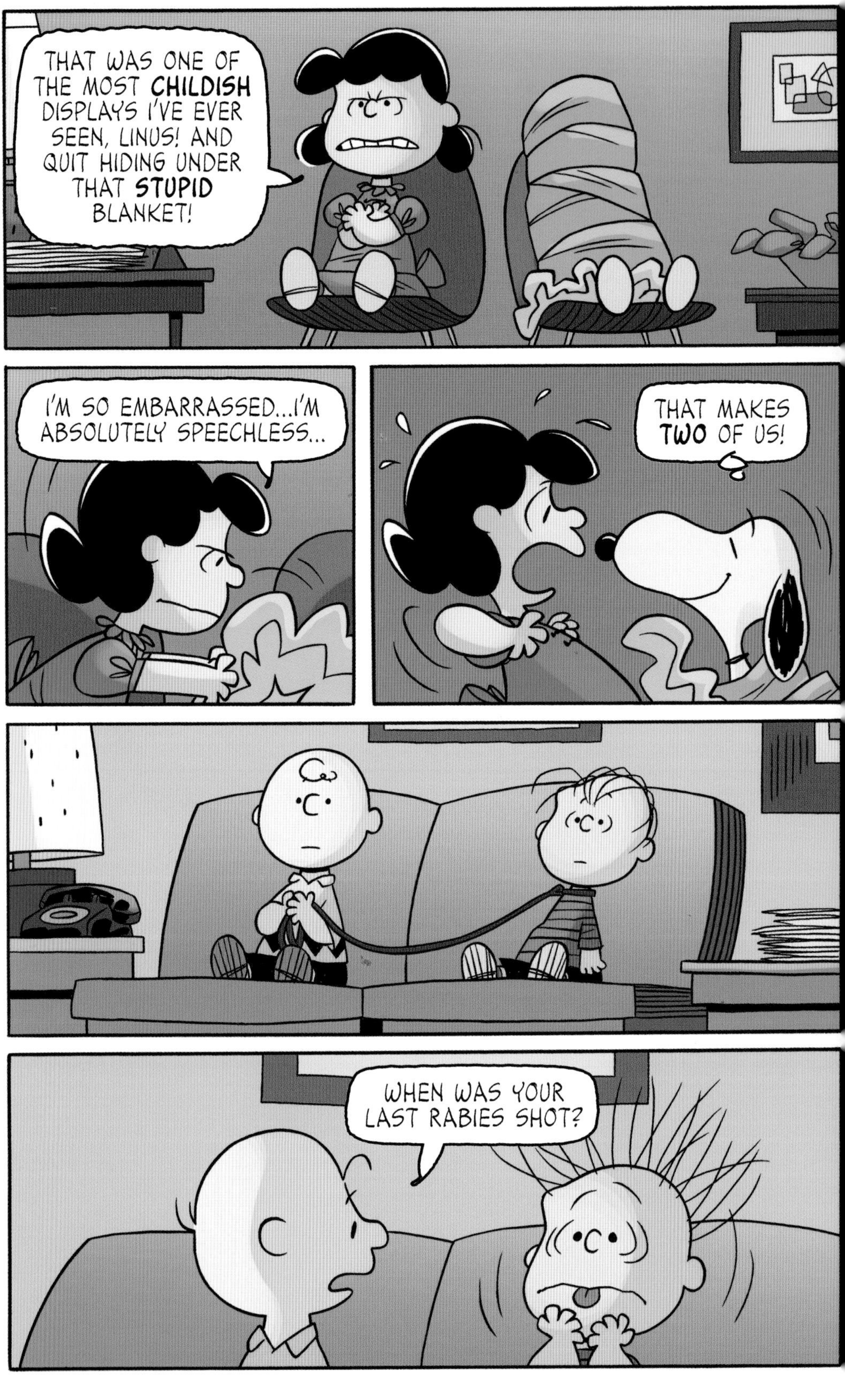
THAT WAS ONE OF THE MOST **CHILDISH** DISPLAYS I'VE EVER SEEN, LINUS! AND QUIT HIDING UNDER THAT **STUPID** BLANKET!
I'M SO EMBARRASSED...I'M ABSOLUTELY SPEECHLESS...
THAT MAKES **TWO** OF US!
WHEN WAS YOUR LAST RABIES SHOT?

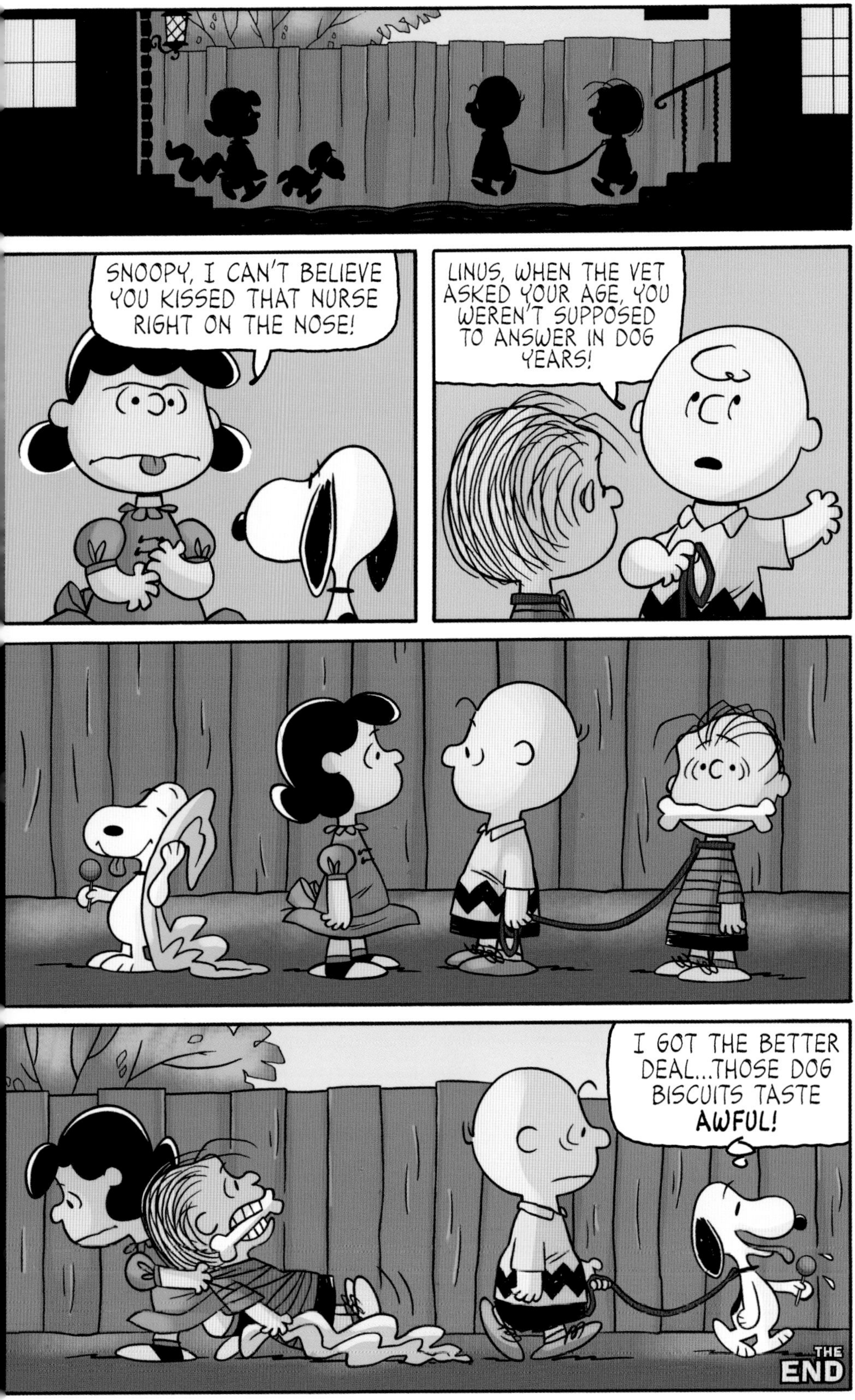
SNOOPY, I CAN'T BELIEVE YOU KISSED THAT NURSE RIGHT ON THE NOSE!
LINUS, WHEN THE VET ASKED YOUR AGE, YOU WEREN'T SUPPOSED TO ANSWER IN DOG YEARS!
I GOT THE BETTER DEAL...THOSE DOG BISCUITS TASTE AWFUL!
THE END

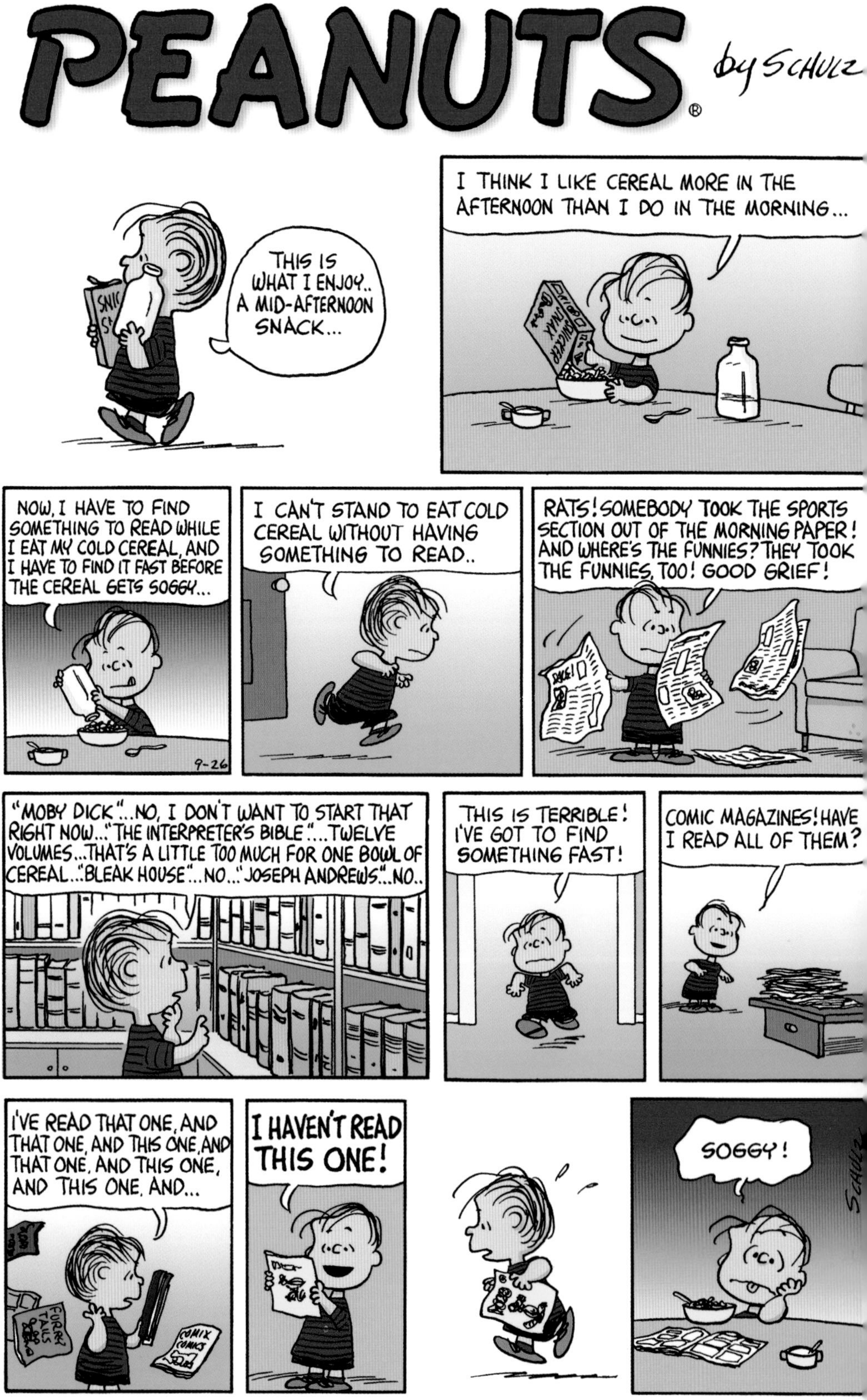
PEANUTS
by SCHULZ
THIS IS WHAT I ENJOY.. A MID-AFTERNOON SNACK...
I THINK I LIKE CEREAL MORE IN THE AFTERNOON THAN I DO IN THE MORNING...
NOW, I HAVE TO FIND SOMETHING TO READ WHILE I EAT MY COLD CEREAL, AND I HAVE TO FIND IT FAST BEFORE THE CEREAL GETS SOGGY...
9-26
I CAN'T STAND TO EAT COLD CEREAL WITHOUT HAVING SOMETHING TO READ..
RATS! SOMEBODY TOOK THE SPORTS SECTION OUT OF THE MORNING PAPER! AND WHERE'S THE FUNNIES? THEY TOOK THE FUNNIES, TOO! GOOD GRIEF!
"MOBY DICK"...NO, I DON'T WANT TO START THAT RIGHT NOW..."THE INTERPRETER'S BIBLE"....TWELVE VOLUMES...THAT'S A LITTLE TOO MUCH FOR ONE BOWL OF CEREAL..."BLEAK HOUSE"...NO..."JOSEPH ANDREWS"...NO..
THIS IS TERRIBLE! I'VE GOT TO FIND SOMETHING FAST!
COMIC MAGAZINES! HAVE I READ ALL OF THEM?
I'VE READ THAT ONE, AND THAT ONE, AND THIS ONE, AND THAT ONE, AND THIS ONE, AND THIS ONE, AND...
COMIX COMICS
I HAVEN'T READ THIS ONE!
SOGGY!
SCHULZ

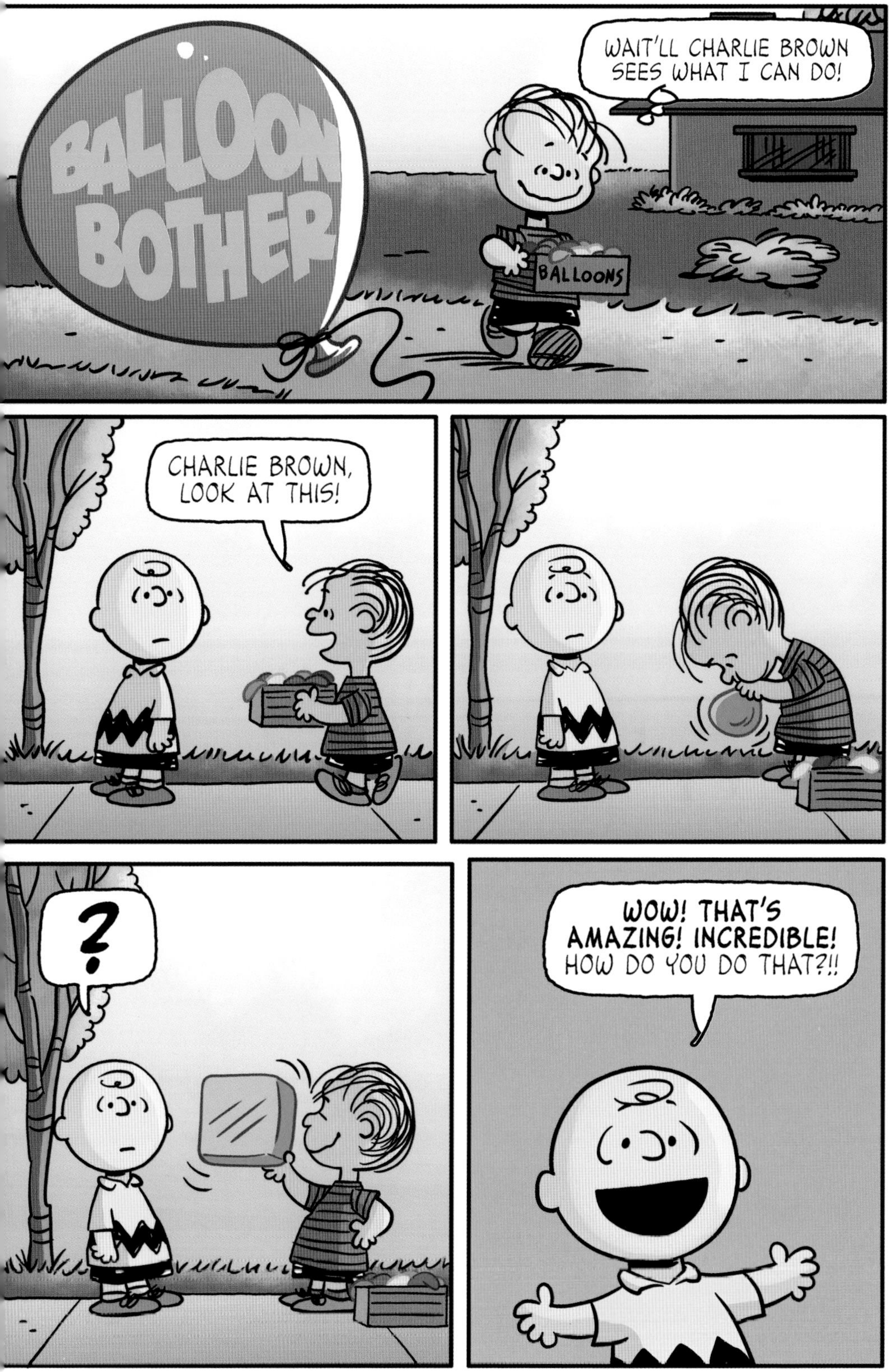
BALLOON BOTHER
WAIT'LL CHARLIE BROWN SEES WHAT I CAN DO!
BALLOONS
CHARLIE BROWN, LOOK AT THIS!
?
WOW! THAT'S AMAZING! INCREDIBLE! HOW DO YOU DO THAT?!!

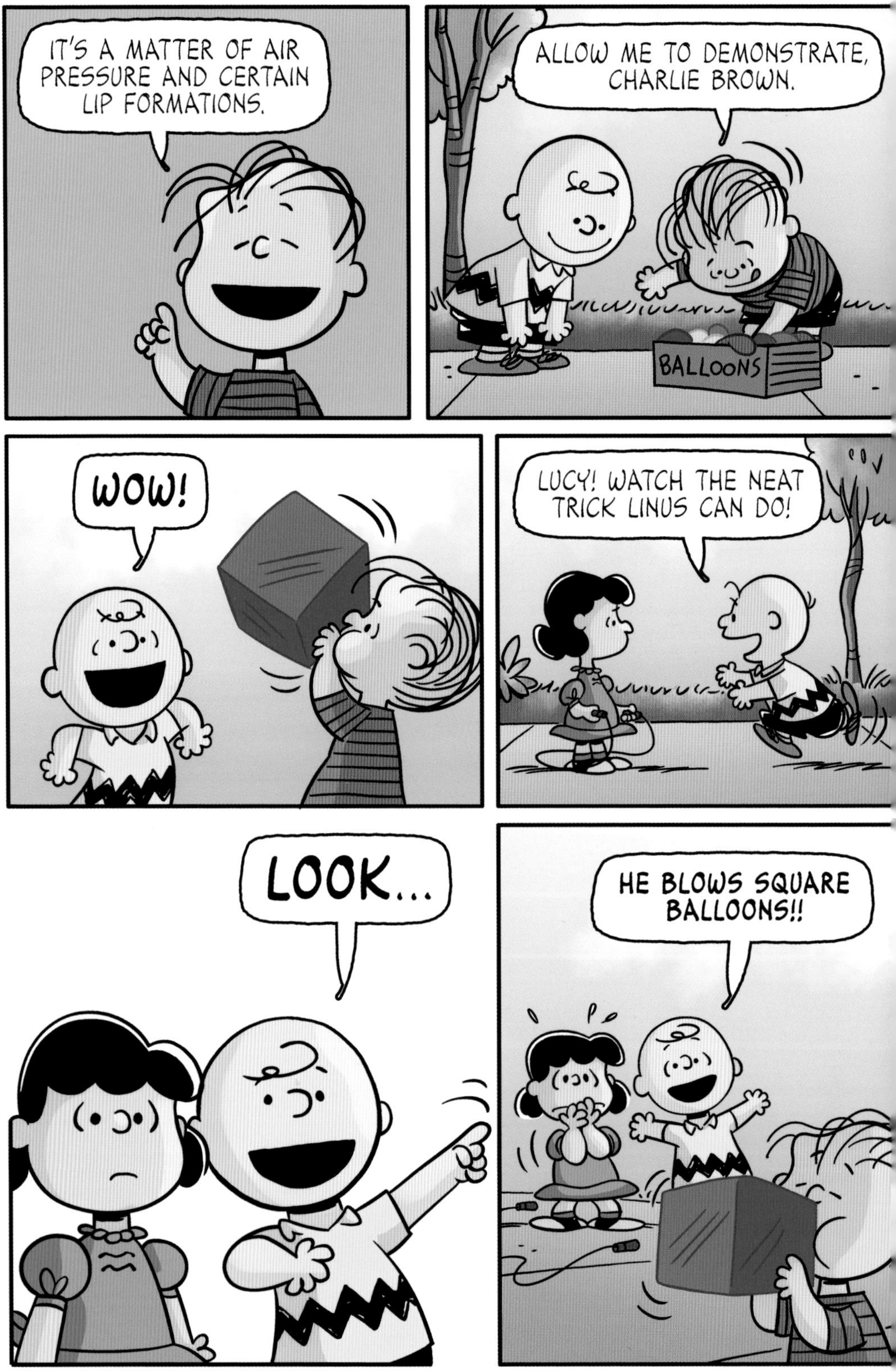
IT'S A MATTER OF AIR PRESSURE AND CERTAIN LIP FORMATIONS.
ALLOW ME TO DEMONSTRATE, CHARLIE BROWN.
BALLOONS
WOW!
LUCY! WATCH THE NEAT TRICK LINUS CAN DO!
LOOK...
HE BLOWS SQUARE BALLOONS!!

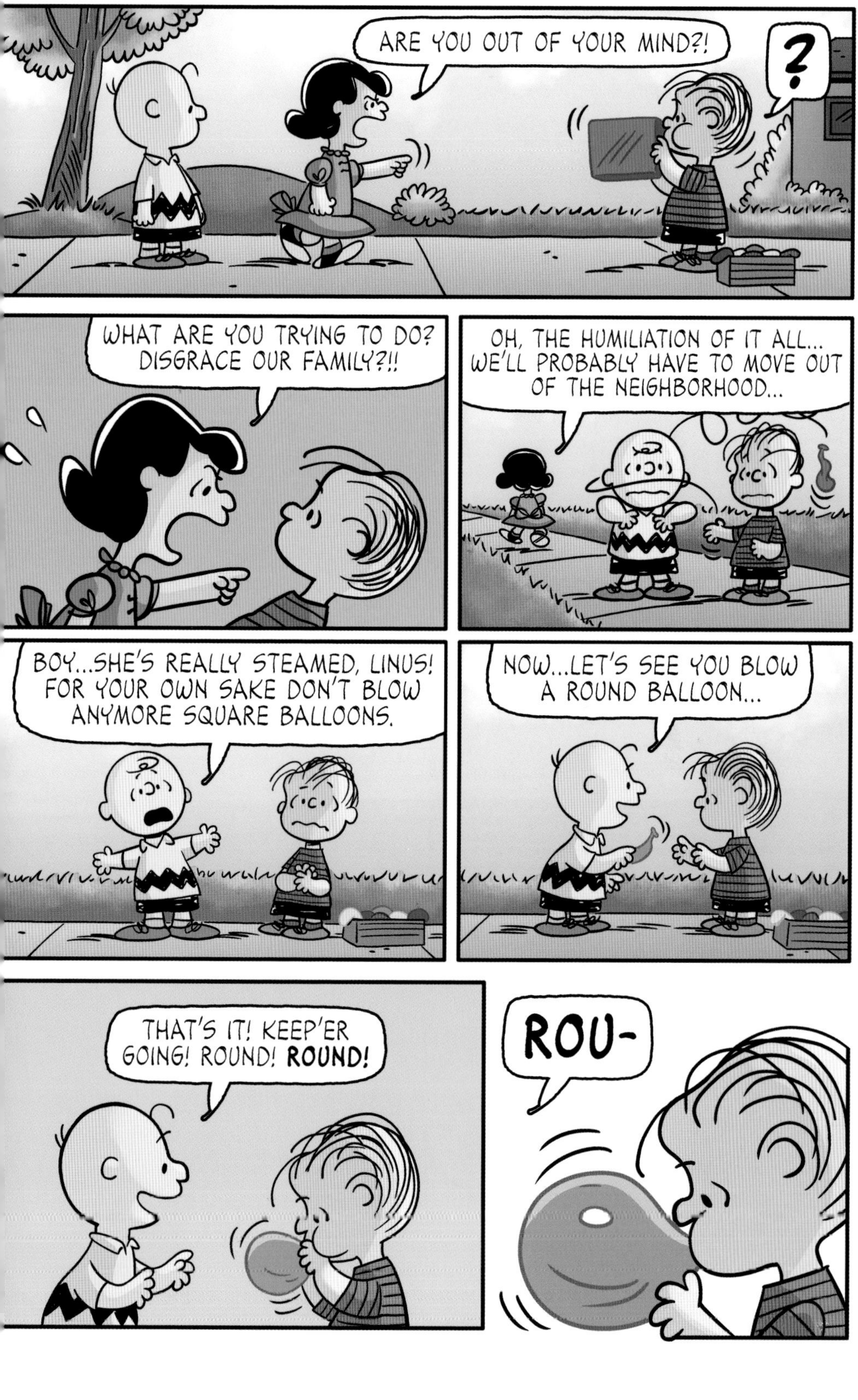
ARE YOU OUT OF YOUR MIND?!
?
WHAT ARE YOU TRYING TO DO? DISGRACE OUR FAMILY?!!
OH, THE HUMILIATION OF IT ALL... WE'LL PROBABLY HAVE TO MOVE OUT OF THE NEIGHBORHOOD...
BOY...SHE'S REALLY STEAMED, LINUS! FOR YOUR OWN SAKE DON'T BLOW ANYMORE SQUARE BALLOONS.
NOW...LET'S SEE YOU BLOW A ROUND BALLOON...
THAT'S IT! KEEP'ER GOING! ROUND! **ROUND!**
ROU-

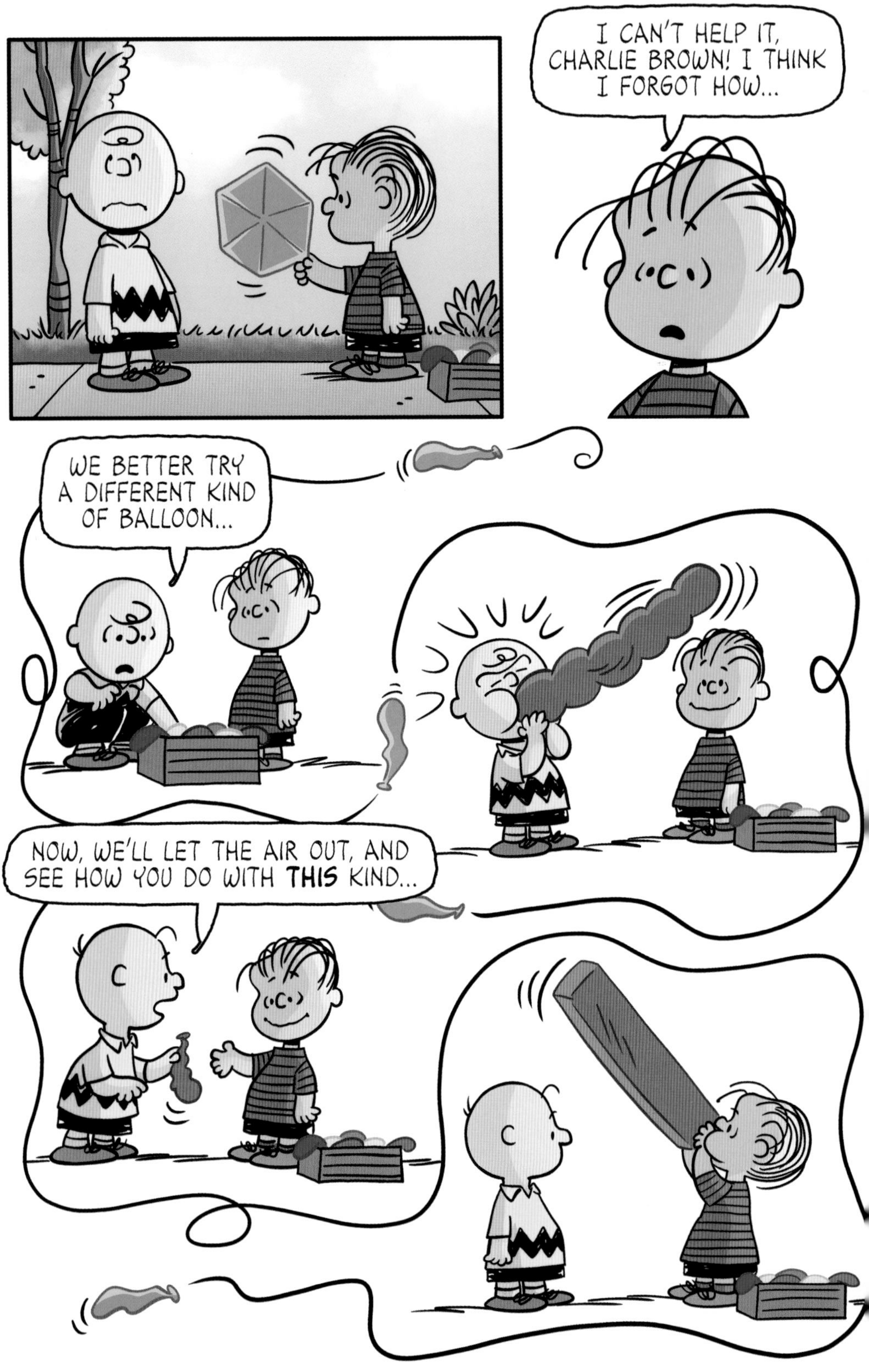
I CAN'T HELP IT, CHARLIE BROWN! I THINK I FORGOT HOW...
WE BETTER TRY A DIFFERENT KIND OF BALLOON...
NOW, WE'LL LET THE AIR OUT, AND SEE HOW YOU DO WITH **THIS** KIND...

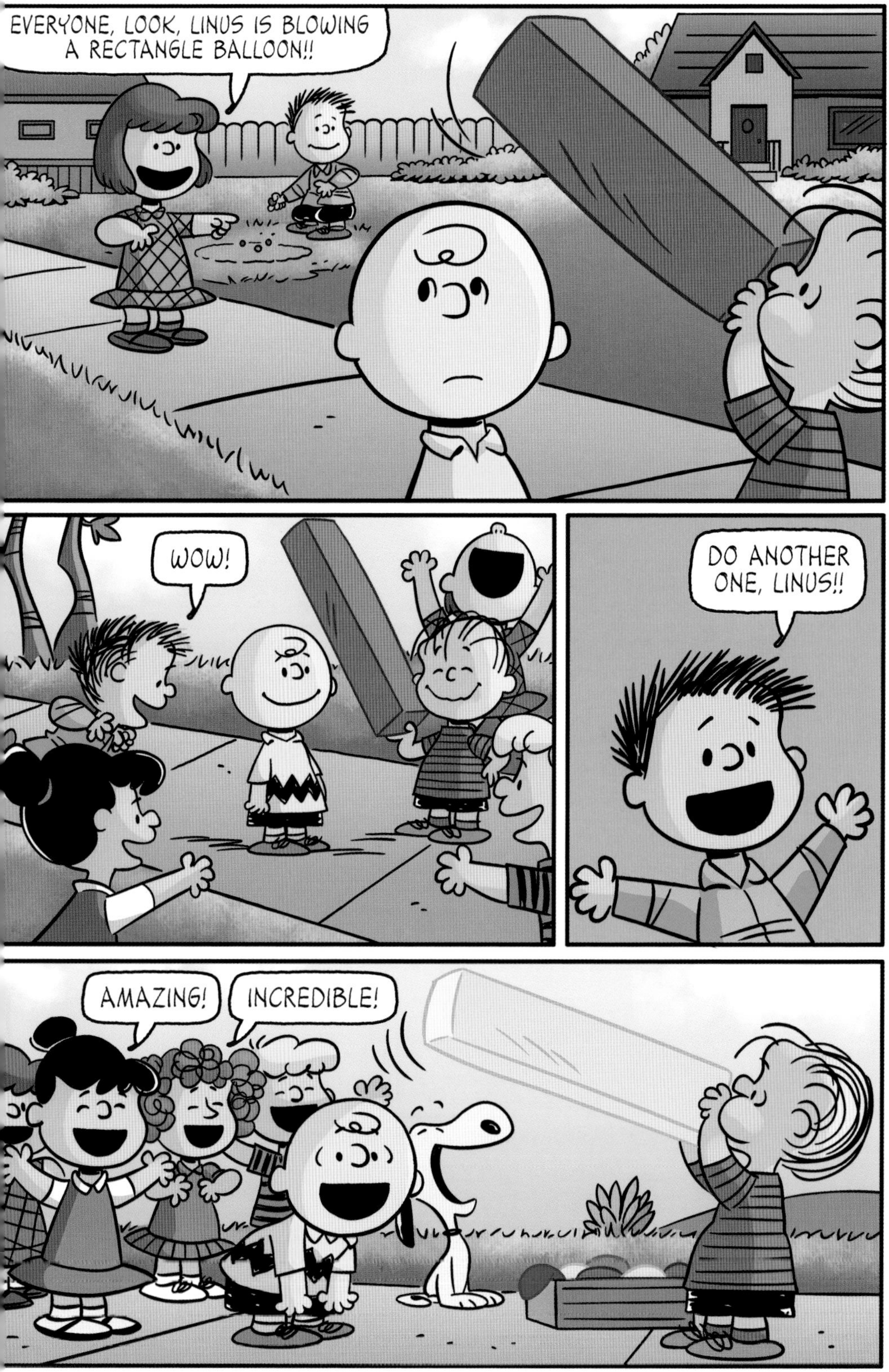
EVERYONE, LOOK, LINUS IS BLOWING A RECTANGLE BALLOON!!
WOW!
DO ANOTHER ONE, LINUS!!
AMAZING!
INCREDIBLE!

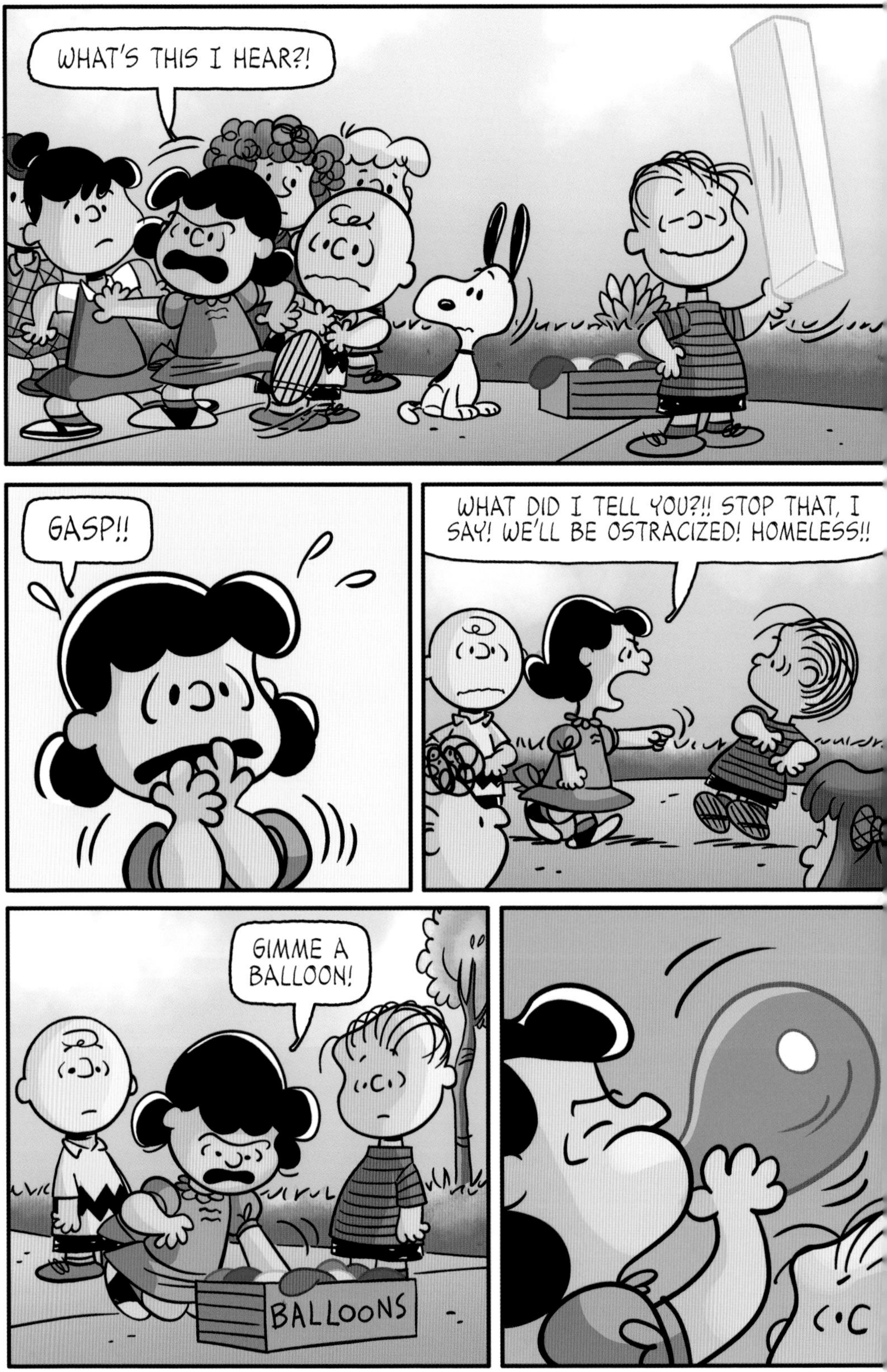
WHAT'S THIS I HEAR?!
GASP!!
WHAT DID I TELL YOU?!! STOP THAT, I SAY! WE'LL BE OSTRACIZED! HOMELESS!!
GIMME A BALLOON!
BALLOONS

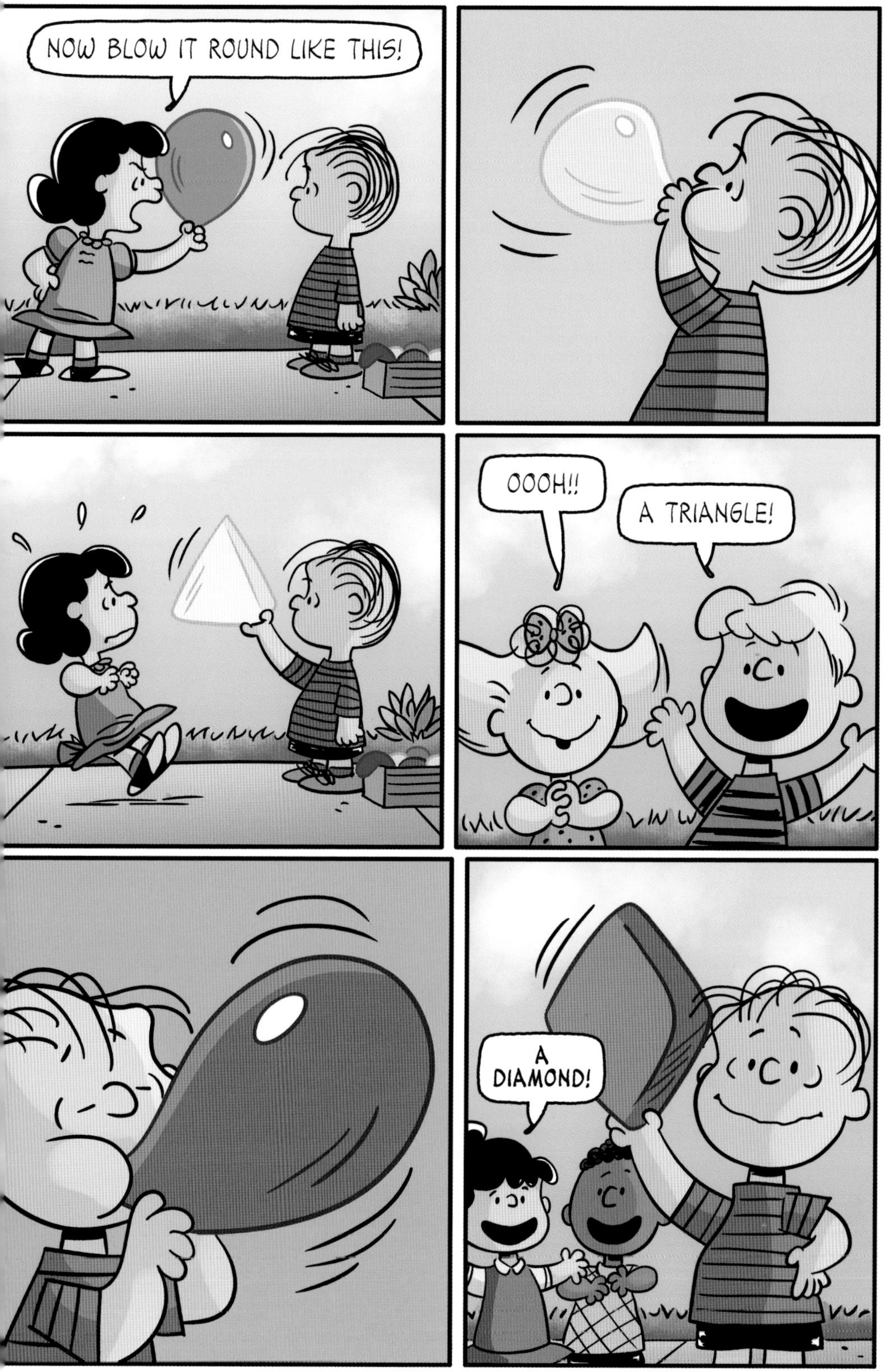
NOW BLOW IT ROUND LIKE THIS!
OOOH!!
A TRIANGLE!
A DIAMOND!

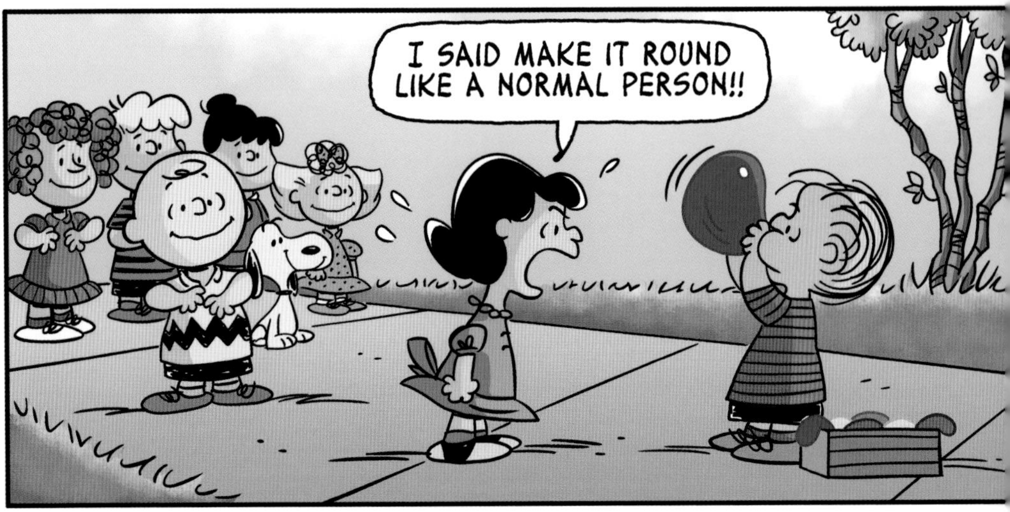
I SAID MAKE IT ROUND LIKE A NORMAL PERSON!!

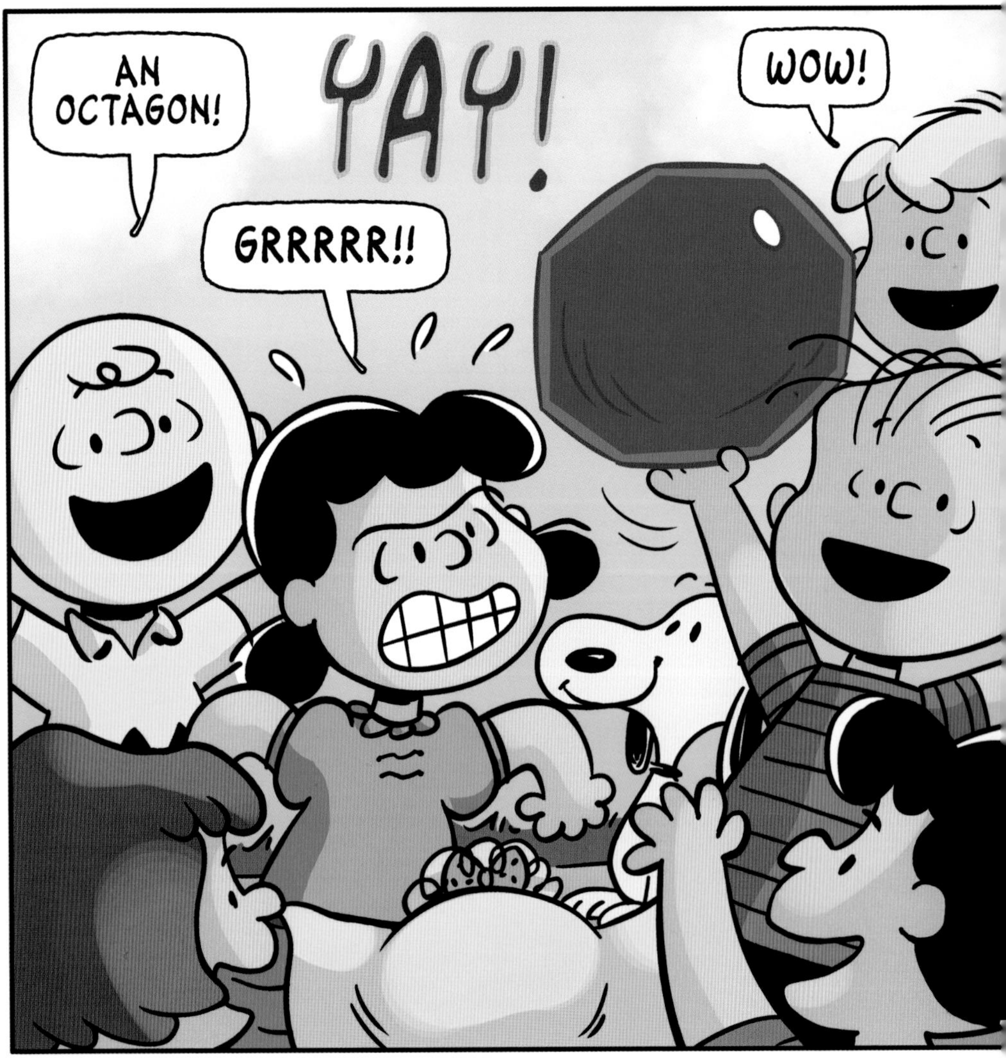
AN OCTAGON!
YAY!
WOW!
GRRRRR!!

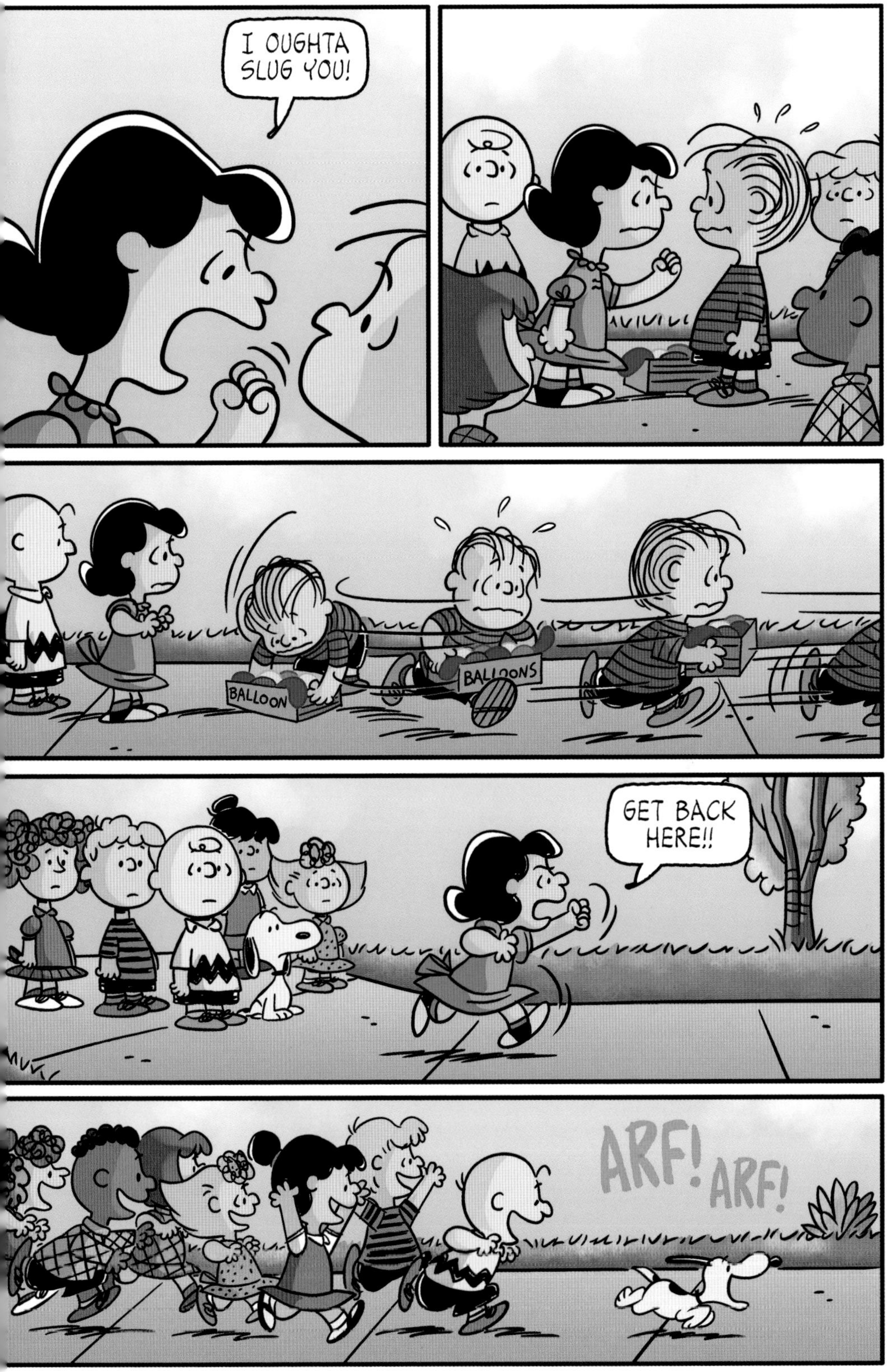
I OUGHTA SLUG YOU!
BALLOON
BALLOONS
GET BACK HERE!!
ARF! ARF!

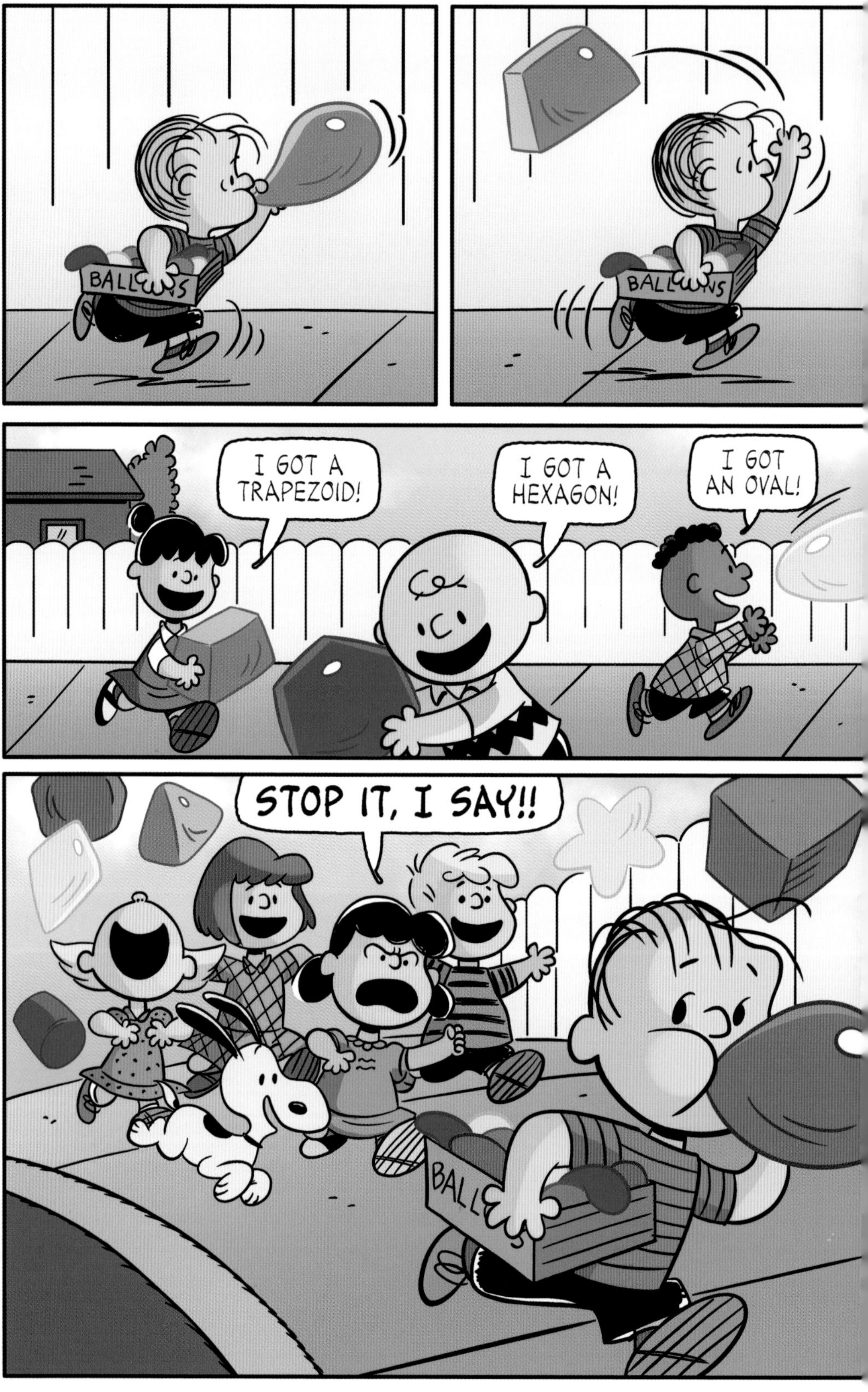
I GOT A TRAPEZOID!
I GOT A HEXAGON!
I GOT AN OVAL!
STOP IT, I SAY!!

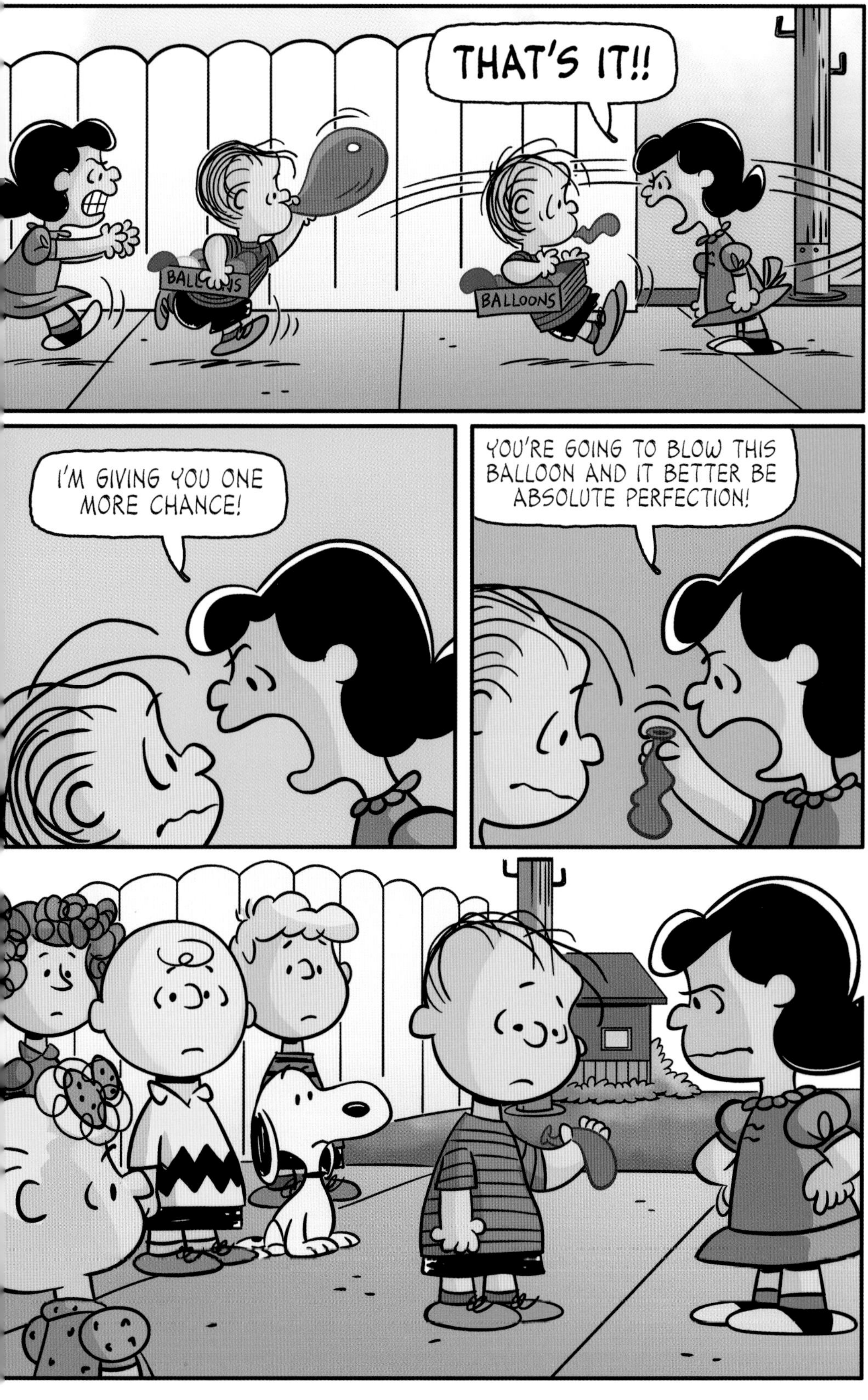
BALLOONS
BALLOONS
THAT'S IT!!
I'M GIVING YOU ONE MORE CHANCE!
YOU'RE GOING TO BLOW THIS BALLOON AND IT BETTER BE ABSOLUTE PERFECTION!

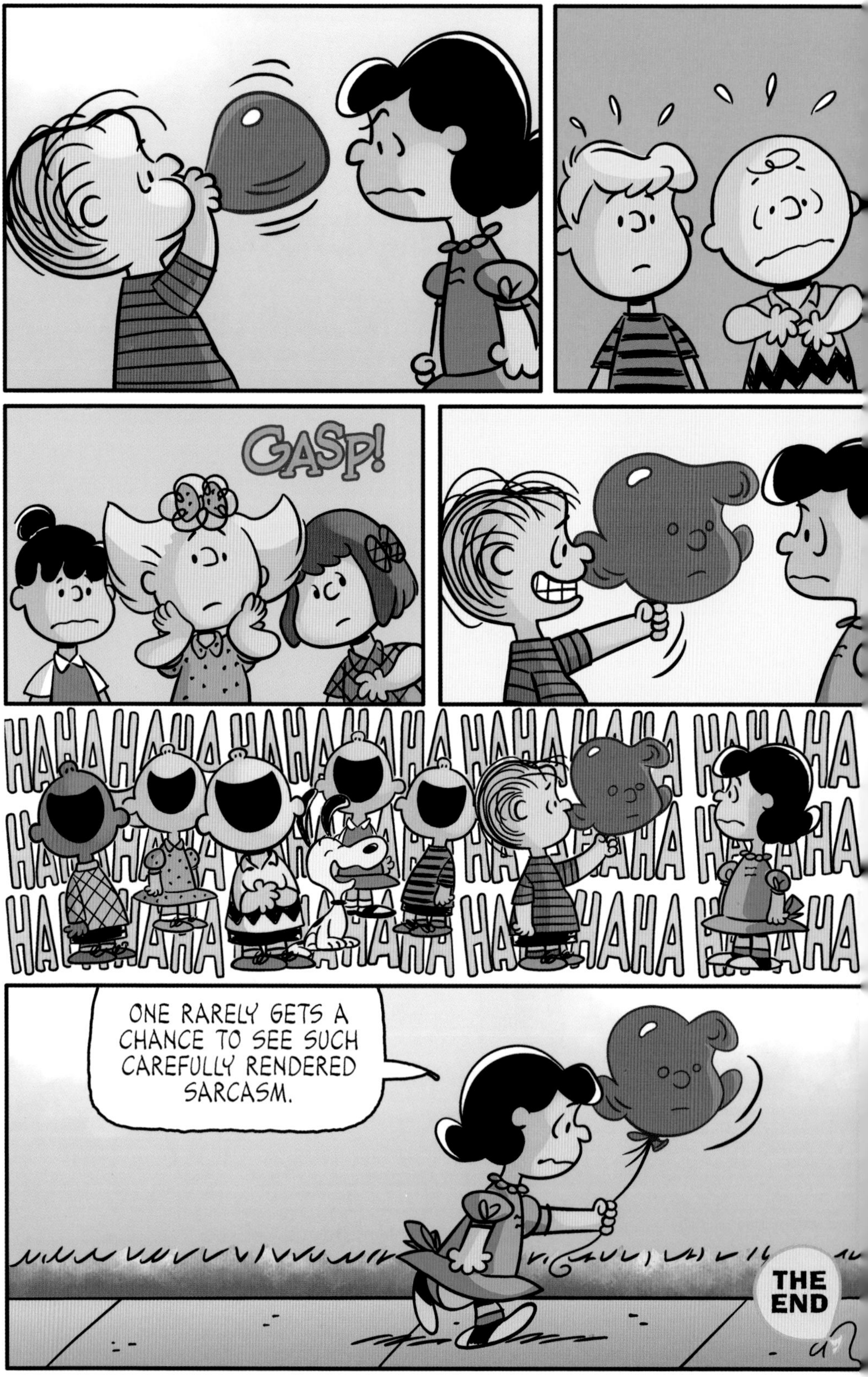
GASP!
HAHAHAHA HAHAHAHA HAHAHAHA HAHAHA
ONE RARELY GETS A CHANCE TO SEE SUCH CAREFULLY RENDERED SARCASM.
THE END

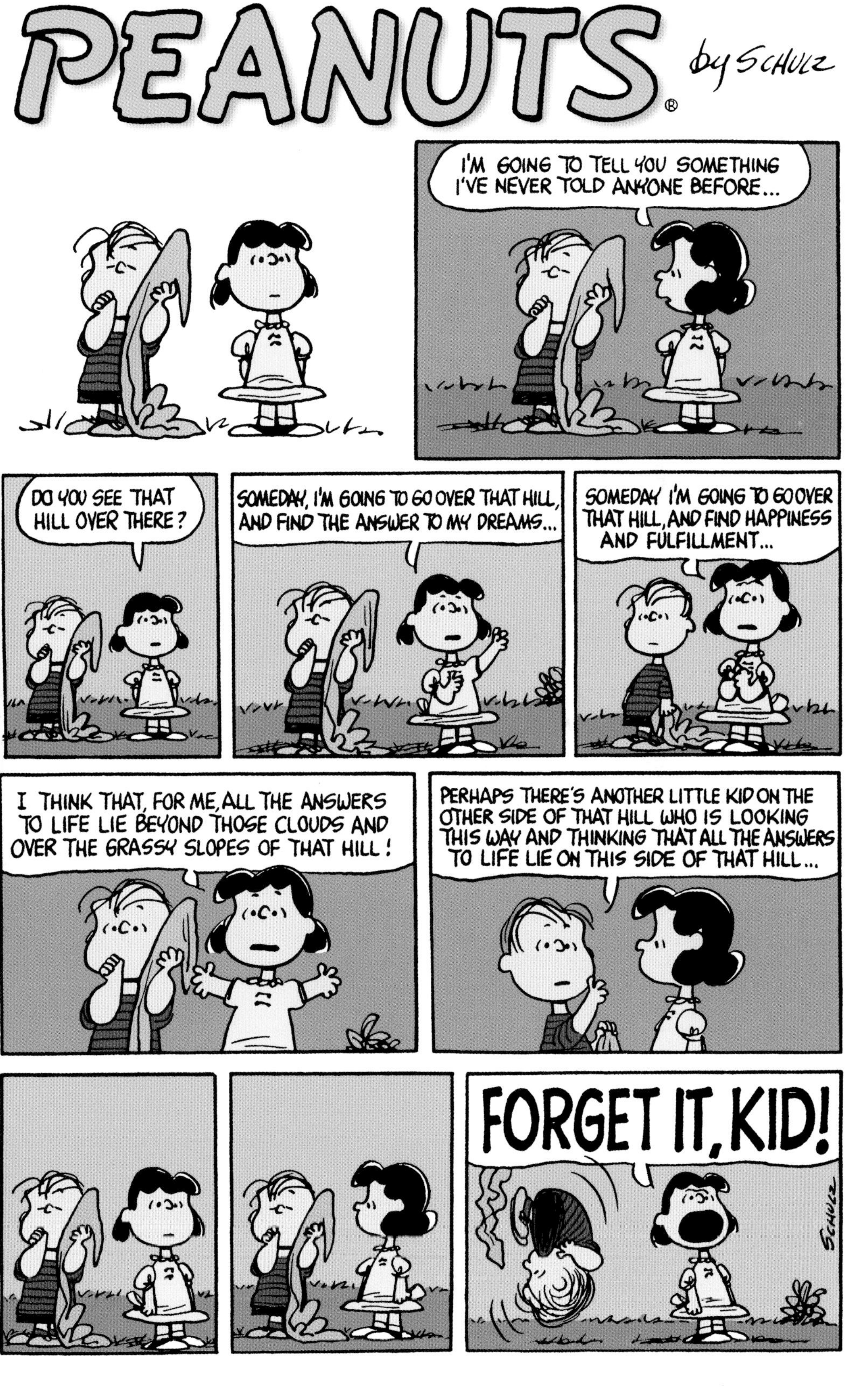
PEANUTS
by SCHULZ
I'M GOING TO TELL YOU SOMETHING I'VE NEVER TOLD ANYONE BEFORE...
DO YOU SEE THAT HILL OVER THERE?
SOMEDAY, I'M GOING TO GO OVER THAT HILL, AND FIND THE ANSWER TO MY DREAMS...
SOMEDAY I'M GOING TO GO OVER THAT HILL, AND FIND HAPPINESS AND FULFILLMENT...
I THINK THAT, FOR ME, ALL THE ANSWERS TO LIFE LIE BEYOND THOSE CLOUDS AND OVER THE GRASSY SLOPES OF THAT HILL!
PERHAPS THERE'S ANOTHER LITTLE KID ON THE OTHER SIDE OF THAT HILL WHO IS LOOKING THIS WAY AND THINKING THAT ALL THE ANSWERS TO LIFE LIE ON THIS SIDE OF THAT HILL...
FORGET IT, KID!
SCHULZ

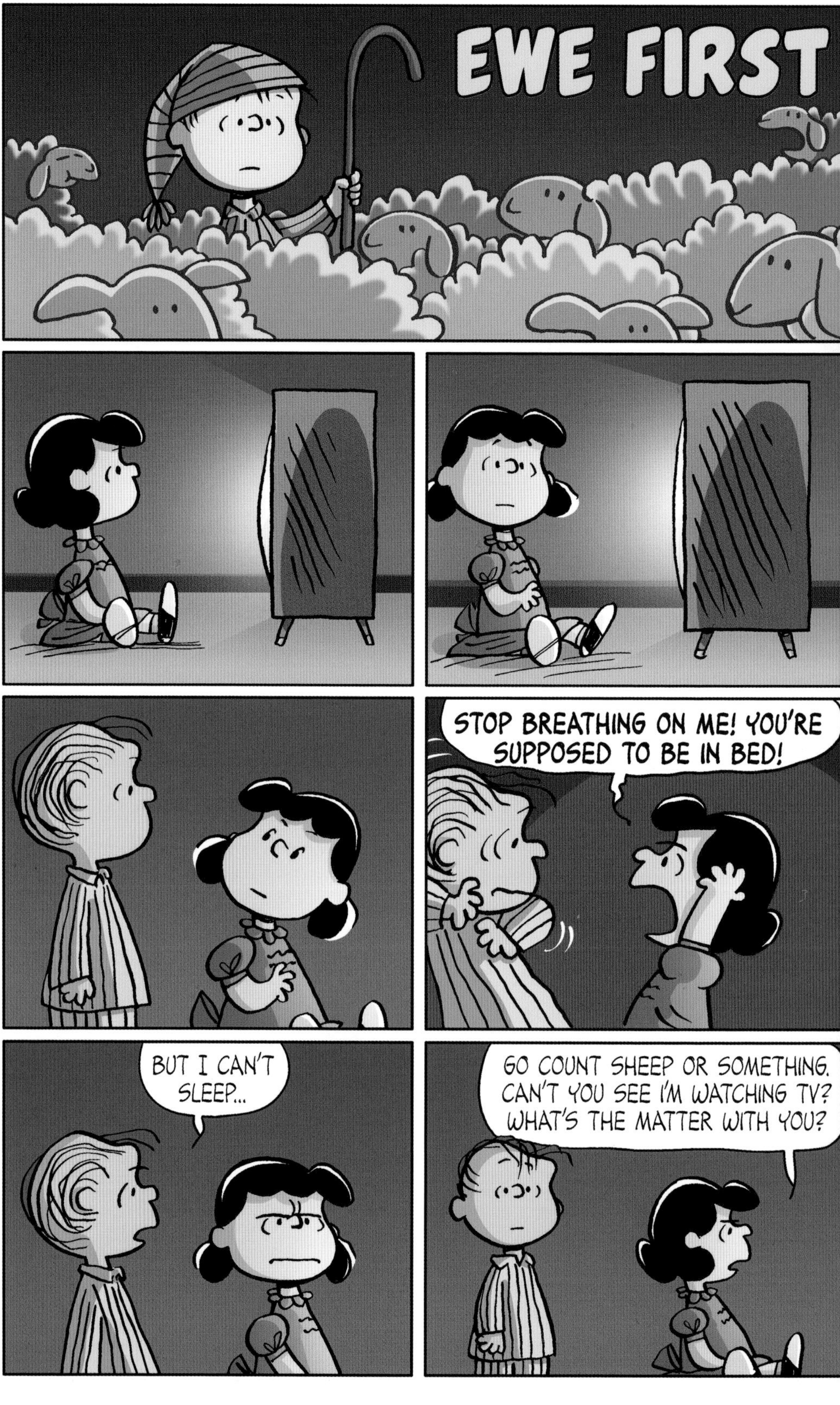
EWE FIRST
STOP BREATHING ON ME! YOU'RE SUPPOSED TO BE IN BED!
BUT I CAN'T SLEEP...
GO COUNT SHEEP OR SOMETHING. CAN'T YOU SEE I'M WATCHING TV? WHAT'S THE MATTER WITH YOU?

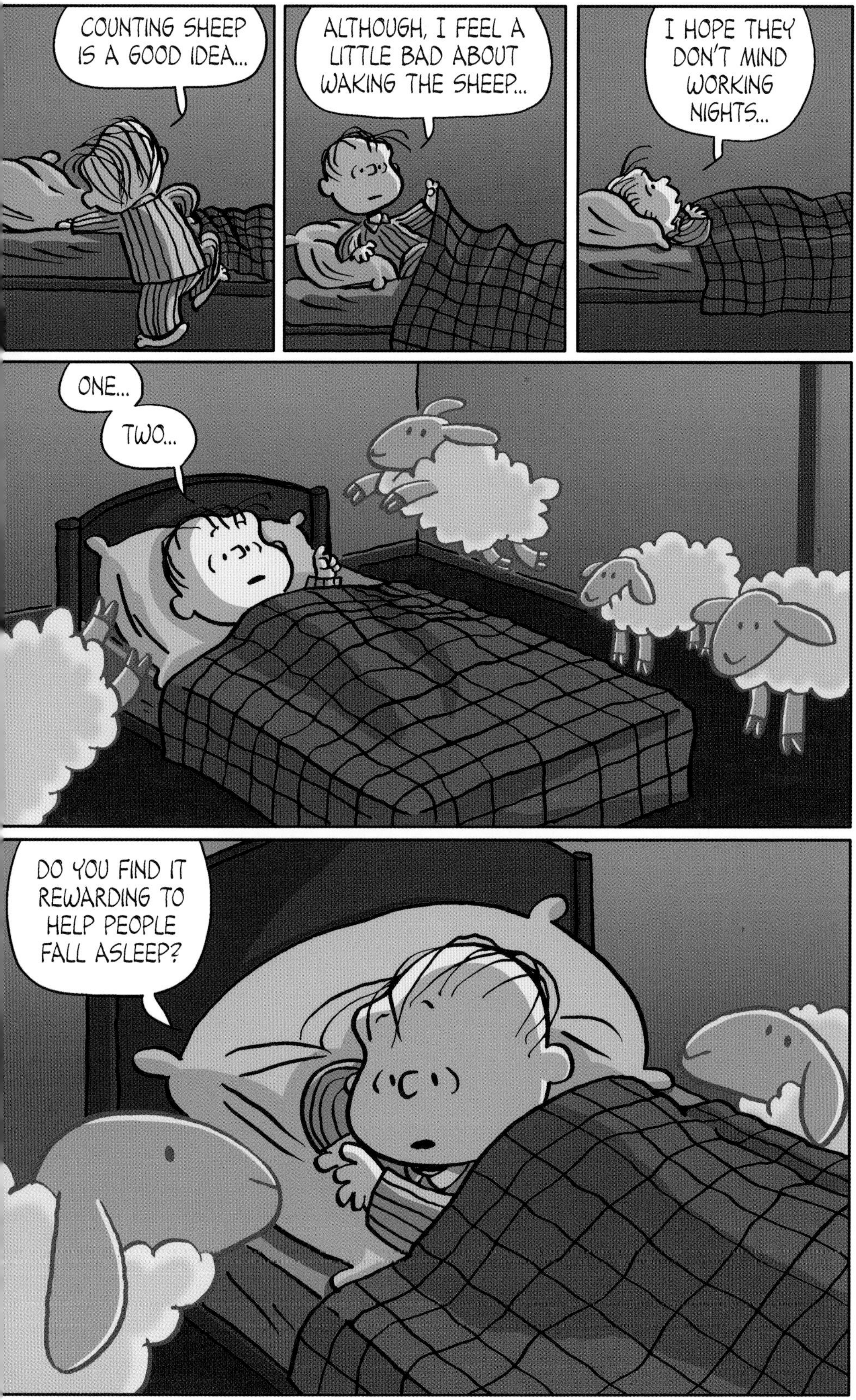
COUNTING SHEEP IS A GOOD IDEA...
ALTHOUGH, I FEEL A LITTLE BAD ABOUT WAKING THE SHEEP...
I HOPE THEY DON'T MIND WORKING NIGHTS...
ONE...
TWO...
DO YOU FIND IT REWARDING TO HELP PEOPLE FALL ASLEEP?

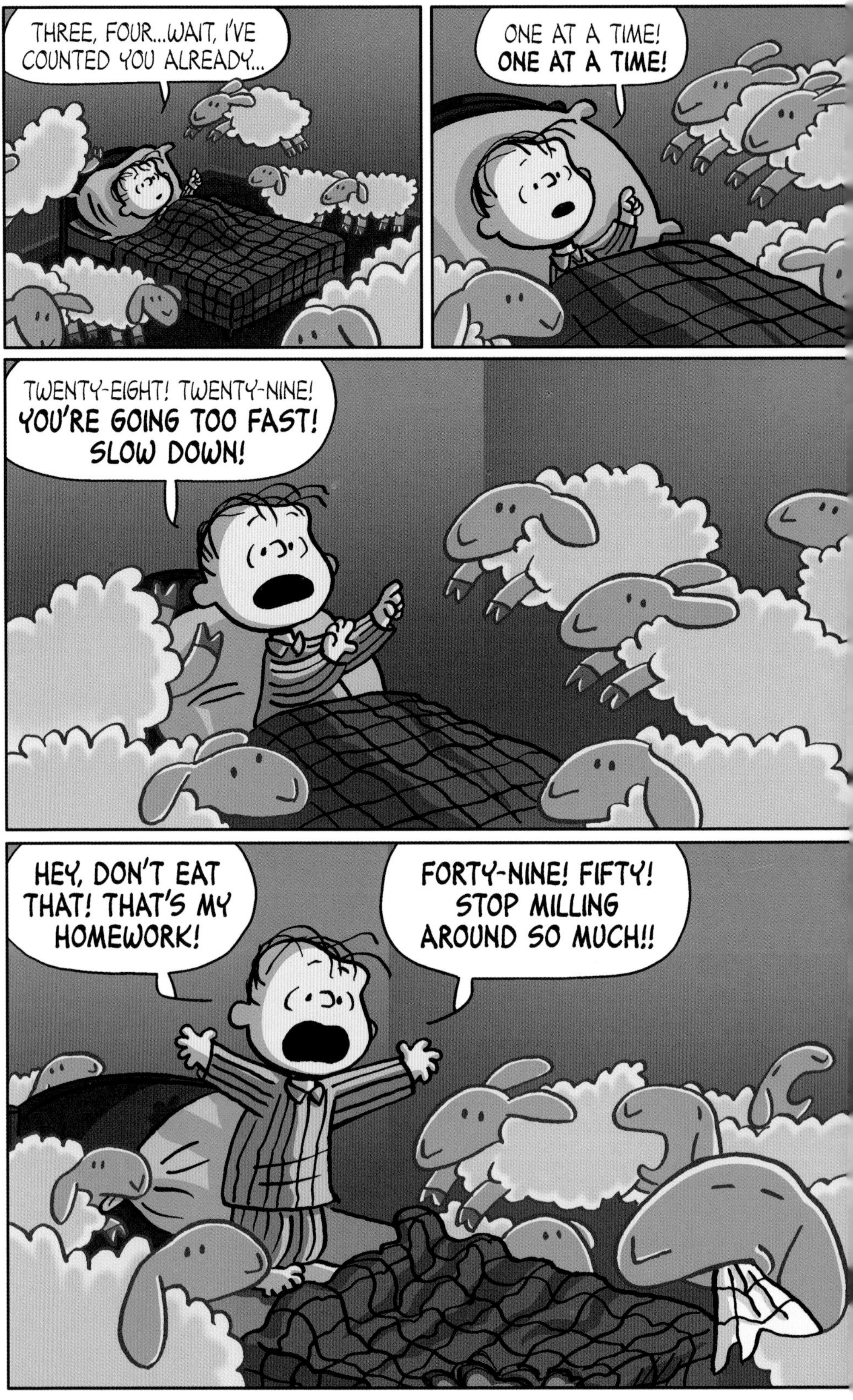

THREE, FOUR...WAIT, I'VE COUNTED YOU ALREADY...
ONE AT A TIME! **ONE AT A TIME!**
TWENTY-EIGHT! TWENTY-NINE! **YOU'RE GOING TOO FAST! SLOW DOWN!**
HEY, DON'T EAT THAT! THAT'S MY HOMEWORK!
FORTY-NINE! FIFTY! STOP MILLING AROUND SO MUCH!!

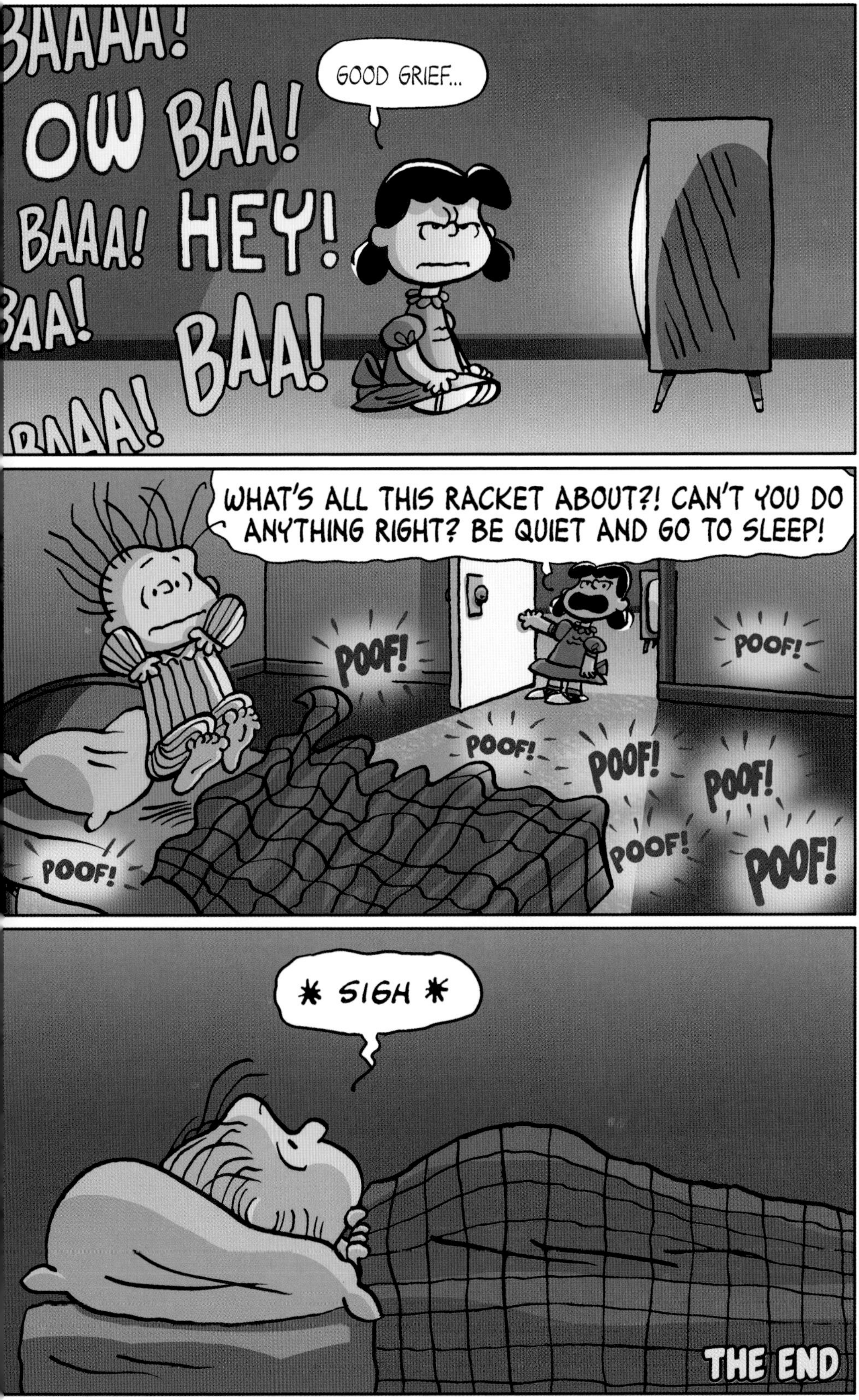
GOOD GRIEF...
OW BAA!
BAAA!
HEY!
BAA!
WHAT'S ALL THIS RACKET ABOUT?! CAN'T YOU DO ANYTHING RIGHT? BE QUIET AND GO TO SLEEP!
POOF!
POOF!
POOF!
POOF!
POOF!
POOF!
POOF!
POOF!
* SIGH *
THE END

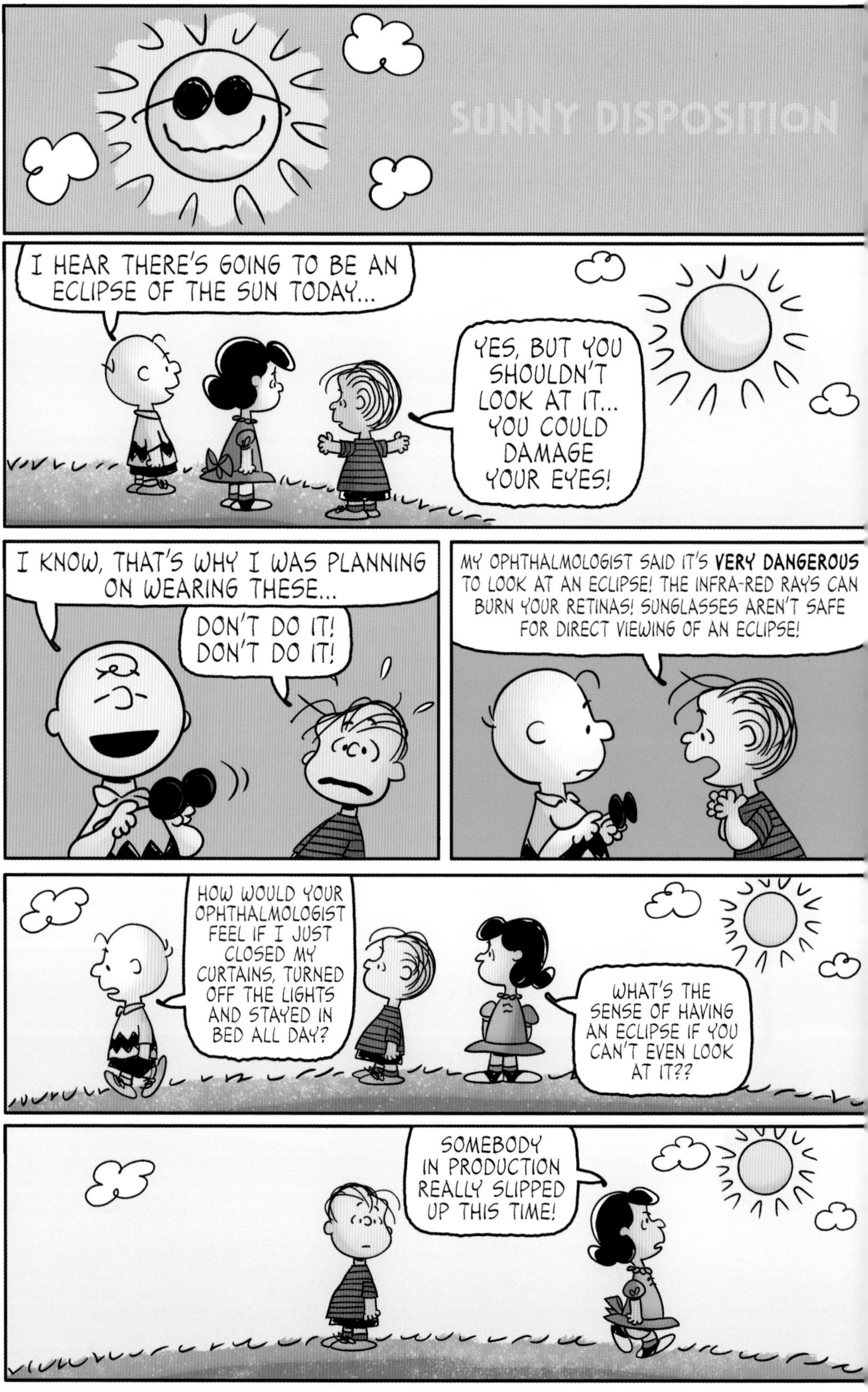
SUNNY DISPOSITION
I HEAR THERE'S GOING TO BE AN ECLIPSE OF THE SUN TODAY...
YES, BUT YOU SHOULDN'T LOOK AT IT... YOU COULD DAMAGE YOUR EYES!
I KNOW, THAT'S WHY I WAS PLANNING ON WEARING THESE...
DON'T DO IT! DON'T DO IT!
MY OPHTHALMOLOGIST SAID IT'S **VERY DANGEROUS** TO LOOK AT AN ECLIPSE! THE INFRA-RED RAYS CAN BURN YOUR RETINAS! SUNGLASSES AREN'T SAFE FOR DIRECT VIEWING OF AN ECLIPSE!
HOW WOULD YOUR OPHTHALMOLOGIST FEEL IF I JUST CLOSED MY CURTAINS, TURNED OFF THE LIGHTS AND STAYED IN BED ALL DAY?
WHAT'S THE SENSE OF HAVING AN ECLIPSE IF YOU CAN'T EVEN LOOK AT IT??
SOMEBODY IN PRODUCTION REALLY SLIPPED UP THIS TIME!

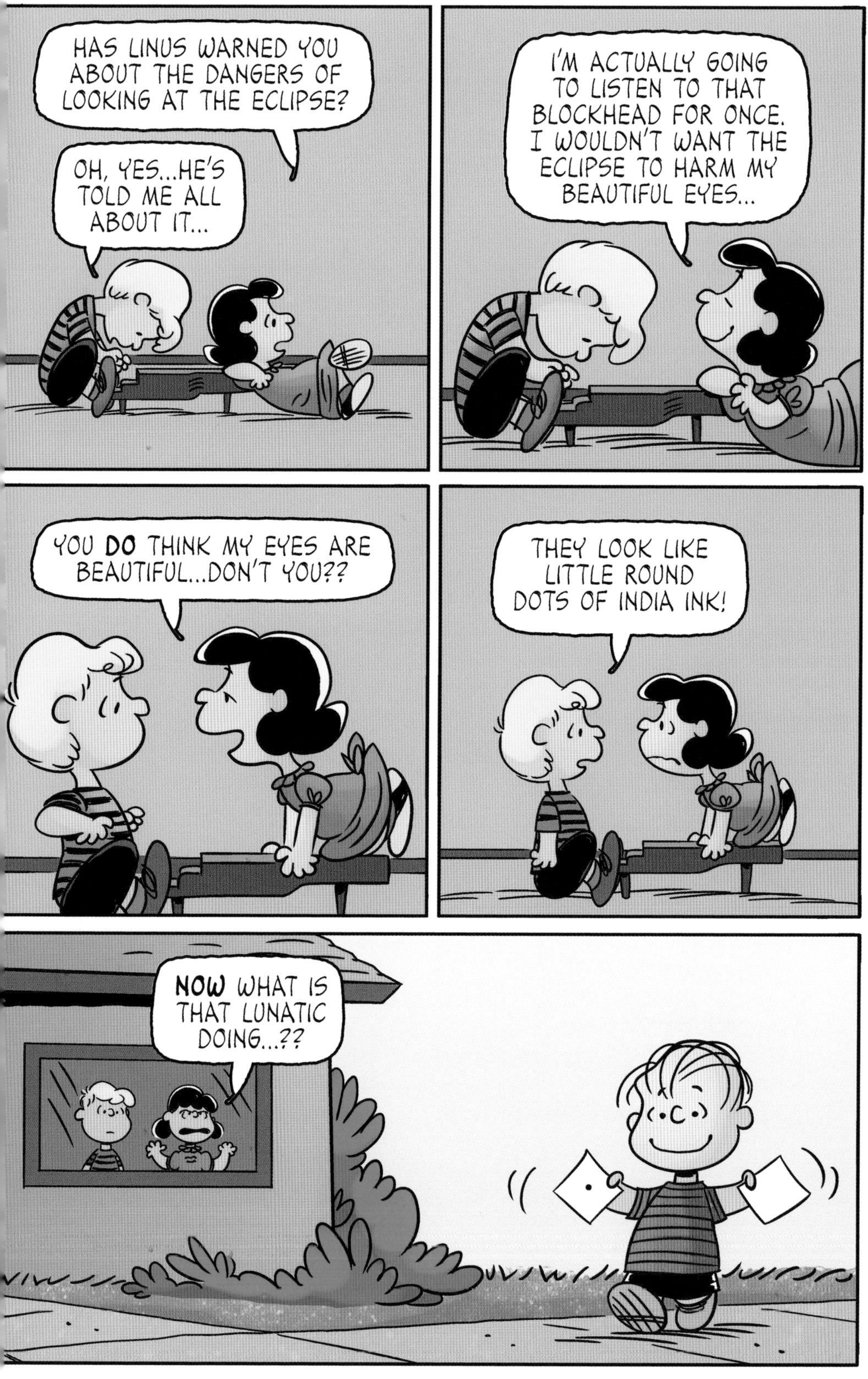
HAS LINUS WARNED YOU ABOUT THE DANGERS OF LOOKING AT THE ECLIPSE?
OH, YES...HE'S TOLD ME ALL ABOUT IT...
I'M ACTUALLY GOING TO LISTEN TO THAT BLOCKHEAD FOR ONCE. I WOULDN'T WANT THE ECLIPSE TO HARM MY BEAUTIFUL EYES...
YOU **DO** THINK MY EYES ARE BEAUTIFUL...DON'T YOU??
THEY LOOK LIKE LITTLE ROUND DOTS OF INDIA INK!
NOW WHAT IS THAT LUNATIC DOING...??

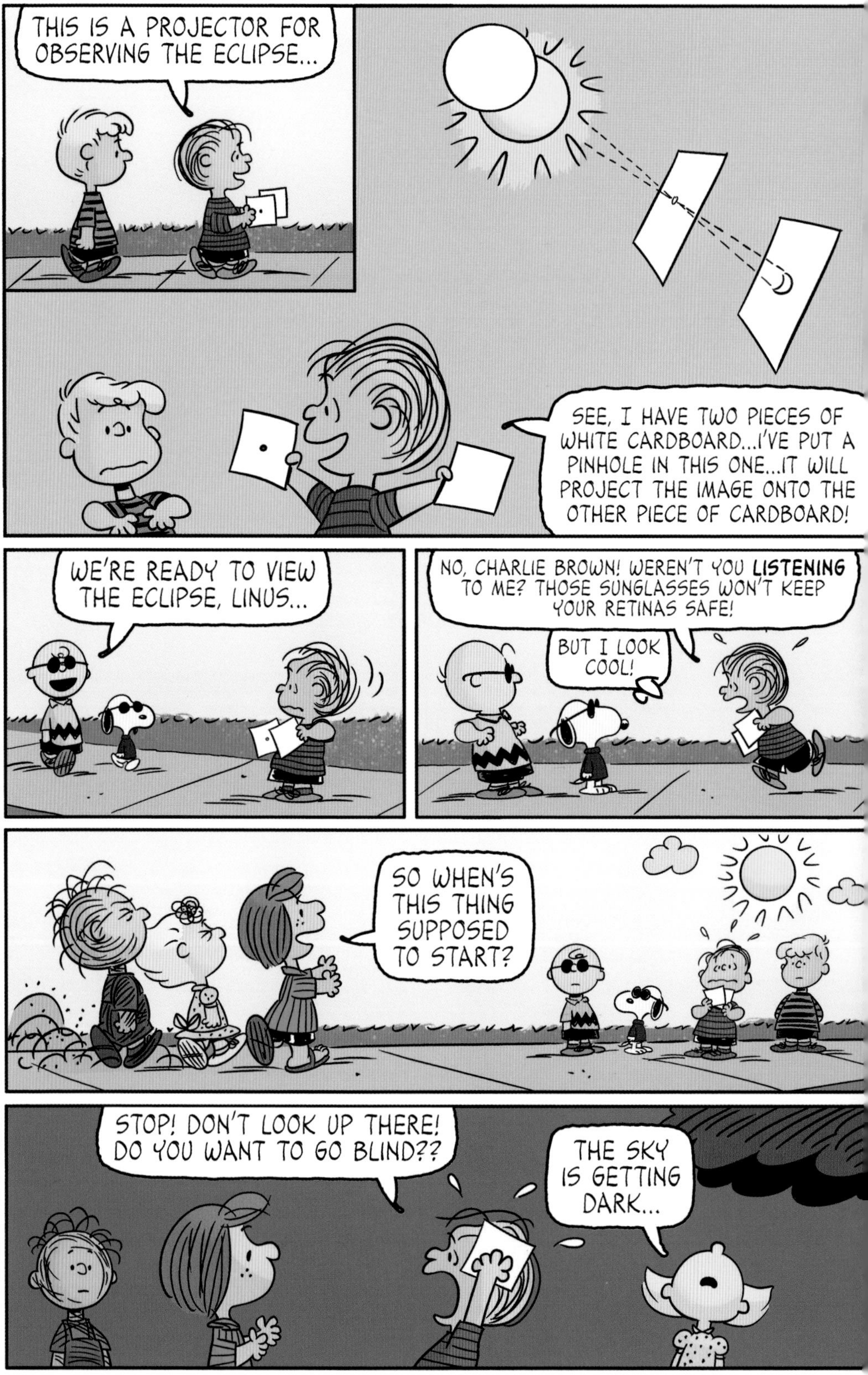
THIS IS A PROJECTOR FOR OBSERVING THE ECLIPSE...
SEE, I HAVE TWO PIECES OF WHITE CARDBOARD...I'VE PUT A PINHOLE IN THIS ONE...IT WILL PROJECT THE IMAGE ONTO THE OTHER PIECE OF CARDBOARD!
WE'RE READY TO VIEW THE ECLIPSE, LINUS...
NO, CHARLIE BROWN! WEREN'T YOU LISTENING TO ME? THOSE SUNGLASSES WON'T KEEP YOUR RETINAS SAFE!
BUT I LOOK COOL!
SO WHEN'S THIS THING SUPPOSED TO START?
STOP! DON'T LOOK UP THERE! DO YOU WANT TO GO BLIND??
THE SKY IS GETTING DARK...

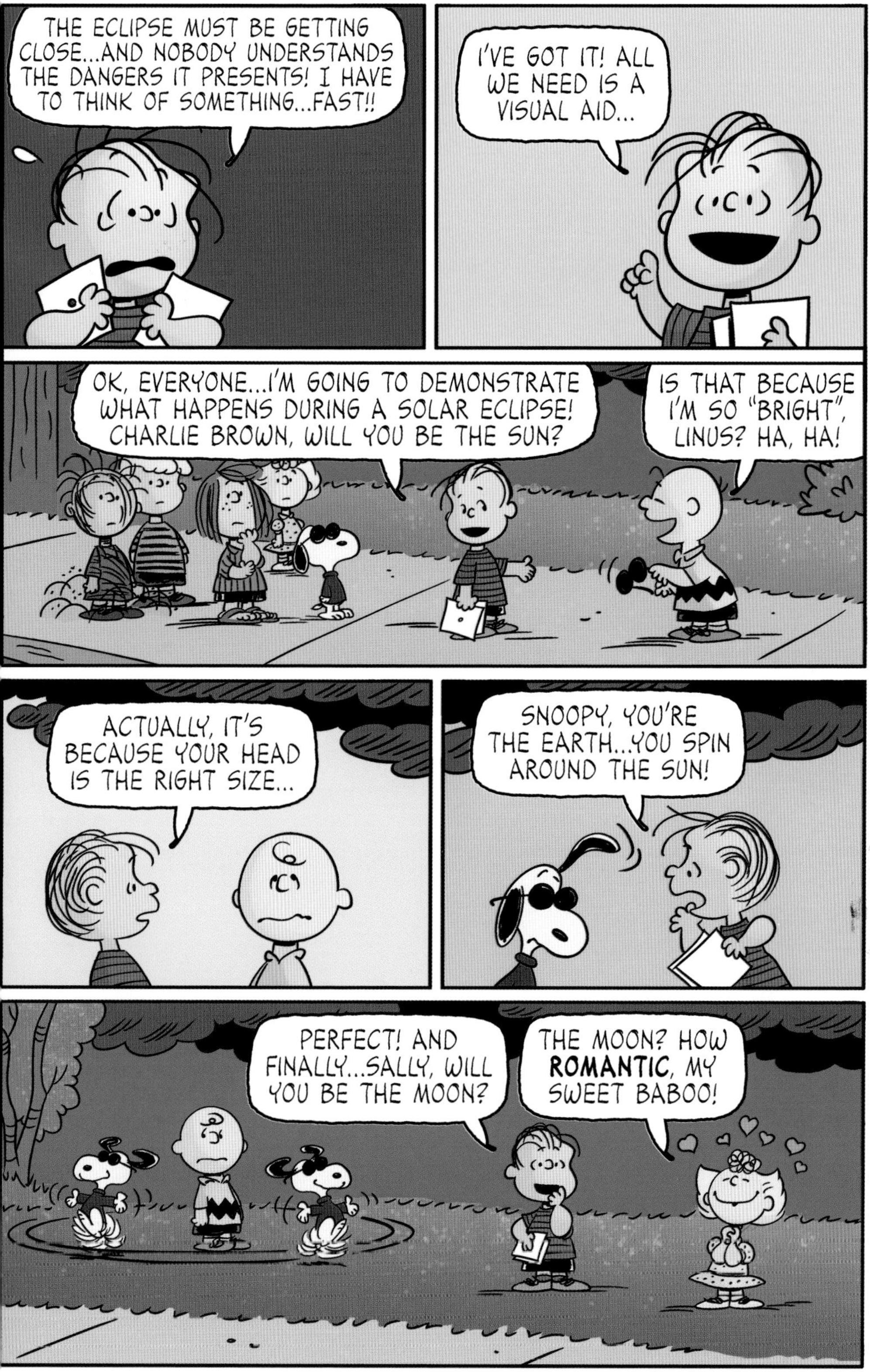
THE ECLIPSE MUST BE GETTING CLOSE...AND NOBODY UNDERSTANDS THE DANGERS IT PRESENTS! I HAVE TO THINK OF SOMETHING...FAST!!
I'VE GOT IT! ALL WE NEED IS A VISUAL AID...
OK, EVERYONE...I'M GOING TO DEMONSTRATE WHAT HAPPENS DURING A SOLAR ECLIPSE! CHARLIE BROWN, WILL YOU BE THE SUN?
IS THAT BECAUSE I'M SO "BRIGHT", LINUS? HA, HA!
ACTUALLY, IT'S BECAUSE YOUR HEAD IS THE RIGHT SIZE...
SNOOPY, YOU'RE THE EARTH...YOU SPIN AROUND THE SUN!
PERFECT! AND FINALLY...SALLY, WILL YOU BE THE MOON?
THE MOON? HOW **ROMANTIC**, MY SWEET BABOO!

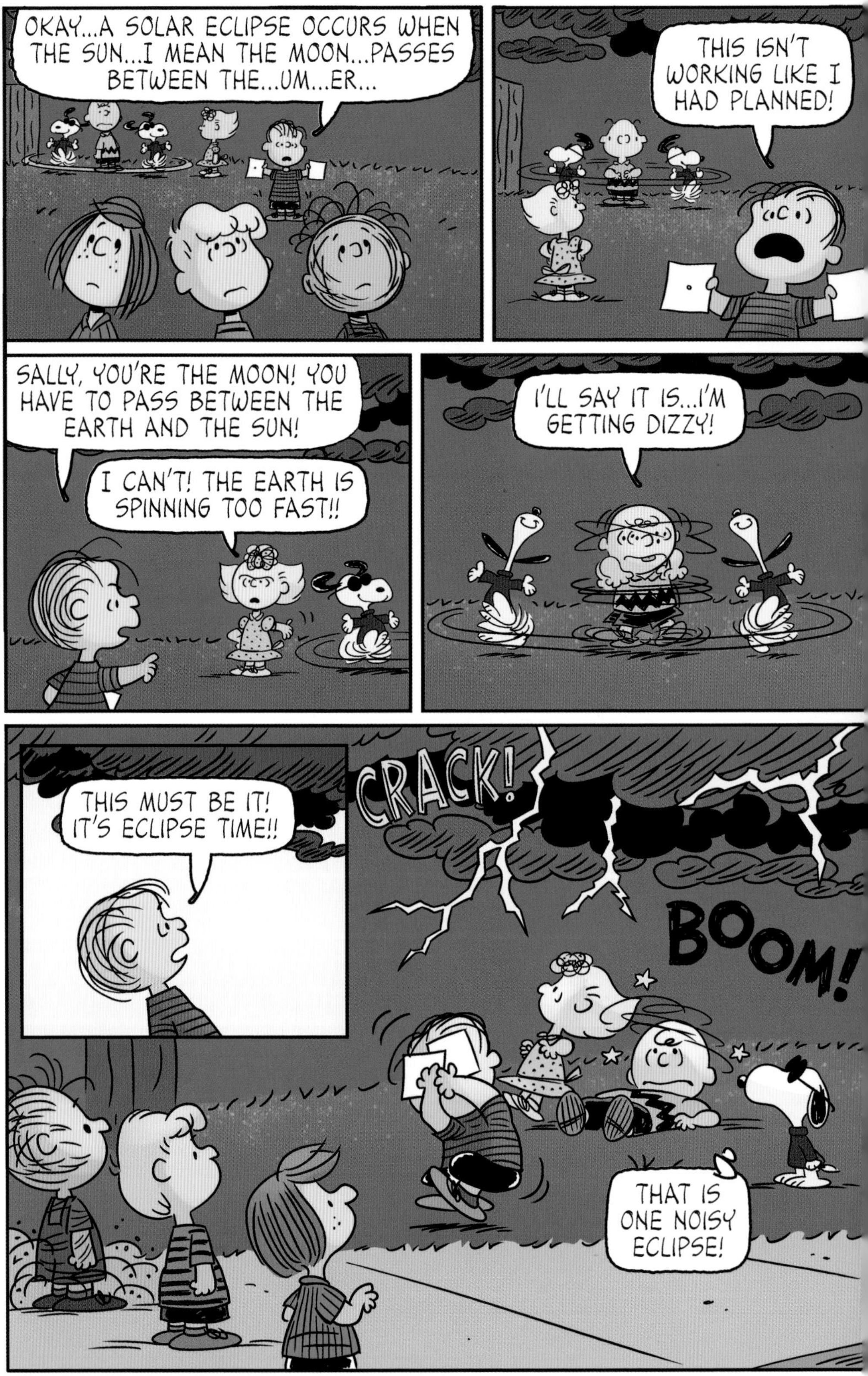
OKAY...A SOLAR ECLIPSE OCCURS WHEN THE SUN...I MEAN THE MOON...PASSES BETWEEN THE...UM...ER...
THIS ISN'T WORKING LIKE I HAD PLANNED!
SALLY, YOU'RE THE MOON! YOU HAVE TO PASS BETWEEN THE EARTH AND THE SUN!
I CAN'T! THE EARTH IS SPINNING TOO FAST!!
I'LL SAY IT IS...I'M GETTING DIZZY!
THIS MUST BE IT! IT'S ECLIPSE TIME!!
CRACK!
BOOM!
THAT IS ONE NOISY ECLIPSE!

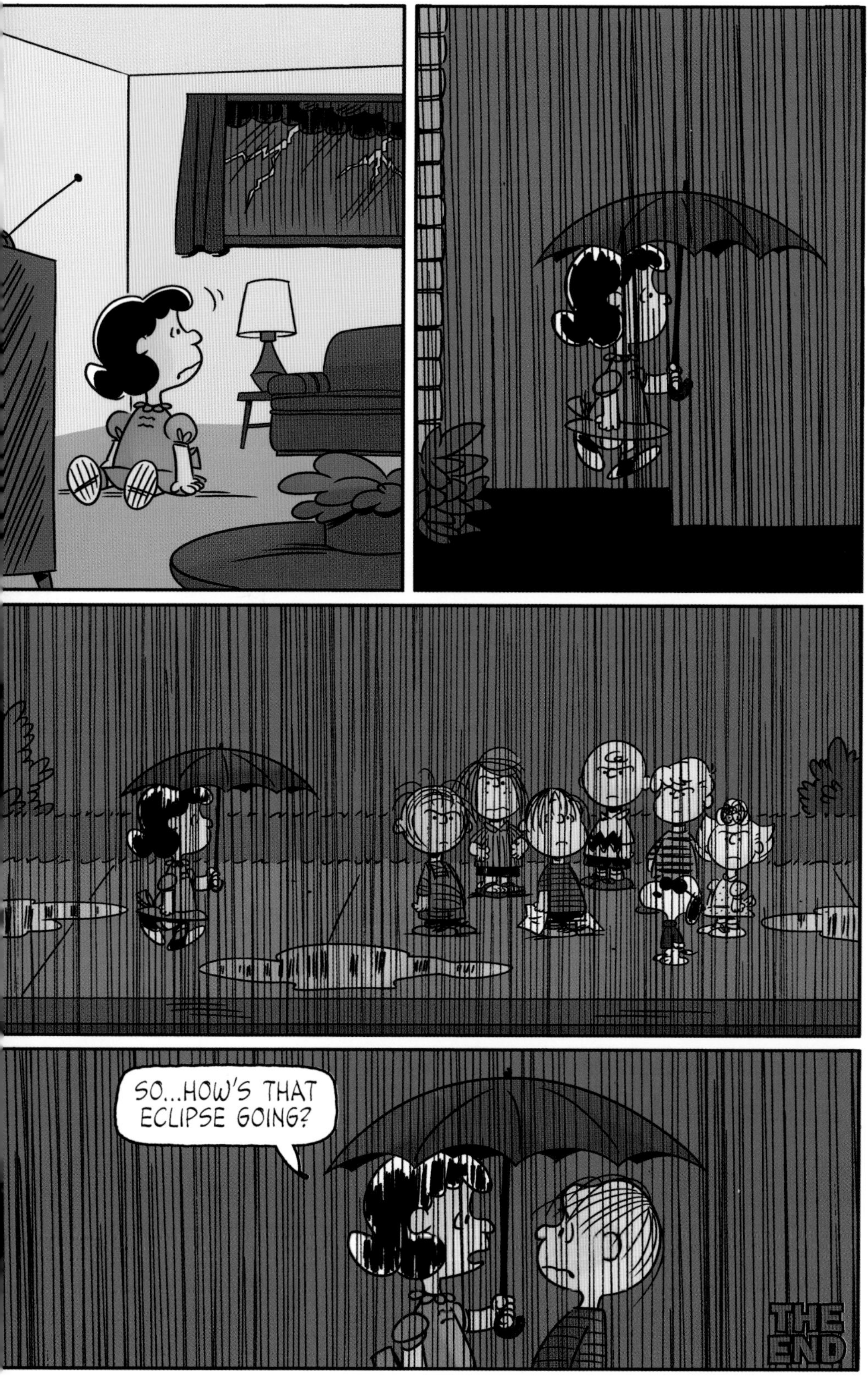
SO...HOW'S THAT ECLIPSE GOING?
THE END

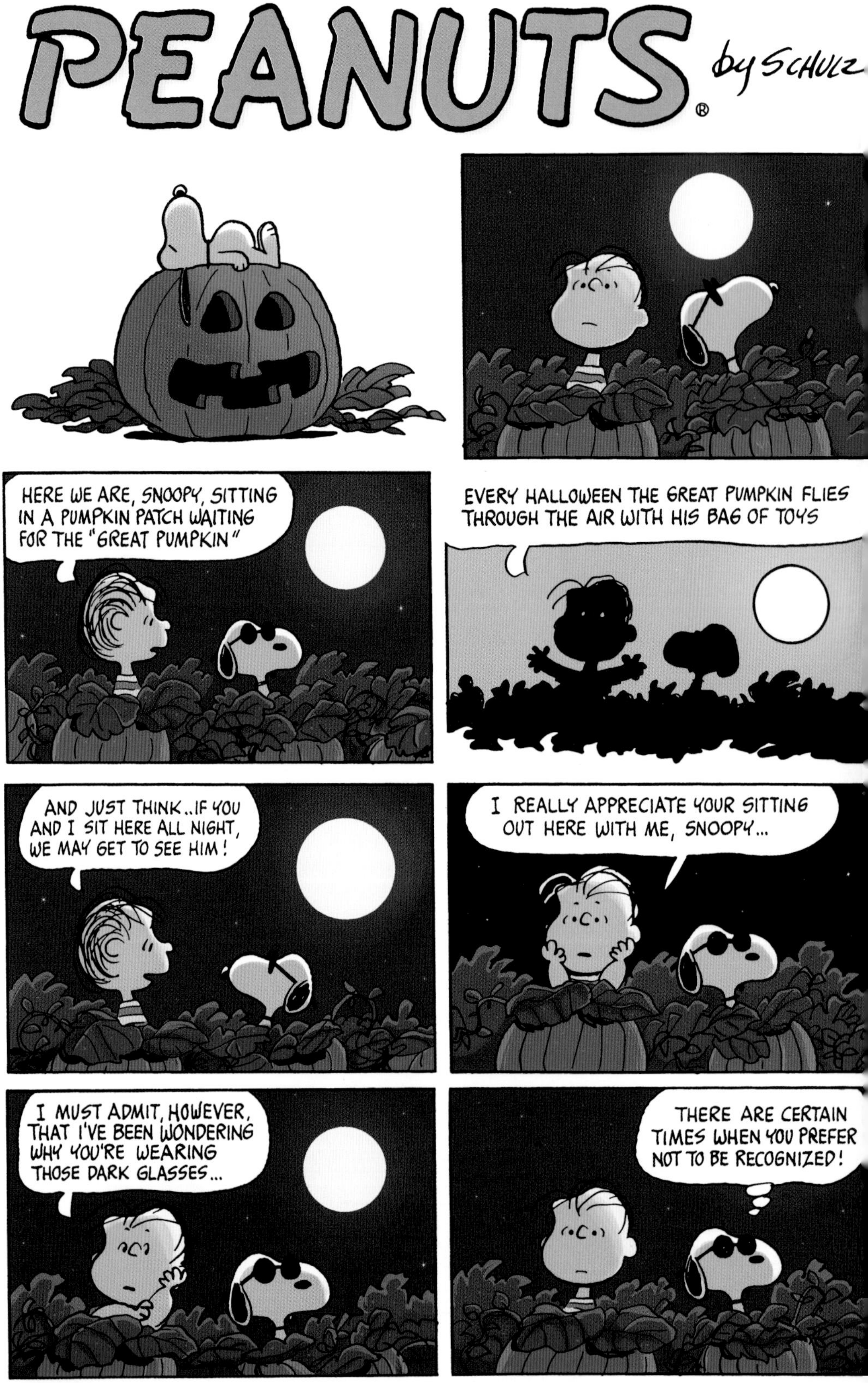
PEANUTS
by SCHULZ
HERE WE ARE, SNOOPY, SITTING IN A PUMPKIN PATCH WAITING FOR THE "GREAT PUMPKIN"
EVERY HALLOWEEN THE GREAT PUMPKIN FLIES THROUGH THE AIR WITH HIS BAG OF TOYS
AND JUST THINK..IF YOU AND I SIT HERE ALL NIGHT, WE MAY GET TO SEE HIM!
I REALLY APPRECIATE YOUR SITTING OUT HERE WITH ME, SNOOPY...
I MUST ADMIT, HOWEVER, THAT I'VE BEEN WONDERING WHY YOU'RE WEARING THOSE DARK GLASSES...
THERE ARE CERTAIN TIMES WHEN YOU PREFER NOT TO BE RECOGNIZED!

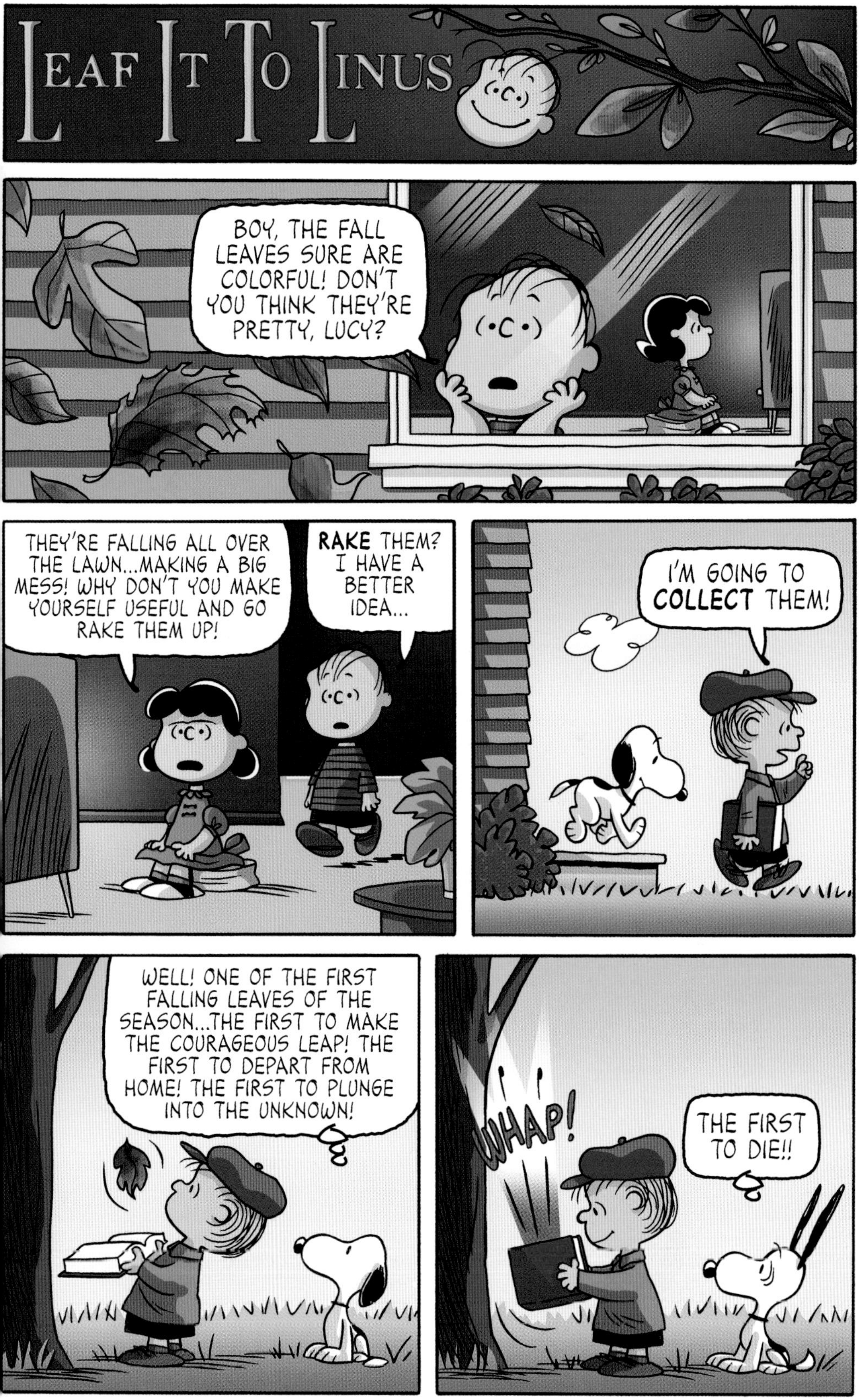
LEAF IT TO LINUS
BOY, THE FALL LEAVES SURE ARE COLORFUL! DON'T YOU THINK THEY'RE PRETTY, LUCY?
THEY'RE FALLING ALL OVER THE LAWN...MAKING A BIG MESS! WHY DON'T YOU MAKE YOURSELF USEFUL AND GO RAKE THEM UP!
RAKE THEM? I HAVE A BETTER IDEA...
I'M GOING TO COLLECT THEM!
WELL! ONE OF THE FIRST FALLING LEAVES OF THE SEASON...THE FIRST TO MAKE THE COURAGEOUS LEAP! THE FIRST TO DEPART FROM HOME! THE FIRST TO PLUNGE INTO THE UNKNOWN!
WHAP!
THE FIRST TO DIE!!

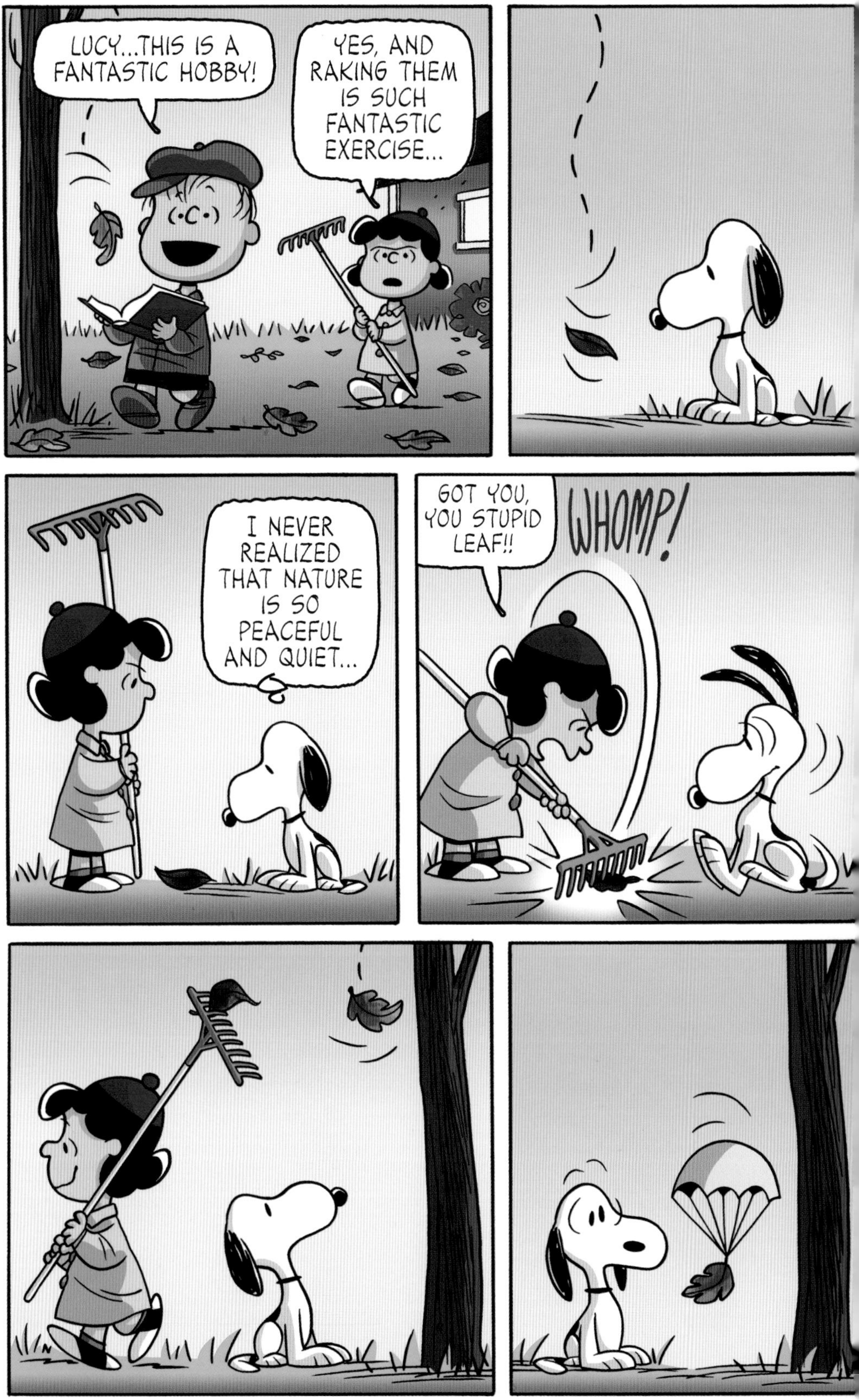
LUCY...THIS IS A FANTASTIC HOBBY!
YES, AND RAKING THEM IS SUCH FANTASTIC EXERCISE...
I NEVER REALIZED THAT NATURE IS SO PEACEFUL AND QUIET...
GOT YOU, YOU STUPID LEAF!!
WHOMP!

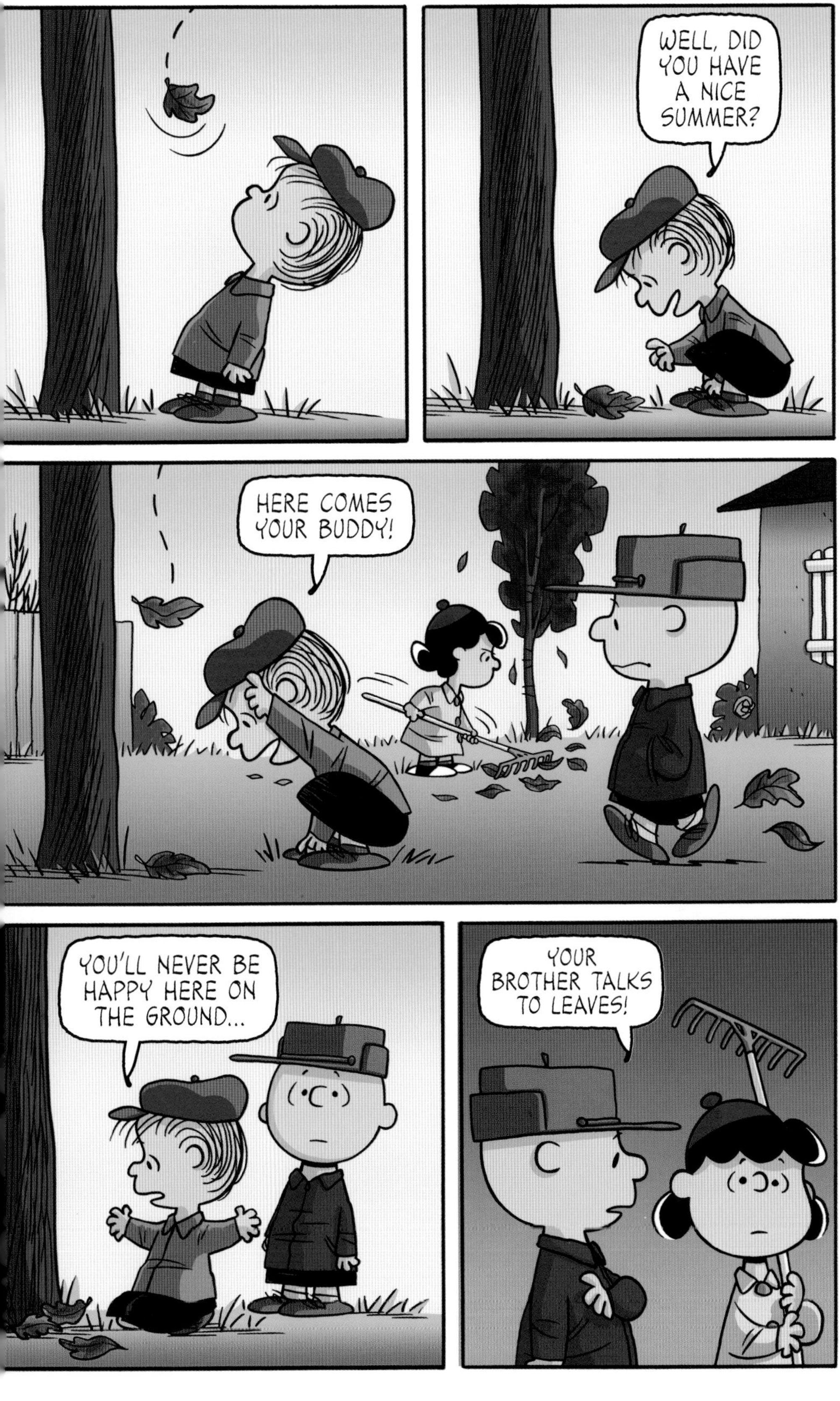
WELL, DID YOU HAVE A NICE SUMMER?
HERE COMES YOUR BUDDY!
YOU'LL NEVER BE HAPPY HERE ON THE GROUND...
YOUR BROTHER TALKS TO LEAVES!

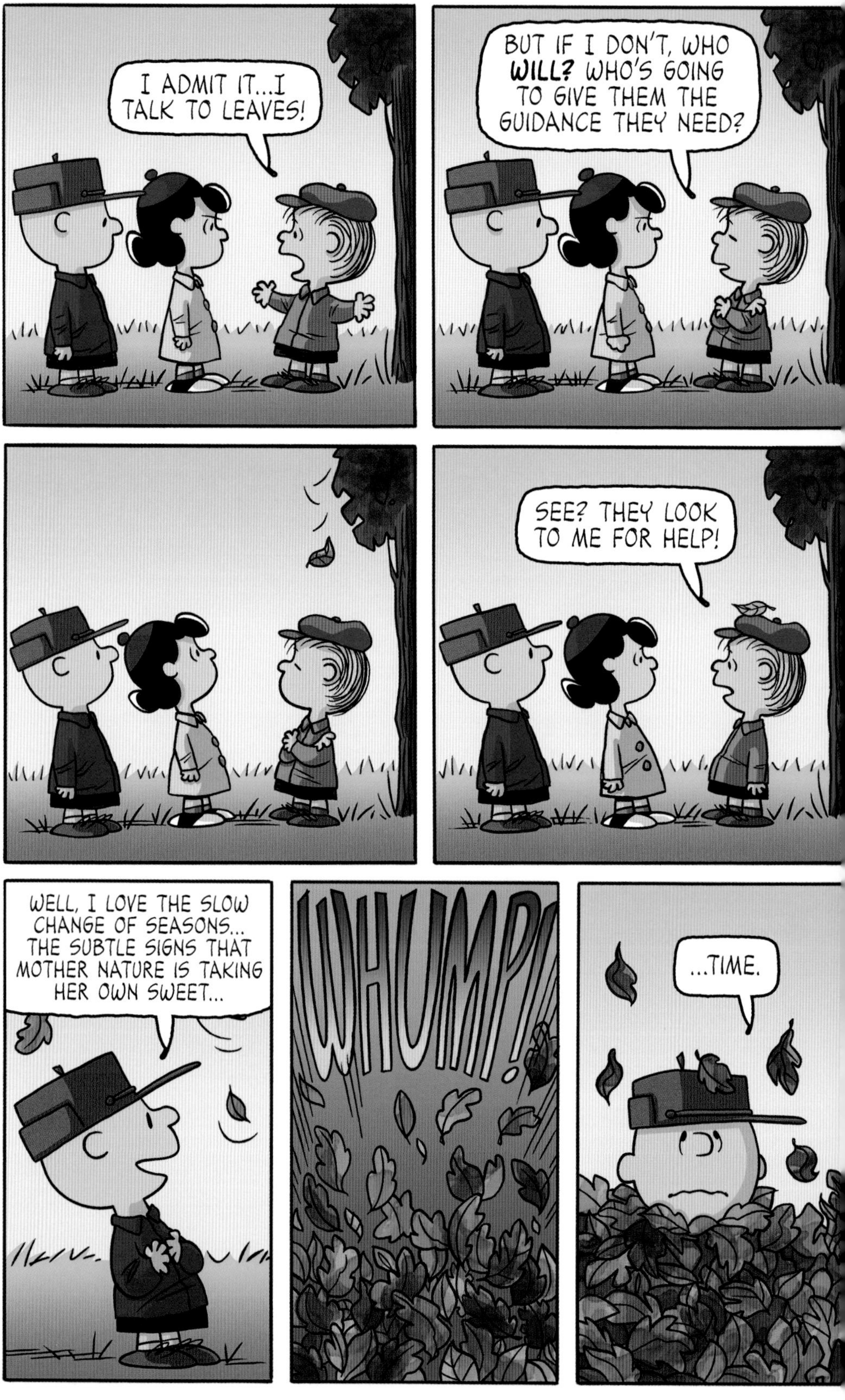
I ADMIT IT...I TALK TO LEAVES!
BUT IF I DON'T, WHO **WILL?** WHO'S GOING TO GIVE THEM THE GUIDANCE THEY NEED?
SEE? THEY LOOK TO ME FOR HELP!
WELL, I LOVE THE SLOW CHANGE OF SEASONS... THE SUBTLE SIGNS THAT MOTHER NATURE IS TAKING HER OWN SWEET...
WHUMP!
...TIME.

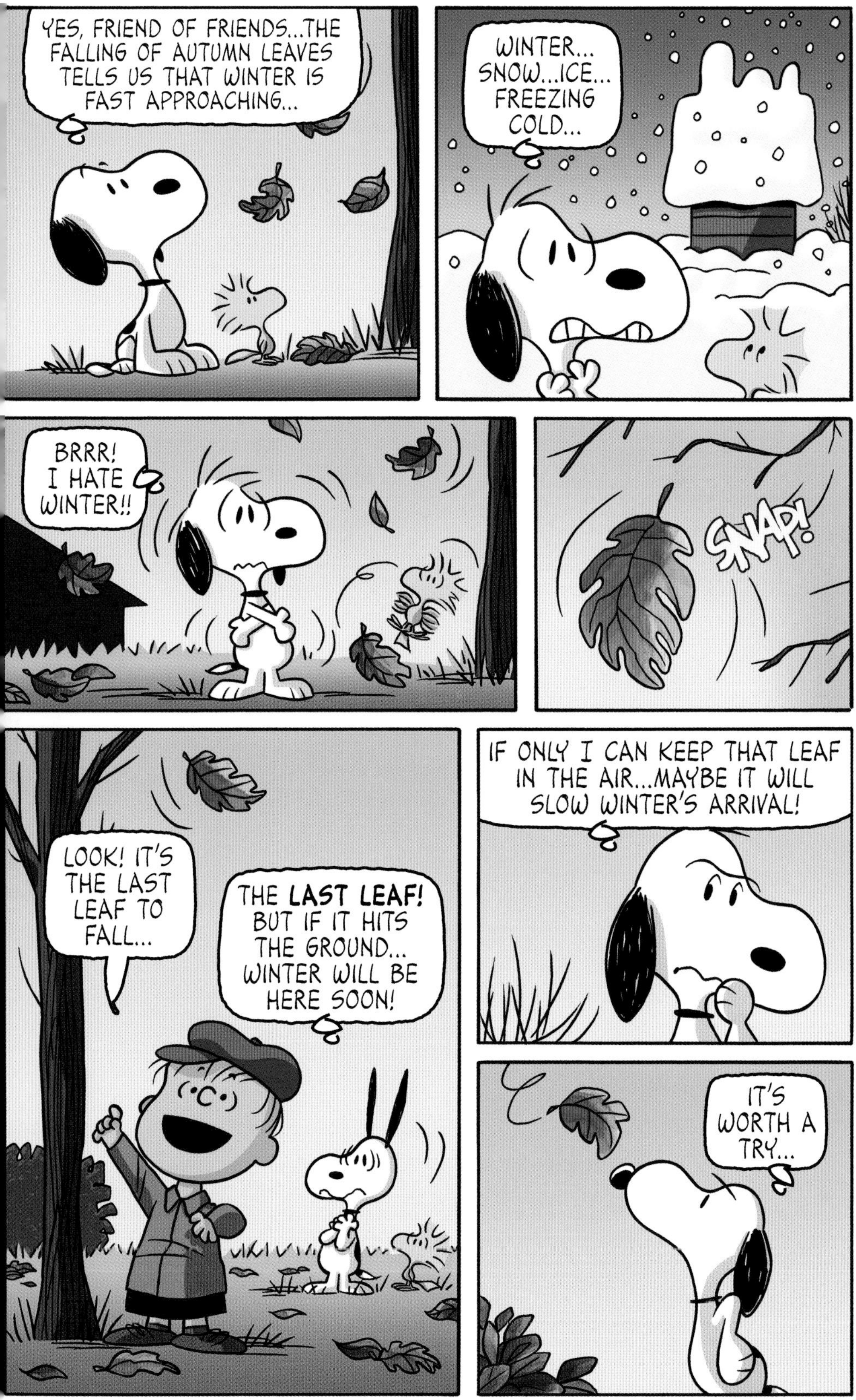
YES, FRIEND OF FRIENDS...THE FALLING OF AUTUMN LEAVES TELLS US THAT WINTER IS FAST APPROACHING...
WINTER... SNOW...ICE... FREEZING COLD...
BRRR! I HATE WINTER!!
SNAP!
LOOK! IT'S THE LAST LEAF TO FALL...
THE **LAST LEAF!** BUT IF IT HITS THE GROUND... WINTER WILL BE HERE SOON!
IF ONLY I CAN KEEP THAT LEAF IN THE AIR...MAYBE IT WILL SLOW WINTER'S ARRIVAL!
IT'S WORTH A TRY...

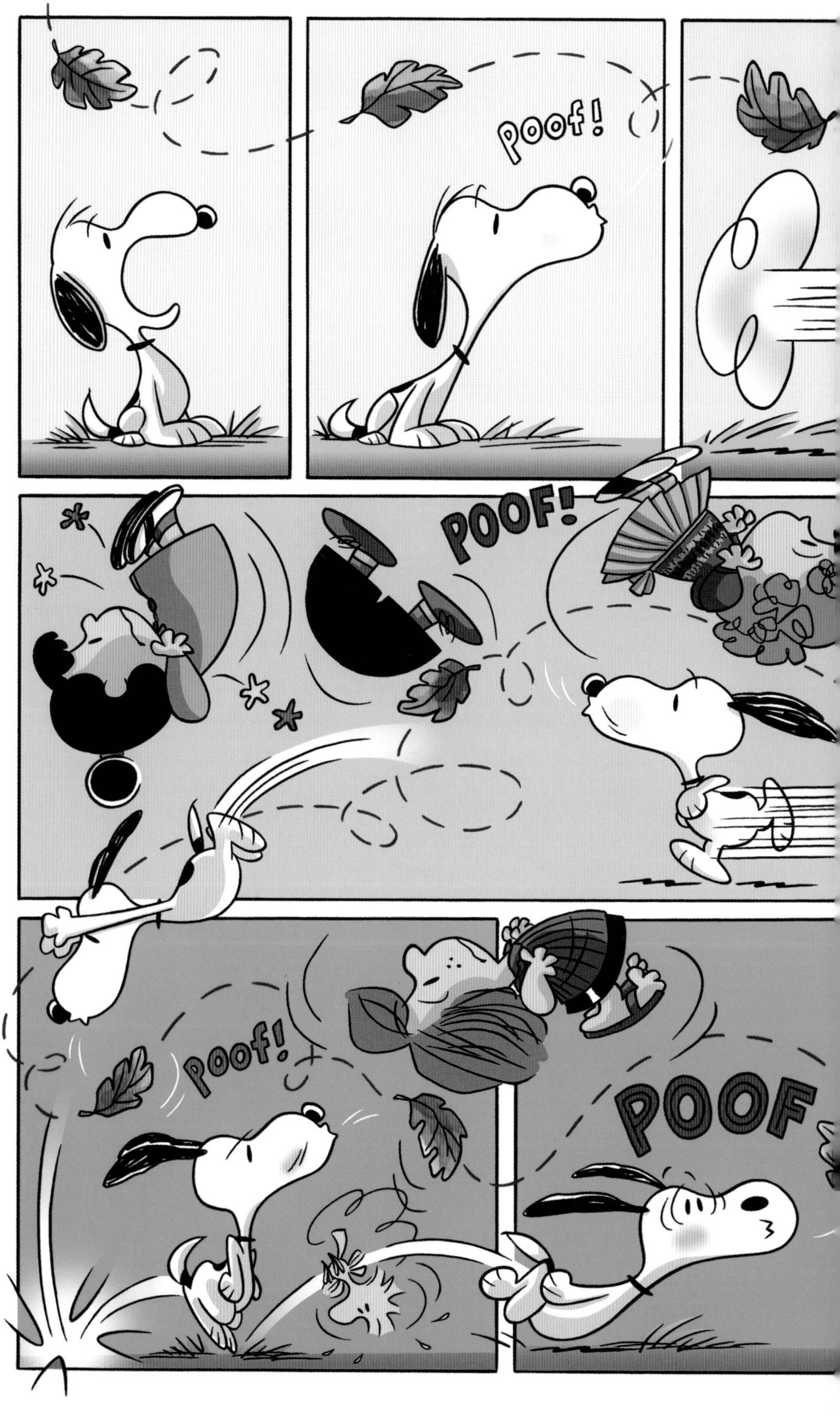
poof!
POOF!
poof!
POOF

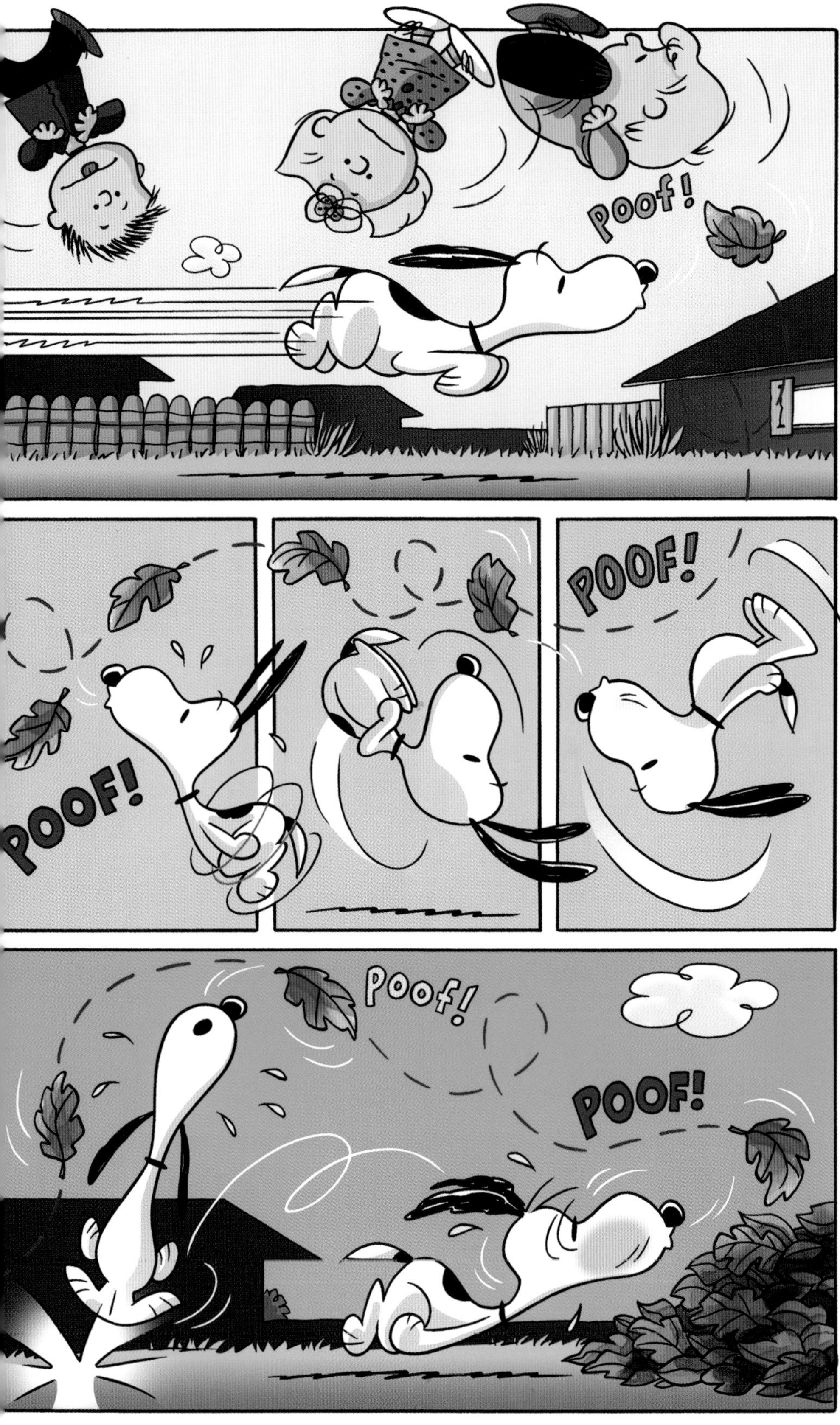
POOF!
POOF!
POOF!
Poof!
POOF!

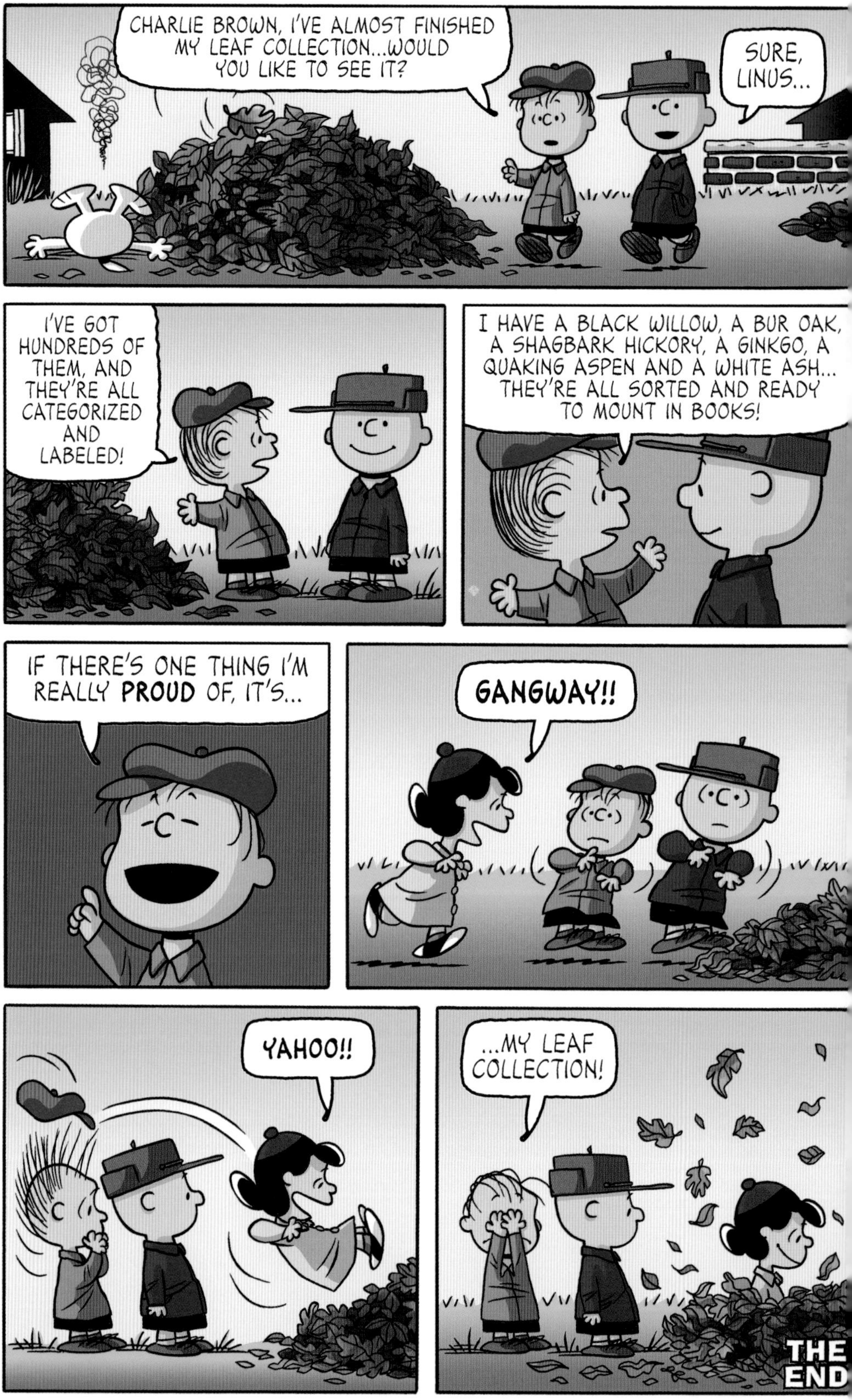
CHARLIE BROWN, I'VE ALMOST FINISHED MY LEAF COLLECTION...WOULD YOU LIKE TO SEE IT?
SURE, LINUS...
I'VE GOT HUNDREDS OF THEM, AND THEY'RE ALL CATEGORIZED AND LABELED!
I HAVE A BLACK WILLOW, A BUR OAK, A SHAGBARK HICKORY, A GINKGO, A QUAKING ASPEN AND A WHITE ASH... THEY'RE ALL SORTED AND READY TO MOUNT IN BOOKS!
IF THERE'S ONE THING I'M REALLY **PROUD** OF, IT'S...
GANGWAY!!
YAHOO!!
...MY LEAF COLLECTION!
THE END

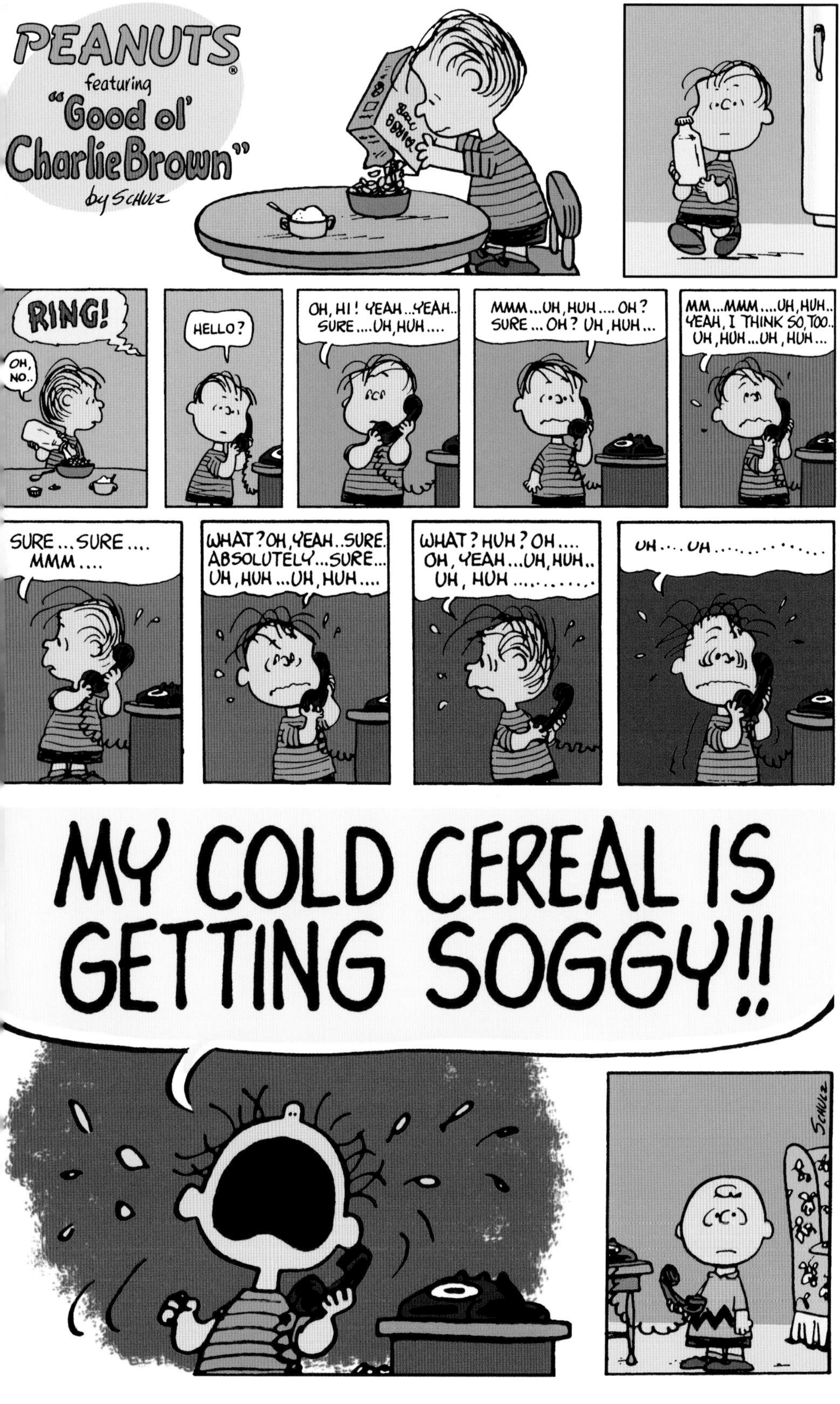
PEANUTS®
featuring
"Good ol' Charlie Brown"
by SCHULZ
RING!
OH, NO..
HELLO?
OH, HI! YEAH...YEAH.. SURE....UH, HUH....
MMM...UH, HUH....OH? SURE...OH? UH, HUH...
MM...MMM....UH, HUH.. YEAH, I THINK SO, TOO.. UH, HUH...UH, HUH...
SURE...SURE.... MMM....
WHAT? OH, YEAH..SURE. ABSOLUTELY...SURE... UH, HUH...UH, HUH....
WHAT? HUH? OH.... OH, YEAH...UH, HUH.. UH, HUH ....
UH.... UH..............
MY COLD CEREAL IS GETTING SOGGY!!
SCHULZ

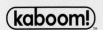